RED RUNNING DEEP

ALSO BY BETH BARANY

JANEY MCCALLISTER MYSTERY SERIES

Into the Black

Lured By Light

Gone Green

HENRIETTA THE DRAGON SLAYER SERIES

Henrietta The Dragon Slayer

Henrietta and The Dragon Stone

Henrietta and the Battle of the Horse Mesa

TOUCHSTONE OF LOVE SERIES

Touchstone of Love

A Christmas Fling

Parisian Amour

A Labyrinth of Love and Roses

A Cupcake Christmas

RED RUNNING DEEP

A JANEY MCCALLISTER MYSTERY, BOOK 4

BETH BARANY

FIREWOLF
BOOKS

FIREWOLF BOOKS
771 Kingston Ave., #108
Piedmont, California, 94611
www.firewolfbooks.com

SIGN UP HERE FOR NEW RELEASE NEWS:

http://bethb.net/rrd

PUBLISHER'S NOTE: This is a work of fiction. Names, characters, places,
and incidents are a product of the author's imagination. Locales and public
names are sometimes used for atmospheric purposes. Any resemblance to
actual people, living or dead, or to businesses, companies, events,
institutions, or locales is completely coincidental.

COVER DESIGN by Nada Orlic
BOOK DESIGN by Beth Barany

ISBN: 978-1-944841-42-3 (ebook)
ISBN: 978-1-944841-43-0 (print)

❀ Created with Vellum

For all who are dealing with the loss of a loved one.

ONE

It all happened so fast.

Janey scrubbed her face and said to Rhea, "Mom's Code Red."

Her personal AI assistant wired into her quarters spoke in a soothing female voice, "Right away, Janey. On it."

And just like that, her Code Red triggered Rhea to send the prepared messages to the right people. To her boss, Chief Daniel Milano, the head of the security team, went the emergency family leave request. To her security team, two weeks' worth of shift assignments. She was leaving L'Étoile, the hotel-casino space station, for an unforeseen amount of time. Milano could assign an acting lead investigator in her absence if one was warranted.

The video chime had woken her up out of a deep, dreamless sleep. She'd instinctively rushed to the vid screen across the room in the kitchenette, where Auntie Teresa gave her the unsettling but not unexpected news. Mom had taken an abrupt turn for the worst.

What next?

By the stars!

Mom's sudden health decline—Mom didn't want to eat or drink, even open her eyes.

Janey's heart couldn't stop racing, and her hand shook.

It was a normal response to stress, she knew that, but the knowledge didn't make it any easier to get dressed as fast as she could. Standard work clothes would do. Had to. No time to plan the perfect travel wardrobe.

She slipped on her full-body protective gear and then layered on a pretty clean pair of black slacks and her favorite cobalt blue blouse. Lastly, she slipped into her sweeping light long coat full of useful hidden pockets and her sturdy ankle boots. Without thinking, she seated a laser-sighted pistol into her belt holster, a small ladies ceramic-graphene handgun into one boot, and a sheathed four-inch black carbon steel blade in the other boot. You never knew. Besides, the weapons made her feel a micron better. She'd take what she could get.

Only one thing left to do. She had to do it herself.

"This is Lead Investigator Janey McCallister, requesting a seat on this morning's departure." Her throat was dry. She sipped her room coffee she didn't remember making. Orlando must have. She glanced about her quarters, but he wasn't there. When had he left?

A high-pitched voice she didn't recognize came through the vid wallscreen.

"What? Who is this? Where's Scott?" Janey clenched her fists and glanced about for something to throw, but her quarters were already a mess. What was the point? Why was she so angry?

Stars.

Would she get there in time?

"Ma'am, you know me. Hannah Chadwick, hangar security guard duty number—"

"I don't need to know your duty number, Chadwick." Of

course, she knew her. Good worker. Always a quiet, steady presence at karaoke night. Always working on a needlepoint of some kind.

Random, so random.

She growled at the frustration overtaking her and tried to take a calming breath. It wasn't working. It had been a long time since she'd felt this angry. She hated it. She hated the control slipping away. But you couldn't stop death. It arrived on its own timetable.

"I said the jet couldn't be ready for another hour, at least," Hannah said, her tone even, firm yet conciliatory. Her famous calm wasn't rubbing off on Janey.

"Hannah, I need to depart ASAP." StarEl, the space elevator, would be so damn slow. It took five days to arrive planetside.

"Investigator McCallister, another hour, ma'am. We posted the delay to all departments, as per SOP. Did you see it?" Right, of course, standard operating procedures.

"No." Of course, she hadn't. She'd been too busy freaking out to read the day's memos, even though she was trying hard not to.

Janey commed off, shoved out a breath, and checked the contents of her go-bag one more time. All there. Then she took the staff elevator to Hangar One. So what if she had to wait another hour or so.

In the small staff waiting room inside the cavernous hangar, she sipped a bland cup of coffee from the food crafter. Only staff waited here. The guest lounge had much better snacks, softer couches, but she didn't want to be around strangers. She tried to ignore how the walls seemed to close in on her as if they could fold her into a tiny box like she was a teensy newborn flower. She scrubbed her face again to rid her mind of such odd images.

Janey paced, tried to think of nothing, and then paced

some more. Her wrist comm pulsed a few times. One message was from Orlando, checking on her departure time.

She replied, "IDK." I don't know. The other messages were from staff marked non-urgent. She was on leave and could answer them later.

Orlando had disappeared at some point in her mad dash to leave her quarters. He'd checked with her, asked if she'd wanted him to stay. She didn't remember what she'd said to him, only remembered him saying he had an incredible lead that needed his attention but would be at the hangar to see her off. Promise. She wasn't holding her breath. She was numb. Was she even breathing?

Finally, the jet was ready to depart a few minutes after seven. She hustled up the steps. At the top of the stairs, she ducked to cross the threshold into the sleek space jet. Her comm pinged her with an urgent call. It was Orlando. She opened the audio link.

"Are you boarding?" he asked.

"Yes, I was in such a hurry." Janey hustled to a seat toward the back of the half-full cabin.

Several jet staff were preparing the cabin for takeoff.

"Me, too. I know, sweetie. Try to relax. That lead—it's a doozy. I had to catch it." He blew out a breath. "That's why I called. I can't see you off."

Venus hells.

"When it rains—" She slipped into a seat, the space jet nearly empty of passengers except for her. A few members of the senior casino staff were already seated in the front, chattering amongst themselves. A few guests returning Earthside read their holos, probably corporate types off to meetings.

"It drenches. You know how it is. Hard work suddenly bringing the harvest in." He was holding back his excitement on her account.

The jet engines rumbled to life, a low vibration like an enormous purring tiger.

"I know," Janey said. "I need to go. Gave family leave request to Milano. Mom's—" She strapped in.

"Sweetie, I heard your Code Red. You want me to come with?" His voice was low and soothing.

Janey shook her head against the lump in her throat and finally managed to say, "No."

"I'll be here when you get back," he said with certainty. But with his job, she never knew. His mysterious spy work for the Sol could call him away without notice.

"Don't know when that is, though." She stared out the window at the massive hangar, its portal to space bleached out by the sun-bright flight beams.

"I know," Orlando said. "That's okay. I'm not going anywhere."

He sounded so sure. How could he be so sure?

Three more people rushed aboard the jet—kitchen staff from the world-class casino restaurant on L'Étoile, the Phoenix. They nodded in greeting to her and took seats in the middle of the cabin.

Another comm channel beeped, her private line, requesting a vid call. Probably Teresa calling, wondering why she hadn't departed yet. The space jet was leaving over an hour later than it normally did. With the time it took to clear customs at the spaceport, flag down a private transport—the train would be too slow—and get to Mom's, she'd be there over an hour later than she wanted to be.

"I need to take this other call, Orlando." Janey stared at the flashing blue icon of a flower on her wrist comm, her mother's choice. Blinked. A sparkle of hope. Mom was calling?

"Go, *mi corazon*. Go." Orlando commed off.

Her heart squeezed at his term of endearment and at what this next call might be.

She switched to privacy mode and answered.

All she heard was sobbing. Not Mom.

"Teresa, is that you?" Janey's voice was pitched high, forced past the painful rock in her throat. "What's wrong?"

Just then someone called her name. A sharp, loud feminine voice shouting for Investigator McCallister.

One of the jet attendants, a young man, looked at her sideways, quizzically, and mouthed, "That for you?" The cooks and casino staff glanced at her.

The young jet attendant knew who she was. Everyone did. She was the chief investigator for the security department and recently interim chief. She signed off on background checks for all staff before they were allowed on board.

From outside the jet, the woman shouted again, as loud and commanding as any drill sergeant Janey had trained under back at the Space Wing training academy.

Janey nodded at the staffer, grabbed her go-bag from the seat beside her, and rushed toward the space jet exit. She brushed past a woman jet attendant standing in the doorway beside the portable stairs leading to the flight deck. The attendant waved her finger in the air in a circle, a distracted expression on her face as if she were listening to her comms. The jet was prepping for takeoff soon.

Janey held up a finger for them to wait.

The young woman drew her fingers close together. A short wait. Then the flight attendant frowned and spoke into her comm.

Janey couldn't worry about that and trotted down the stairs and off the jet, back to the grey, wide hangar level.

Teresa was still sobbing in her ear.

"Titi, what is it? How's Mom?" She squeezed the words past the pressure in her chest and shivered. There was a breeze coming from somewhere in the cavernous space. She fastened the neck warmers on her jacket.

A few meters away, one of her new security recruits and trainee investigators, Anahi Prentice, hands on her hips, was about to yell again. Eager Beaver Prentice, other security staff had dubbed her, was a recent Space Wing Academy graduate with frizzy red hair and lots of freckles.

Janey shook her head at Prentice and pointed to her head comm. Prentice snapped her mouth shut, her lips tight. She shifted and gazed at Janey with urgency and excitement.

"She's gone, Janey," Teresa finally said, her voice muffled by sadness. "She's gone. It was painless. One minute she was with us, the next gone. So fast. Too fast. There wasn't anything we could do."

"What?" Janey said dumbly. "Gone?" She turned away from Prentice. Just because she knew this day would come, it didn't make it any easier.

The hangar's grey floor pulsated and slipped sideways, her visual field malfunctioning. A stress response from her ocular implant. She pressed a hand against her eyes to block out all input.

"The doctors never did help her," Janey said through gritted teeth.

All those experimental treatments for her mom's rare illness.

She wanted to throw something. Instead, she gripped her go-bag tighter.

"And the storms—" Teresa started.

"What storms?"

"Category five dust devils they say, blanketing the whole southwest, spreading as far east as Dallas."

An alert flashed on Janey's ocular implant screen that the flight was being re-routed, no new destination posted yet, and the departure could be delayed…again.

7

No, not happening. A sound like a moan escaped. Was that her?

"Janey-dear, so, so, sorry," Teresa continued in a muted voice, "but the spaceport has been shut. Too dangerous for folks on the ground they said, to be outdoors. Train service has been suspended, too."

Janey could take the spacejet to wherever they were re-routing, take a highspeed train toward Las Cruces, but who knew how close she'd get?

"Excuse me, ma'am," Prentice said from a discreet distance. "So sorry to interrupt your leave but—"

Janey opened her eyes and held up a finger to Prentice.

Janey went into extra-privacy mode with her call by pressing a finger to her ear and turned away again from her new trainee.

"Teresa, what happened? Are you sure I can't land?"

Jupiter's balls, that sounded lame.

Teresa sobbed, muffled.

Prentice stepped closer to her, just inside her peripheral view.

Janey swallowed against the pain in her throat of unshed tears. "Titi, can you hold for one minute?"

"Sure, but aren't you on the jet already?" Teresa asked. "I thought you knew about the storm, that they'd be rerouting you already, that you could get here before the storm, but..."

"The jet was delayed. I'm still on the station." She should have called Teresa earlier. A wave of disorienting lightness passed through her head as if she was being pitched into zero-gee. She swayed. Someone, probably Prentice, righted her.

"Oh," Teresa said in a low voice. "I'm so sorry, Janey."

"Just a moment, titi." Janey wiped her face and blinked her ocular implant to reset it. It was Prentice beside her, one hand on her arm, concern on her face. "Yes, Prentice, what is it?"

"I'm glad I caught you before you left." Her eagerness seeped into her voice. "A guest was found dead in his quarters. Kim wants you on scene." Kim Iona was the Security Office Manager, incredibly efficient, and warm, and Janey's best friend on L'Étoile.

"What?" Janey exclaimed. "I-I have family leave. She should know that."

Everyone should know that.

Prentice blinked, gulped, a little pale. "Yes, she knows that. It's just—" She glanced away, shifting from foot to foot. Caught Janey watching her. Stilled her fidgeting. Gulped again.

"Spit it out, Prentice," Janey said.

"Investigator," the jet attendant called from the top of the stairs, "we're at final boarding call. You need to take your seat. We have to seal the craft. We're re-routing to Prince Albert."

What? Saskatchewan?

From the security checkpoint, two more kitchen staff dashed up the stairs for their seats, empty market bags over their shoulders.

"Janey, the whole area is in lockdown. Even we're grounded. Thank the stars we were all here," Teresa said, voice full of tears. "No one knows when the storm will lift. I am so, so, sorry. The storm delays everything." The storm would delay getting the death certification, the cremation, and the funeral rites.

Then Janey heard her whispering through the audio. Probably the other aunties listening in and conferring.

Prentice fidgeted with her uniform collar.

Janey spoke in a whisper, past the lump in her throat, "I really want to come home."

"Querida sobrina," Teresa said, a bit more energy in her voice as if the rest of the aunties gave her strength. "The rest of the gang is here. We're prepared to—to handle the details —the plan. When the storm lifts."

"The plan?" Her brain wasn't engaging.

"Investigator?" the jet staffer called. "We need to go. Storm front approaching at our landing site."

Where wasn't there a storm?

"We can't find Milano," blurted Prentice. "Chief Milano is missing."

"Missing?" Janey blew out a breath.

Even stormy weather on-station.

Venus hells, and Jupiter's balls.

"What's the matter?" Teresa asked. Then more whispering, conferring among the aunties. "Janey, I'll send you the plan. Dana didn't want to bother you with it. Everything is in hand. Go, do what you need to do, querida sobrina. I know you want to be here. We want you here, but…"

Janey shook her head, gulped. This couldn't be happening. Yet here she was.

The staffer on the spacejet stairs frowned at her. Prentice hovered. And titi let her make up her own mind, as she always had, as Mom always had. Mom. Mom would understand and not want her to suffer through who knew how many layovers. The aunties could handle… well, anything. They'd raised her along with their gaggle of kids on the far side of the tracks.

She blew out a long breath, her gut tight, her grief lodged there like a stone.

Decision made, Janey shook her head, no, to the staffer, who gave a thumbs-up of understanding and rolled up the flight stairs.

"Teresa, with the storm, the shutdowns, the delays…and I'm being called to a case. They need me here. No one else is trained up." That sounded lame to her ears, though Mom had never faulted her for making work the center of her life.

"I know. It sucks," Teresa said. "Your mother knew how much you loved your work. She was so proud of you. Always. She came back from her visit raving about you and the great job you're doing." She sniffled and then resumed, "We girls know what to do. Implement the plan. Your mom's plan. We have this in hand." Teresa blew her nose. "Your mother loved you very, very much. Now go do your job, querida. We're okay. Sad, but okay. You come when you can."

"Maybe I should come anyway..." Janey scanned the vast hangar, staring at the sleek space jet that could whisk her to the Prince Albert, Saskatchewan Spaceport instead of the Las Cruces Spaceport in just under two hours. Everywhere was two hours from the hotel high above the planet. Then she'd have to lay over until the trains ran into Las Cruces. Or she could catch another flight. Once there, in days hence, she would be able to breathe the crisp desert air and say goodbye to her mom properly under the stars they all loved so much.

Mom, I'm coming.

"Maybe I could—" Janey started.

"What would you do here, bake biscochitos and drink Jack Daniels with the rest of us while we waited for the storm to pass?" Teresa said, a teary smile in her voice.

"What about arrangements, talking to the doctors, the funeral rites?" Stars, she wouldn't know where to begin. The cremation, too.

Teresa huffed out a breath. "We'll have to wait on things. Don't worry. We have it in hand, Janey." She whispered, "I am so sorry, querida, for your loss."

"Thank you. And yours. Are you sure? I could be there in a few days..." Maybe. The travel delays, ugh. And then the gravity of the situation—Chief Milano AWOL, the need for her to investigate—was tugging at her. The pressure to solve, to fix—she couldn't do that at home.

"Go get the bad guys. Come once your case is wrapped up. The storm should be lifted by then, and we'll celebrate Dana's life and invoke the joyous funeral rites under the constellations." With that, Teresa commed off.

"I will…" Janey said to a closed connection and glared at the wavering walls of the huge hangar, not hearing anything except for the buzz of a billion sacred bees. Grey, wavy lines clouded her vision.

"Investigator McCallister, sir?" Prentice said. "Are you okay?"

The woman who liked to call her "sir" as they did at the Space Wing Academy regardless of gender seemed to be in a glow, all her tones—her red hair, dark skin with freckles, and violet eyes—technicolor bright and wavering like ripples on the wide Rio Grande.

Janey blinked to reset her implant, again, and Prentice's image reset to normal. The buzz dissipated.

But then all the other colors in the hangar came out tinged in grey. That wasn't right. She shook her head. That didn't help. She swallowed against a queasiness rising. She could manage. She had to manage. "Lead on." She'd be more of use here. She hoped.

Prentice headed for the elevator. Janey followed, her legs weighing a ton.

Had she made the right choice?

She envisioned turning around and making a run for the jet that was now heading toward the gravity barrier, its engines revving at a higher pitch, but her body didn't follow the vision. Instead, she moved into the elevator after Prentice. Its walls vacillated, shadows rippling across them like crows dashing across the bright and wide desert sky.

If she hurried, she could maybe still catch the jet.

She should call Orlando, tell him. But he was busy with his case, his hot lead.

She dropped her go-bag on the floor and scrubbed her face with both palms. Eyes closed, she swayed, put her hand on the wall to steady herself, and banged her hand on the railing. She sucked in a breath at the sharp pain.

"Sir, are you okay?" Prentice's voice sounded far away... tinny. "Should I call someone? You look a little pale. Sol Investigator Valdez, perhaps."

A muffled boom sounded. The jet had just taken off.

Jupiter's balls.

She shivered, unreasonably cold, and then squatted in front of her bag, zipped it open, rifled inside, and pulled out her vacuum flask. She clicked the On button and rolled the vacuum flask between her hands as the water heated to near-boiling.

"Fine, Prentice. Fine. I just need a moment."

"Yes, sir."

The doors closed on them. Prentice requested the seventh floor, which contained high roller suites for L'Étoile's most exclusive guests. Guests who demanded and received the best of the best—dedicated housekeeping and kitchen staff, anytime made-to-order meals from the Phoenix, the restaurant rated six out of six stars in the Xajak Review, and perks like on-call private security. One of her team was with a hotel guest acting as their undercover security. Her boss's boss, the owner of the hotel, had his own suite on the top level, a large sprawling affair with a sitting room and a living room. Such irrelevant details jangled in her mind.

She sighed. "Anahi, call me Janey. Don't need formalities. Not right now."

Prentice squatted beside her. "Yes—Janey."

Janey's vacuum flask clicked. The tea was ready. She drank right from the canister, gulping the hot liquid. The licorice aroma and the rich, orange tangy flavor triggered in her a deep sigh. She shivered with the hot electricity of the tea's medicine and stood, strength flooding her limbs, her spine, and her neck and head. The vibrant warm beige walls hugged her. The freckled pale recyclo-flooring sparkled. The silver elevator doors reflected her back—sober, grounded, present.

Prentice stood, too. The elevator stopped, and its door slid open.

Down the hall, Clark Alexander Bernard and Jintao Cho, two of her security staff, stood at attention on either side of a suite door.

She approached them, strength in each step of her long stride. She could do this.

TWO

AT THE HOTEL DOOR, JANEY SPOKE, STRENGTH IN her voice—thankfully. "Clark, Jintao, report."

"Sir," Jintao said and flashed a smile at her, then glanced at Clark. They exchanged a gleeful look.

What had they been cooking up this time?

These two were always clowning and scheming up staff pranks. A regular two-man circus. They were good people and hard workers despite their nonstop jokes. A jolly demeanor and a love of exchanging bao recipes with everybody, Jintao was a head shorter than tall, gangly Clark, full of irrepressible confidence and an air of mischief.

Clark nodded, repressing his smile. He saluted with his silver prosthetic hand, then sobered. He must be reading on his implant screen about Janey's emergency leave. "Are you okay, Janey?"

"Fine. For now. Anyone else on the floor besides us?" Janey was pleased to hear her voice was robust. Her shock had cleared.

"No," Clark said. "All guests accounted for in their suites, as per usual at this hour. Except for the deceased,"

15

"Housekeeping found him when she delivered his breakfast. She—" Jintao added.

"She who? Who served him?" Janey snapped.

Unfazed, Jintao consulted the security console on the wall.

Janey sipped her tea. She had to tone it down.

"Mai Chen," Jintao said.

Right. Mai Chen had said something the other night at karaoke that she'd been promoted to the high rollers floors to cook and personally serve her delicious world-class meals. They'd all teased her about becoming a specialist—something she swore she wouldn't become—and then drank to her success with China Fight Cocktails. Mai's favorite.

"Where is Mai?" Janey asked.

"Suite Acorn," Jintao said. "Two doors down."

"And the victim?"

"Mr. Hampton Nel. His suite is the first one down the hall. Suite Berry."

Who named these suites?

"Did you call medical?

"They're on their way," Jintao said.

"I'm surprised they're not here by now," Clark mused.

"Check on their ETA," Janey said.

Clark waved into his comm. "Five minutes, ma'am."

Janey nodded her thanks and headed for the victim's suite, reviewing Nel's hotel record on her ocular implant screen as she went.

Hampton Nel was a Pan African national, a professor based in the Gaborone Granton. He'd checked in four days ago, entering the hotel with the evening's jet arrivals. The only charges to his room were three days' worth of meals. No casino or asteroid race betting. Not a big spender.

At the threshold, she turned to Prentice and held out her

go-bag. "Can you run this down for me to our conference room and stow it in the side room?"

Prentice didn't move to take her bag. "But, sir, I was hoping to walk the scene with you. Learn from you. If you don't mind."

Janey eyed her, considering. "Okay."

"Yes, sir. Perhaps Bernard or Cho can guard it for you for now?"

"No, I want it in as few hands as possible." That sounded strange, perhaps, but she was particular about her stuff. Janey set the bag down outside the suite, her vacuum flask too, and then palmed open the door. "No one is coming up here except medical and our people."

From the elevator, Jintao nodded at her. He'd keep an eye on it.

At the suite entrance, a sweet odor hit her first like her mother's homemade cherry pie. Then the chaos of the room, loose data sheets and papers everywhere—on the plush carpet, the large real-mahogany table for six, and the dark wood side armoires, low finely carved coffee table, and blue velour couch. Bright galaxy swirls in vibrant reds, greens, and oranges displayed on wall screens. The clusters of stars didn't move as they would on a decorative wall panel. No music either. Most guests programmed their walls with bright images coordinated to move with the latest hyped jazz or electronica. Not here. Here the room with no soundtrack was still, stifling. Even in her quarters, she usually had soft water nature sounds or Baroque music playing. Maybe that was where she should be right now, lying down with a cool, soothing compress over her eyes.

Janey stifled a sigh and turned her attention back to the case at hand. At the long dining table near the door, a man was slumped in a chair as if the air had gone out of him. He'd been studying documents, by the look of the mess in front of him. From a few feet away, the man appeared to be sixty years of age. He wore a royal blue long-sleeved shirt adorned with sunburst patterns and black slacks.

Janey took one step toward the table and took air samples with her wrist comm. Prentice saw what she was doing and followed suit.

"What do you think that sweet smell is? Like peaches," Prentice whispered, excited.

"What do you notice?" Janey stared at the readings, not comprehending the chemical compounds at first.

"$C_{12}H_{22}O_{11}$. Hmmm." Prentice studied her holo screen, projected brightly above her wrist comm. "Chemistry wasn't my strongest subject. I'm a mechanical engineer like you, but I seem to remember this as table sugar."

"Smells like burnt sucrose," Soren Stinson said from the open door, the station's lab tech, dressed in his standard black jumpsuit, a toolkit around his waist full of sensor wands. "A disaccharide, usually from sugar beets or sugar cane, when not lab-grown. Hello, McCallister, Prentice. Kim sent me." He glanced about and asked Janey, "Milano is MIA? And where's Valdez?" He gave her a long look as if studying her for odd symptoms.

She ignored the look. She was as fine as she could be under the circumstances. "I don't know about Milano. Orlando is working his own case."

She hadn't told Orlando about her mother yet. A pang in her chest. She'd tell him later.

Soren nodded, his long blond bangs falling into his eyes, one strip a blue sparkly shade, the latest fashion. He brushed it away with the back of his gloved hand. "Cause of death yet?"

A tall Nordic blond with hazel eyes and a short, spiky haircut, Soren Stinson was a Science Tech Level Five—which meant he was wicked smart and could work anywhere in the

Sol. He chose to work on L'Étoile. All the best toys for his lab, he said.

Janey frowned. "We just got here, too."

"Of course." He eyed her, waiting. Finally, he said, "Where do you want me? The usual?"

"Sweep and document the room." Janey approached Nel, his body slumped in a chair, over the loose papers—the paper and the plastic digital kind. Rigor hadn't set in. She'd bet his skin hadn't cooled off very much yet. This man died less than two hours ago, was her guess. She slipped on the gloves Soren handed her. Of course, she didn't have her standard kit.

"On it," Soren said. "Shall I close the door?" He gave her a concerned look, probably wondering why she hadn't shut it herself to hide the scene from any guests who might wander by at this early hour.

"Please."

He did and started his scan of the entrance area.

"Thanks." Janey moved closer to the body. "Nel has no puncture marks on his skin. No visible defensive wounds, either."

"His lips are purple," Prentice said, her hands in crime scene gloves. "And his right hand is curled tight around a fork." She glanced at Janey as if for approval.

Soren arrived at the body, mapping it with his wrist comm. "No other utensils, or plates, for that matter."

"What does that mean?" Prentice asked breathlessly.

"He was getting ready for a meal?" Soren conjectured. "Weird that he's clutching it if the food hasn't been delivered yet."

"Right, yes, really weird," Prentice said.

"I agree." Janey eyed Prentice. "Mai Chen discovered him when she delivered his breakfast. What else do you notice?"

"There are no other marks on his body."

"Good. Document the whole scene with Soren. Detailed notes. Images and vid, too." She headed for the door. "I'll go speak to Mai Chen."

"I want to go with you."

"One step at a time, Prentice. Stay here and work with Soren. Direct medical when they arrive. But don't let them transport the body yet. Doc needs to see the victim in situ." Janey focused straight ahead, focused on her breathing, focused on staying upright.

"Yes, sir," Prentice called out.

Janey strode two doors down the hall to Suite Acorn and knocked. Without waiting for a reply, she used her security clearance—a palm on the door to a reader guests couldn't detect—and opened the door. Mai Chen sat at the dining table of the tidy living room, studying her holo.

Mai stood, a guilty expression on her face, replaced by one of compassion, and brushed her short black hair behind one ear, revealing four rainbow-themed crystalline studs pierced up her earlobe. "Janey! I thought you were heading off the station. How's your mom?"

Janey paused in her stride across the room. "How did you know?"

"You told me. This morning. Don't you remember?" Mai Chen rushed to her and gripped Janey's hands in hers. "Are you all right? Your mom—"

Janey shook her head, unable to speak. Breath coming too short. She had to get out of here. She spun toward the door. "Be right back."

Mai Chen called out her name, but Janey let her legs clobber the carpet in a fast run, eating up the space between her friend's concern and away, compelled by a force more powerful than her. She just couldn't. Everything.

The corridor curved gently. She huffed and strode and tried to only focus on the luscious grey air plants and overflowing bright green ferns that hung along the wall. She passed Clark and Jintao and felt their gazes on her but didn't look up to verify. She passed Nel's suite, arrived at Suite Acorn, and entered it again. Within six and a half minutes, she'd made a complete circle of the floor.

"You okay?" Mai Chen reached out a hand.

"Let's keep this professional right now, okay?" Janey let Mai pat her arm for a second, then sat back out of reach. It was all so much. Why hadn't she boarded that jet?

Mai Chen nodded and folded her hands on the table in front of her, a breakfast tray at her elbow—a silvery carafe, a pastry, and a fruit platter on colorful porcelain, and a small, covered brown crockery pot.

Janey started with the basics and waved to the tray. "You were delivering breakfast to the victim. At what time?"

"7 a.m."

"A Mr.?"

"Don't you have that?"

"Yes, just corroborating everything."

"Mr. Hampton Nel." Mai Chen checked her wrist comm's holo screen. "He likes—he liked—his breakfast at the same time every day and always the same thing. A carafe of double Turkish coffee, croissants and cantaloupe, and oatmeal seasoned with butter, cinnamon, and a dash of cumin."

Janey nodded, a question not kicking in.

Mai volunteered more information. "Today was my first day bringing him breakfast. Just started."

"Who are you replacing?"

Mai looked at her funny like it was a dumb question. Maybe it was, but Janey's brain wasn't firing on all cylinders.

"Jonas Hazari."

"What happened to him?"

"Janey, you can just check the records for that."

"Humor me."

21

"He transferred out. Deciding to switch careers, he said."

"To what?"

Mai Chen shrugged. "Real estate, I think. Don't really know. What does this have to do with what happened to Mr. Nel?"

"Just covering all my bases."

"Janey, it's me. You don't have to be so—"

"So, what? Formal? Unemotional? I just lost my mother, how am I supposed to do my job."

"I am so sorry." Mai made to stand and lean across to give her a hug.

Janey held up a hand. "Can we just focus on work? There will be time to grieve later."

Mai sat back down, shook her head. "It was hard when my ama died. She practically raised me."

There was a knock on the door. Janey unlocked it, and the door slid open soundlessly.

"The M.E. is here, sir," Prentice said from the open threshold. "She's asking after you. Well, barking really." Prentice suppressed a grin.

"Tell Doc I'll be there in a few minutes," Janey said. "Finishing up here."

Prentice gave a snap nod and left. Janey turned back to Mai, eyed her friend, and found her bearings. "Describe what you saw when you arrived at Mr. Nel's suite."

"He didn't answer my hail at the door, but he didn't have the Do Not Disturb indicator on, so I let myself in, as per protocol for him." Mai checked her holo screen.

"Something else?"

"Just thought you'd like to see the protocol. Not sure if you have access."

"We probably do, but show me anyway."

Mai showed her the details on her holo screen. Janey read: Nel likes to work at odd hours and wants his food delivered, even if he can't answer the door. Place tray on the table and do not disturb him in his work.

"Quite specific," Janey said. "I wonder what work he's doing."

"They're all like that. Well, not all. Some." She shrugged. "Why someone would come here to work I'll never understand."

Janey pounced on the first part. "Some or all are like what?"

"Everyone on this floor has…idiosyncrasies."

"Like?" Janey prompted.

"Some want their meals every four hours. Some call in requests just to dare us with outlandish dishes, which is fine. Some want us to bypass the food crafter programming, so they order off-menu. We don't do that, of course. They should just order directly from the restaurant, but no." Mai shrugged.

"Then what did you do?"

"I stepped into the suite and saw him slumped in his chair. I called to him, stepped closer, but then I saw he wasn't breathing. I left and called security."

"Not medical."

Mai shook her head.

"Why not?"

"I've been around you too much." Mai aimed a small smile at her.

Janey couldn't reciprocate. "Bad influence."

"Don't say that. Comes with the territory." Mai clasped her hands on the table in front of her and breathed, long and slow, meditative almost. "Are you sure you don't want to talk about it? Your mom, I mean."

Janey sighed and found her breathing was slowing to match Mai's. Clever friend. "Let's just stick to work. Gives me something to focus on, other than my powerlessness against death." Her vision blurred. "If I can't prevent death, I can at least solve mysteries like these." Janey blinked to clear her vision. Her best friend, Christine. Now, Mom. All links to the past gone.

"I know, sweetie." Mai patted her hand, lightning-fast, ignoring the frown Janey threw her way. "What other questions do you have for me?" Mai sat back in her chair, relaxed. She seemed more concerned for Janey's well-being than anything else, not on edge like she'd been the first time Janey had questioned her over a year ago on her first major case on the station.

Janey checked her holo screen, though there wasn't anything useful there. "Did you set the tray down when you checked Mr. Nel?"

"I did. But just for a second."

"Show me."

Mai stood and lifted the tray. "Here?"

"Yes." For now. Later she would walk the scene with Mai.

With tray in hand, Mai went to the door, turned around, and approached the table, pretending her empty seat was Mr. Nel. "I stopped about here." She stood a foot away from the back of his chair.

"Why there?"

"I could see something was wrong. I called out his name, came around him, and put the tray down, wrinkling my nose at the smell." Mai set the tray down and scrunched up her face as if the smell was rancid.

"What smell?"

"Something overly sweet and burnt like custard left too long in the oven. Or on the edge of going bad, turning into alcohol."

"We smelled it too when we entered his suite. Then what?"

"I bent over him, about to touch his neck, but then I remembered." She glanced at Janey.

"Remembered what?"

"Something you said about trace evidence. I didn't want to be caught up in all that. So, I grabbed the tray and hustled out of there."

"When did you call security?"

"As soon as I stepped out of the suite. I'm sure it's time-stamped."

"I'm sure it is."

"This floor isn't—" Mai paused and eyed Janey sideways.

"Isn't what?"

"Don't be mad at me. I know we're not supposed to know..."

Janey crossed her arms, fatigue pressing her down into her chair. "Know what? Spit it out, Mai."

"There are cameras and sensors everywhere, even on this floor, that aren't supposed to be there. Ones that the hotel guests aren't supposed to know about."

The guests knew they were being monitored for their safety in the casino and other public areas of the hotel, but the hallways and suites weren't supposed to be monitored by the station's security vids.

"What do you know about that?" Janey stood.

"Only whispers." Mai stood, too. "Rumors. Some engineers in the machine shop went looking—"

"And?"

"They found some dot cameras in the casino and lobby," Mai said. "But I don't remember who they were. I don't want to get anyone in trouble."

"Why do you bring this up?"

"Well, if there are cameras and sensors, you can check my timeline that way. I can't be in any trouble, can I? I didn't do anything wrong. In fact, according to what I've learned from you, I did everything right." She leaned in conspiratorially. "If there was a killer, you could see him, or her. On the hidden cams."

"You did everything right." Janey stared at Mai, without seeing her. A part of her was delineating a to-do list for her team. Another part of her was numb, watching, wondering what in all the stars she was doing here. And why hadn't someone on her team already checked the footage of the hallway? Maybe they already did, and she didn't absorb that information. "We'll check everything."

"I think you need to see Medical," Mai said.

"Not yet. Besides, we have the Doc on scene."

"No, you're not understanding. *You* need to go to Medical. You need to get checked out," Mai said, her voice loud. "I'm worried for you."

"I'm fine." Janey took a step back. When did she stand up? Mai was standing too close. "I'll be fine."

"Can I speak now as your friend?" Mai frowned.

"Haven't you been doing that already?" The pressure on her chest built like she was being squeezed from all sides, darkness at the edges of her vision.

"You aren't fine." Mai crossed her arms. "Why are you here? Why aren't you down there, with your mom?"

"She's gone. There's nothing I can do. Her friends are handling the details. I'll go—later, for the funeral rites—as soon as I close the case." Janey spun and headed for the door, her legs strong, blood pumping, heart beating, and arms swinging. In her body, but also observing it, cataloging each movement. "Besides there's no one else qualified to handle the case." She needed to feel useful. Here she was useful.

Mai followed her and squeezed her with a sideways hug. "I'll look in on you later.

"Okay." She wasn't on her A-game. How could she be?

"Can I go back to work?" Mai waved to her tray on the

table. "I've been sitting here for twenty minutes, and I have more breakfasts to deliver soon. At least one other guest is expecting their breakfast in about thirty minutes. You'll need to open the floor up again. If that's okay. And the killer's not around?"

"Wait until we remove the body. We'll let you know," Janey said.

Mai gave her a look of concern and hustled down the corridor to the prep kitchen on this level. Janey left to join Doc in Suite Berry.

Doc glanced up at her from examining the body. "What's wrong?" Her deep blue turquoise necklace peeked out from her white lab coat.

Janey shook her head. "Later. What do you have?" She had to stay focused.

Doc squinted at Janey and then turned back to the body. "Aside from the slight discoloration of his lips and strong burnt sugar smell coming from his body, nothing yet."

"The smell's coming from him? I thought it was coming from somewhere in the room." Janey glanced about at the wide floor plan, the mess of paper sheets, and the living room furnishings. Three staff from medical waited by the door with the hover stretcher.

Soren glided to Doc's side. "I checked the suite. It's not coming from the hotel room. It's got to be coming from Nel."

"Agreed." Doc surveyed the suite, missing nothing in her sharp eagle gaze, all fodder for her analysis. "I'll know more once he's on my table."

"Can you give me a preliminary cause of death, Doc?" Janey asked.

"No, but I *would* rule it as a suspicious death."

A grey area. Not enough to warrant locking down the station until they knew more.

"On what grounds?" Janey blinked to stay focused.

27

"According to his medical files"—Doc glanced at her holo—"this man was in perfect health until his odd death."

"I need a definitive call of murder to order a lockdown," Janey said. "I'll inform the chief of your findings."

"Sir, Kim's been looking for him," Prentice chimed in from the hallway to the bedroom where she was taking readings.

"I'm surprised he's AWOL," Soren added. "I thought he was doing better. Renewed purpose and all that."

"I'm not." Janey sighed. Milano had been dealing with his own grief for months. She didn't blame him for being hard to reach, but it was bad timing.

"You'll have to deal with Schoeneman," Doc said, frowning as if she'd eaten a sour candy.

"I know." Venus hells. Janey really didn't want to face Schoeneman right now. He was a piece of work. Doc seemed to think so, though she never gossiped about anyone.

Frederick Schoeneman, the hotel-casino owner, would not be happy to hear the death might be a homicide, especially three months after the last murders during an attempted heist. If it was murder, they'd have to shut down the station to all incoming and outgoing traffic. Schoeneman hated that, but she would do what had to be done.

"If only..." Doc shook her head, not finishing her thought.

She was about to ask Doc what was on her mind when Janey's comm chimed. It was the security staff office manager, Kim Iona.

Instead of relaxing at the sight of her friend calling, Janey replied professionally. "McCallister here." Maybe Kim had found the chief. He could be in Kim's office, overhearing, waiting for Janey's reply.

"Janey, I heard. Oh dear," Kim said. "How are you?"

"I—my tia—the storm—I couldn't—" She tried to speak

past the block of granite that clogged her throat. Wasn't happening. Doc supervised the medical staff as they lifted the body with practiced moves onto the hover stretcher. They'd shroud it so anyone glancing at it wouldn't see it for what it was—a dead body. Doc then nodded a goodbye to Janey and followed the stretcher and the medical staff out of the suite.

"Wait. How did you hear? Did Mai tell you?"

"No, you did. Your emergency message and then we talked. You don't remember?"

"No." Kim was the second person she'd spoken to after she'd received the first call from Teresa that she didn't remember. Was she experiencing blackouts? She'd need to get checked out in Medical, but later.

"Janey?" Kim asked softly. "You okay?"

"The last few hours have been a blur. Like I've already lived two days." Janey blew out a breath and surveyed the room. Soren and Prentice still worked the scene, scanning and documenting the kitchenette and wide sitting area.

"Why are you still here? Why didn't you leave?" Kim asked again.

"Later." Janey didn't want to go there.

"I understand. I called to give you an update. Is now a good time?" Thank goodness for her steadiness.

"Yes."

"I haven't been able to track down Milano and didn't want to send staff all over as we're stretched thin. Antonia has stepped in to coordinate the case from here. So, send her all the case details."

"She was prepared to take lead on the case, wasn't she?"

"But then I saw you were here, and we agreed—"

"When you couldn't find Milano—"

"I panicked."

"I get it," Janey said. The timing felt absurd. Surreal. If the jet had left earlier... If there wasn't a storm planet-side...

"Did you check the spa?" She'd had to track guests before. People took off their trackers to swim or use the sauna.

"Yes, we put in a call. They're checking discreetly," Kim replied. "I feel bad for you, Janey."

"Let's focus on the case."

"Yes, how bad is it?

"Bad. Doc's ruling it a suspicious death. We may have to lockdown the station. We should know more soon. Once Doc —" Janey scrubbed her face.

"Completes her autopsy. Oh dear. Just say the word and I'm on it."

"Thanks." The weight of it. What kind of person killed and left no mark? And why? She needed to know more about the victim. "Have Antonia call up all station and personal records for Mr. Hampton Nel, Suite Berry, and let me know if anything flags. Prentice and Stinson are finishing up here. I'll be down shortly to go over everything with her and whoever we can spare."

"You got it," Kim said. "And I'm here for you. *We're* here for you."

"Thanks, Kim. Let's wrap this case up—"

"So, you can go home."

Janey commed off and turned to Soren and Prentice, who busied themselves studying their holos as if they hadn't been eavesdropping. "What do you have?"

THREE

PRENTICE DOVE IN. "IN ALL THIS MESS"—SHE waved to the papers and loose data screens strewn about on every surface, the place looking as chaotic as a college dorm room—"we only found Nel's DNA." She looked to Soren, who nodded in confirmation.

"That's it? Between the two of you?"

Soren studied his holo and specialized scanner, then glanced up at her. "Well, there was some trace of sugar particulates in the air, but they dissipated with the removal of the victim to insignificant parts per million."

Janey glanced about. "What are all these papers and screens about? Who was Nel? What have you learned?"

"From these notes, I gather he was working out some scientific theories about quantum mechanics, string theory, and black holes," Prentice read off her holo. "Something about mirror universes, galaxies colliding, notes about an FTL drive. That's faster-than-light. Far out." Prentice glanced at Janey for approval. "A theoretical physicist."

"Look at you! Nicely done," Soren said approvingly. He turned to Janey. "Don't you think?"

Janey nodded, not finding the enthusiasm to smile. "Anything else?"

Maybe she'd slipped into a mirror universe.

Soren eyed her strangely and opened his mouth to speak.

Prentice jumped in, "He arrived here three days ago, traveling alone, and he took all his meals in his room. He didn't use the casino, not once." She glanced up at Janey. "Maybe he came here to stargaze. And do his research. Why else come here and not gamble? The views *are*..."

"...out of this world." Soren grinned. Then he schooled his expression.

Not as subdued, Prentice practically pranced with excitement, giddy with using the hotel's catchphrase.

"Speculation, Prentice," Janey said. "Confirm, double-check, and start a timeline of his whereabouts, everyone he met, including staff and other guests. Work with Antonia."

Prentice grinned, her eager-beaver attitude in full swing. "Yes, sir." She waved her hand over her wrist comm to take notes into her holo screen, then dictated into it in a low voice.

"Who would want him dead?" Soren frowned. "A brainiac like him."

"It is a suspicious death, but not yet a murder," Janey said. "Are you sure there's no trace of anyone else being in this suite?"

"I am sure. None, whatsoever," Soren said. "Though there is a fine sheen of particulates on some of the surfaces."

"Standard dust." Prentice turned back to them and bounced on her toes. "I took a baseline from my quarters when I first arrived."

"Nicely done," Soren said.

"Thanks. Looks like he didn't let room service in to clean in the three days he was here," Prentice added. "Not that my

32

quarters are dusty. Housekeeping does a good job. As clean as any recruit's barracks."

Prentice liked to talk. Janey rubbed her temples. "Supposition on the standard dust, but likely. Check with housekeeping to confirm."

"Yes, sir." Prentice headed for the door, practically skipping. Telling the probie to tone down her walk seemed out of line, but Janey was tempted.

"I'll head back to the lab to double-check everything." Soren glanced about the main room as if looking for something.

"What is it?" Janey asked.

"I've never been in one of these high-roller suites, but aren't they supposed to be bigger, multi-room affairs?"

"Right." Prentice stopped and glanced about, too. "This suite only has a kitchen, bathroom, and this main room, plus a bedroom. Shouldn't it be bigger? More rooms?"

"Check on that as well," Janey said to Prentice. To Soren, she asked, "Are you going somewhere with this idea?"

"Not sure. Just noticing."

"Good noticing. I want to take another look around." Janey glanced at the kitchenette recessed at the far wall. It was tiny—nearly as small as hers. Normally, as Prentice and Soren pointed out, kitchens for this level were bigger and classier.

"Okay, boss," Prentice said, but when Janey didn't hear the door whoosh open and shut, she glanced back. Prentice squirmed like a puppy as if she wanted to offer to stay, to watch Janey work.

Soren, in his graceful still way, watched her with concern.

"Go, both of you. Clock's ticking."

"Isn't it always?" Soren said, rhetorically.

"So exciting," Prentice whispered as they left the suite.

Finally, she could be alone. She turned her attention back

to the kitchenette. You learned a lot about people by what they ate. She needed to know more about Nel. Perhaps he ate something from the food crafter that poisoned him. Standard in every guest suite and staff quarters, the food crafters offered a limited menu. Maybe something had gone wrong with this one.

Embedded in the wall, a dirty food crafter sported crumbs and a few days' worth of residue. On the food crafter's readout screen, she ran through its history of recent meals. Then she asked it to run a diagnostic in the background and send the data to her comm when it was done. In addition to his daily breakfast from the Phoenix Restaurant, like the one Mai had delivered this morning, Mr. Nel favored cayenne lentils and basmati multivitamin rice twice a day. A staple meal in many parts of the world, including where he came from.

She scanned with her ocular implant and holo to confirm the crumbs on the food crafter and the espresso maker, even though Soren or Prentice had done the same. She needed to keep focused, stay busy. Nothing odd showed up in her scans. No poison there. Besides, Soren would have told her.

The narrow kitchen counter housed the sink containing dirty bowls and espresso shot glasses. A non-standard espresso maker occupied the rest of the tiny space, sprinkled with dark fine granules. Perhaps he'd brought it from home. Her team could track that down.

She didn't see anything out of place, yet something about this case didn't add up, namely how a studious man who kept to himself and had been in perfect health died in this hotel room this morning. All guests had to pass a rigorous health check before departing for L'Étoile.

Even so, maybe he'd had a cardiac arrest or stroke. With today's health medicine, it was statistically improbable, though not impossible.

She needed to talk it out. She strode to the middle of the paper-strewn room and commed Orlando.

He didn't pick up. She tried again.

Jupiter's balls.

He usually picked up by the second call. No matter what he was doing. Unless he'd left the station to follow up on a lead for his top-secret case. Like when he'd pulled one of his disappearing acts. He was supposed to leave her a sign—a coffee mug on her bedside table. His spy work was so top-secret he didn't want to leave any digital footprints unless absolutely necessary. And telling her he was leaving to investigate a lead Earth-side or on another space station didn't fall under such absolutely necessary conditions.

She thought-commed her room AI, Rhea.

Is there a coffee mug on my bedside table?

The words appeared on her eye implant screen in glowing too-bright pinkish font.

No, Janey.

She blinked to clear the screen. The brightness gave her a headache.

Orlando had to be somewhere on L'Étoile. Into her wrist comm, she waved in the message for him to contact her. No reply. Where was he? Even though she was in a guest suite and at a crime scene at that, she went to a wall screen and open the ident-protected security feeds. She had to see him, speak to him.

There he was, in the environmental controls room, down at the bottom of the station. He was kneeling in a tight space in front of a blocky machine. Maybe the room shielded all comms, so he couldn't receive her messages. Thankfully, the vid cam worked fine. She could see him staring at the machine, but he had no idea she was spying on him.

She closed the feed, guilt pressing on her chest. He had

free rein of the station. And he'd sounded excited, hot on a lead that must have taken him to environmental controls.

Bao Suzuki was the guard on duty in that area. Janey commed him. Bao picked right up. "Ma'am."

A very polite man, he didn't like calling her sir.

"I need you to check on someone and relay a message," Janey said.

"Of course, ma'am. As long as I don't leave my post."

Good on, Bao. He knew his regs.

"Isn't Basco down there, too?"

"Emilio just stepped away for his break. Do you want me to call him back?"

Did ten more minutes make a difference? She'd spoken to Orlando less than an hour ago. He couldn't have gotten himself into a tight spot in that period of time, could he? What was he doing nosing around the environmental controls in the bowels of the station, off-limits except to security and the engineers who worked there?

Environmental controls consisted of a closet-sized area packed full of machines and computers overseeing the whole station's air and water circulation. As far as she knew, no one worked in the cramped space. Controls were monitored elsewhere, mostly on-planet at headquarters. Plus, the room was normally locked. So, how'd Orlando get in?

Janey glanced about Nel's suite with new eyes. Small air ducts, shaped in circles, dotted the walls close to the ceiling, twelve feet up. These suites had higher ceilings than the ten-foot norm. She scanned in closer with her ocular implant. The small circles were about a hand span in diameter, five inches if she wanted to be precise—and she always wanted to be precise—with a thin membrane covering, the ventilation holes one-sixteenth of an inch in diameter. Tiny but enough to pull in stale air and pump back into the suites fresh, recycled air. They'd scrubbed every inch of the air duct system a few months ago after the last case, but maybe they missed something. How that could be possible she wasn't sure.

"Ma'am?" Bao asked, prompting her back to the conversation.

"Wait until Emilio gets back to relay this message."

"Yes, ma'am. What's the message, and who is it for?" Good man. He was on top of it.

"Please go to the environmental controls room. Sol Unified Planets Investigator Orlando Valdez should be there. Have him meet me in the conference room as soon as possible."

Maybe Orlando could help her with her case. Maybe she needed to talk to him for personal reasons. Either way, she needed to talk to him. She didn't want to interrupt whatever Orlando was doing, but he could handle it if indeed Bao managed to discover him in the act of doing whatever spycraft he was concocting.

"Yes, ma'am, but no one works in that room. I didn't see anyone go in. I've been here since 6 a.m."

Strange. But Orlando was a master at sneaking into places he wasn't supposed to be without being seen. One of the things that made him excellent at spycraft.

"I know no one works there," Janey said. "Please check for me anyway. Could there be a back door not on the official schematics?"

"Yes, ma'am," Bao said. "I'll check. And I'm not aware of any back door. I'd have known. Anything else?"

Janey hesitated. How to say this? "Let me know if you see anything suspicious."

"Like what?"

"I'm not sure. You'll know it when you see it."

"Yes, ma'am." Bao commed off.

Was Orlando involved in something hinky? She had

nothing to go on, no evidence, except the tightness in her gut and a feeling of dread unyielding under her breastbone.

Bao commed her back. "Nobody's there, sir. Nothing's out of place. All systems green, from what I can tell. The home office will have to run diagnostics. Engineers say they can't do it on our end."

"Thanks, Bao. I'll handle it," Janey said and closed the comm. She'd wait on contacting headquarters until she knew more.

Orlando had been in an area where no people worked, a locked room he'd entered and apparently exited unseen. They'd have to talk.

An idea hit her. What if whatever had killed Nel had been piped in via the air ducts? And what if Orlando was somehow a part of that? It wouldn't be the first time he'd hidden the details of a case from her, one he was directly involved in.

Venus hells.

Sadness weighed on her. She really didn't want him involved. Not when they'd recently patched up their first major fight. She was starting to fully trust him again. She wanted to trust him.

But she had a case to solve. Focus.

She blinked to clear her thoughts and her ocular implant screen, cluttered with input from Prentice and Soren's data, and spun to study the suite with fresh eyes.

If no one had slipped into Nel's suite, then perhaps something had been piped in via the air ducts that had killed him. How was that possible? No idea, yet. Speculation. She needed more information.

She blinked again to increase magnification and zoomed in on the table where Nel died. Details scrolled on her ocular implant screen, all standard air composition and common particulates. Nothing stood out as a possible cause of death. If Nel had inhaled a foreign substance that had also seeped in through his skin, her implant couldn't pick it up. Or whatever it was had long dissipated and had left no trace.

She wasn't going to find any answers dawdling in the messy suite. Janey exited, shut the door, and installed the security lock. She motioned for one of the guards.

Jintao trotted over. "Sir?"

"Put a code red security screen on the door. No one in except the security staff."

That would make the door invisible to the naked eye, camouflaged to appear as the wall and only visible to those using their holos tuned to a specific frequency. If a guest happened to brush up against it, they'd notice a door—if they were paying attention and weren't drunk.

"Yes, sir. What about guests for the other suites?" Jintao asked. "Can they return to their rooms?"

"That should be fine."

She thought of something else. She had to keep the news of the death out of earshot of the guests, as per regulations and Schoeneman's, the station owner's, clear order. "Do you know what housekeeping told the guests to have them stay off the floor if they weren't already in their rooms?"

"I don't. I can find out."

"No, that's okay. I'll check. Thank you, Jintao."

Housekeeping had probably told guests that there was a temporary maintenance issue on the floor that would keep them from their rooms if they weren't already in them. Though at this hour, most guests would be asleep, having partied into the night. Except for Nel.

If anyone had complained about the inconvenience, no one had told her yet. Good. One less issue to deal with.

Jintao nodded and hustled to a small gear kit beside the elevator door. That reminded her of her go-bag, right where she left it at the entrance to Suite Berry. She grabbed it and her tea vacuum flask, too.

Janey lifted it to her mouth to sip, then paused. Had anyone swept the hall for particulates? She pulled the vacuum flask away from her lips and did the sweep with her holo and implant screen.

Nothing jumped out as unusual. Great. Nothing to go on. A big fat black hole of a case.

What was she doing here?

A leaden blanket pressed on her, pushing her into the carpet, her legs jelly as if she were walking through the desert under a burning sun.

Faint music tinkled from the wall speakers. A wispy light aroma of lavender carried on the slightest of breezes, hinting of the French Riviera—or so she'd been told. The area was turning on for hotel guests. She needed to get back in the game. She could do that. Tea would help. She gulped some from her vacuum flask. Energy and lightness burst through her chest. Coolness flooded her from the inside out.

Yes, she *could* do this.

Jintao and Clark jogged over to the suite door and proceeded to tap up a security screen. If a guest did happen to see it out of the corner of their eye—it happened sometimes that the hall light hit the security screen in just the right way—they'd only see a sign marked "Beautification Project for Your Excellent Comfort" to make it appear as if the room was being worked on. Good.

Jintao turned to her. "Anything else, sir? Do you need us to remain on guard for this floor?"

"No, we've done all we can. Head back to your regular posts." She scanned the twelve-foot-high corridor ceiling. Smaller air ducts were dotted at regular intervals above her and on the wall, a foot down from the ceiling. Scanning in, she could see that the membrane was at one-sixteenth of an inch, too.

Jintao blinked. "But both of us were off-duty. Antonia said

she had to re-jigger the duty assignments per your flight leave orders."

"Right." Flight leave? She'd sent those prepared orders over two hours ago—a lifetime ago. "Good—good on Antonia. Good."

"Are you all right, sir?" Jintao peered at her with kindness. Clark gazed at her too with such concern that she had to glance away.

"My mother died this morning."

"Oh, I was wondering why you were still—" Jintao started until Clark elbowed him in the gut with his metal arm, and Jintao let out an oof.

"We are so sorry, Janey," Clark said, his voice gentle.

Before Clark could ask any questions, she said, "There was nothing I could do. Can do. She was sick for a long time."

"May the stars bless her passing and ease your pain," Clark intoned.

"As the stars be," Janey replied without thinking and reached for the wall that was suddenly too close.

Clark stepped toward her but stopped when Janey righted herself. "I am so sorry, sir. If there's anything I can do…"

"Just your job, Clark," Janey said and headed for the elevator, go-bag and vacuum flask in hand. "Your job."

Inside the elevator, she commed Orlando again, and again, he didn't pick up. She commed several more times with no reply. Now that he'd left environmental controls, where the Jupiter Trojans was he? He hadn't left her the signal that he was off-station, so what the hells?

She was about to comm Suzuki to confirm her message had been delivered when the elevator opened on the security floor, and there he was. In all his smudged glory.

"*Carina*," he breathed and opened his arms to her. "I got your messages but…"

She didn't care about the dusty grey smudges on his high cheeks, across his wide forehead, and all over his light-sucking black-as-night silky shirt. She let herself be enveloped by his warmth and solid chest.

"You left your hot lead, for me," Janey said into his shoulder. At five foot eight inches, she fit perfectly to his six-foot lean, muscular frame.

"It is a dirty one, too." Orlando nuzzled her neck.

"Glad you prefer me over dirt."

"Well…" But she heard the grin in his voice.

"Why didn't you answer my comms?"

"I was in the middle of it—I found—never mind." Orlando hugged her tight. "It can wait. For this. For you."

FOUR

Orlando stepped back and tucked a stray strand of blonde hair behind her ear. She felt his attention on her, studying her. She couldn't look at him.

"What is it?" He pulled her back into his arms. Warmth surrounded her, strength too, and a coiled, pent-up vibrancy as if he could go supernova at any provocation.

Janey shook her head against his chest.

"Your mom?"

She nodded.

"And? ..."

She shook her head, her throat tight.

So much more than that. What was she going to do? She'd only taken the job at L'Étoile to help Mom. Now that she was gone, what kept her on L'Étoile? Even before this job, she'd entered Space Wing and then become a military investigator to support her mother and get treatment for her rare and hard-to-treat illness. Would she stay in this line of work, carry a weapon, carry the risks and the responsibilities? She'd been a high school science and engineering teacher before—before tragedy had struck. Did she want to go back to the safe life of teaching, back on Earth?

Without asking anything further, he hugged her harder as if he felt the so-much-more that was troubling her. After a long moment, he let her go. She turned to head toward the conference room across the corridor. He grabbed her hand.

"Wait. Come on," he said. "Let's get you cleaned up. You'll feel better."

"I have work to do."

"You need a moment to yourself. The case can wait five minutes. You have a team."

"But…" Her protest was weak, and they both knew it.

At his mock stern look, she relented and let him gently guide her in the opposite direction, away from the security offices and toward the part of the curve that housed the personnel quarters. He led her to his own and unlocked the door, blocking her view of the keypad sensors. He still kept some things from her. She was too tired to protest his secrecy yet again. He had his reasons—his high-stakes highly secretive case for the Special Investigations Unit of the Sol Unified Planets Security Office.

He nudged her into his quarters. They were surprisingly clean. Usually, they were a mess—a lot like Nel's suite. When had he had time to clean? In the last week, he'd spent most of his time with her, when he wasn't working at a desk in the office or discreetly running around the station doing stars knew what.

"Hey," Orlando said, "you with me?"

Janey blinked. "How long have I been standing here?"

"Forty-five seconds," Orlando said, his face grey and fuzzy to her.

She blinked to clear the blurriness. His rugged features came into sharp relief, his warm brown gaze on her.

"Go wash your face, *mi corazon*."

"Right." She was his heart. She felt her shoulders release tension. In a daze in Orlando's tiny bathroom, she lathered up her hands, scrubbed her cheeks, and tightened her blonde hair in its ponytail. She splashed cold water on her face and finally peered in the mirror. Blinked. Still thirty-three years old, but now an orphan. Even without clicking into the high-resolution scan of her skin, she could see the tight lines of sadness and grief bracketing her blue-grey eyes and mouth. If she could see her grief, so could others.

How was she going to be able to do her job?

She lifted her chin. She'd do her job, for mom, for herself. Because it was what she knew. But when this case was over… maybe it would be time to leave.

Janey could have worked anywhere with her skill set, somewhere more in line with her values of universal education and health care. Like at one of the space stations run by the Granton Community—the same group behind the San Francisco Granton community where she'd lived since she was eighteen years old. The one she'd thought she'd never leave until she did, after tragedy struck five years ago.

In the Granton communities, everyone's basic needs were met. Every resident received credits to redeem for housing, food, education, and clothing. You could focus on your life's work, earning extra credits to spend however you liked, or just enjoy yourself with leisure activities. She'd loved being a high school science and engineering teacher. Until grief had her fleeing back to her mother's home in Las Cruces Spaceport, New Mexico and to the Space Wing Academy.

Orlando appeared in the mirror, gazing at her with so much love her heart squeezed. She turned, brushed past him, plunked herself down at the table, and activated her holo. She needed to run a diagnostic, find out why she was experiencing the blackouts and fuzzy, psychedelic vision. And then she needed to get back to work.

"Janey," Orlando said, sitting beside her.

She waved into the medical program designed just for her and unstrapped her comm from her wrist. "I need you to scan me."

He took the comm. "Why?"

"Please."

"Just run it over you?"

"My whole body, but mostly my eye." She waved a spot above her right ear where a teensy, one-nanometer computer was embedded under her skull that allowed her to see with her ocular implant.

He gazed at her with concern.

Janey scrubbed her clean face. "It's fine. Doesn't hurt. Come on. You said I need a break. Maybe I need medical, but I'd rather not." She opened her eyes and peered at him, hopefully conveying her pleading. "The sooner I know... the sooner I can get back to the case."

Orlando rubbed the comm wristband as if weighing something.

"Please." She closed her eyes against the throbbing pressure of an escalating headache at her temples.

Something ticked or clicked like an old-fashioned clock. Orlando liked old-fashioned tech, even though he was a wizard at the most advanced tools a spy for the Sol could ever want or need. The few times they'd spent the night in his quarters, it had taken her longer than usual to fall asleep due to the *tick-tick-tick* of an old wind up, even though he'd buried the clock in a drawer of socks.

Now the sound comforted her like the pecking of the red-headed woodpecker outside her mom's home, or like the soft clickety-clack of the commuter auto-train that passed by their house when she was growing up.

With the clunk of her comm being set on the table, she opened her eyes.

Orlando was gazing at her with that concern.

"Please scan me."

"I did. You're fine, I think."

She picked up her comm and reviewed the readings on the holo screen. Her implant was fine, but her electrolytes were low, and—her stomach growled—her salts, too.

Orlando cleared his throat. He crossed his arms and gazed at her sternly but spoke in a soft, gentle tone. "You haven't told me what happened."

"With what?" she snapped, jumping to her feet and pacing his small room. "You're the one who was—"

"Who was what?" Orlando said in a soothing tone. "I was asking about your mom."

She huffed out a breath. No reason to pick on him, not until she had evidence. Besides, he had a right to hear the news from her instead of just reading her emotions, which he was excellent at.

"Just as I was boarding," Janey started, "Teresa called and told me the news. Mom passed away, quickly." She stared at the floor of beige recyclo-tile. "Titi said to stay. Because of the storm. She said plans were made. That Mom made plans. I knew that but..."

"Oh, *mi corazon*." He was there, wrapping his warmth around her again.

She peered up at him. "Did you hear me call Mai and Kim about leaving to see my mom?"

Orlando nodded.

"Weird. I don't remember."

"You're having selective memory blackouts. I've seen this happen before."

"You have?"

"In stressful, life-altering moments." He rubbed her back in comforting circles.

She leaned into his comforting touch. "What do I do?"

47

"I hear hugs are good."

She let herself melt for a long moment, then pulled away from his warmth but didn't step out of the embrace. "How am I going to do my job if I've been forgetting things?"

"Are you forgetting case-related things?"

"Don't know yet. That's why I have a team and triple backups."

"There you go then."

"How can I work and grieve?"

"I don't know." He bent to kiss her, and she tilted her face up to accept the gentle kiss. They fit perfectly. She groaned and let herself melt into his touch again, into his comfort, for another moment. After a moment of heat, he pulled away, his rich brown eyes full of care for her.

"Thank you. You're right. Hug and kisses help."

"You have me. You have your team." He reached out and brushed her cheek. "You could go anyway. You don't have to stay. Nothing is holding you here anymore."

"Leave?!" Despite the warm of his touch, she sucked in a breath and jerked back, even though she'd been having the same thoughts, his words like cold water splashed into her face. "But the storm…"

"I know. You could take your time, travel slow boat and be home in time to help handle the arrangements, the funeral."

"Funeral rites. Oh, Mom wanted a wake." That information popped in suddenly.

"There you go. Arrange her wake. Lots of party planning in those." He smiled gently.

"The girls have it in hand." Janey shook her head. "Teresa and her friends. Average age seventy-two. Girls—that's what they call themselves. The Cherry Girls. My aunties. Titis, I call them." She waved helplessly, talking just to talk, to push the panic away. "All the cherry trees in the area."

"I know." His tone, tender and soothing, calming her heart. "*Carina*, I met them, remember? I loved all the fruit trees in your neighborhood." He caressed her arm, gave her a long adoring look, and then went into the bathroom. The water ran for moment. When he returned, the smudges were gone from his cheeks. "Have you decided what you want to do?"

"Here. I'd be at loose ends down at Mom's." She strapped on her wrist comm and gathered her vacuum flask. She didn't remember putting it on the table. "At least here I'm needed. I'm useful, and I'll be at the wake and for the funeral rites. Need to find out when those are."

Janey waved in a message to Teresa about when the funeral rites and wake were and what she needed to do about her mother's estate. Probably not much really. A small company house Janey paid rent on and a few remaining medical payments. Fat lot of help the doctors had been, except for excellent pain management. Thankfully, Mom hadn't ever suffered from the pain. She'd just hated feeling weaker.

Her mom's things her friends would surely divvy up. All of Janey's worldly possessions she'd moved out of her childhood home many years ago when Mom had moved into the smaller place and Janey had gone to college at Granton San Francisco.

She couldn't think of anything of her mother's that she wanted. Her mother had given her the pearl choker she often wore. Janey touched her neck. She didn't have it on.

For a moment, panic flooded her chest, her breathing coming in too-short bursts. Mom had given her the choker as a high school graduation gift, packed with photos and holos of her childhood. Janey couldn't remember if she packed it in her go-bag. She would have if she'd been thinking straight.

She had her go-bag. There it was by Orlando's door. She pawed through it. Where was it?

"I can't find it."

"What?" He was at her side. He'd been putting the few clothes that had been folded on a chair away into the armoire.

"My choker. The one Mom gave me." A heaviness descended on her like the scraggly Organ Mountain range sitting on her.

He caressed her neck. "*Carina*, you have it on."

"What?" She felt under her protective garment and there it was. She blew out a shaky breath. "I can do this," she voiced to herself, to the Sol, and to the stars all around.

"One foot in front of the other," he added.

She zipped the bag closed. "I need to keep working." She gave the choker one last caress and tucked it under her protective garment once more. "It's weird that I haven't heard from Kim about Milano."

"Let's go check on the chief."

"I need to drop this off first." She picked up her go-bag, no lighter than it had been when she'd carried it to the jet two hours ago. Her quarters were just three doors down.

She could do this.

Had it really been two hours since she'd gotten that final call from Teresa?

Accompanied by Orlando, Janey headed out of his quarters, slipped into hers, and dropped off her bag but kept the vacuum flask. She was going to need its pick-me-up tea today.

They took the curve back to the security section, nameplates beside doors to mark the move from private quarters to the business of security for L'Étoile. On the way to her office, Janey commed Milano. Maybe he'd pick up her comm when he'd ignored everyone else's. It was so unlike him to not let anyone know what he was doing, where he was going. He didn't reply. She stopped outside his office next to hers and waved his security panel beside the door, but still, there was no reply. She tried again. Only silence.

"Milano's one of the most reliable men I know. Never missed a day of work since I've been here," Janey said. "Except...after the last case. But then he let us know he was leaving."

"He could be finally taking more time off to grieve." Orlando lifted an eyebrow to her, his nudge about her work ethic clear.

"Maybe, but he would have let us know." Janey overrode the security on Milano's door. At least, she attempted to. Her bio signals with her security clearance should have done the trick, but the door didn't open.

"I imagine he wouldn't like that," Orlando said mildly.

"I imagine not." Maybe it was some communication delay. Janey waited for a beat, and still, the door didn't open. "Weird. I'll need to get Kim on this. Must be some bigger malfunction than normal if my security clearance can't override it."

"Perhaps, or maybe he really doesn't want to be interrupted," Orlando said. "Let me try."

Janey moved out of the way so he could work on the security panel. After a minute, he moved back. "I can't bypass the lock."

"Now I know something's really wrong if a master thief can't even get in."

Orlando made a face at her. He wasn't used to not being able to get in wherever he wanted.

Janey commed Kim.

"Iona here," Kim said.

"Kim, have you located Milano?"

"Yes, he's here with me." Relief was strong in her voice

and hint of something else, panic, maybe. It took a lot for Kim to lose her cool.

"On my way." Janey commed off and headed to the next door down the corridor, Orlando keeping stride with her. No sense asking questions when she could go see for herself.

The security office door swished open upon her approach.

Milano sat in a chair beside Kim, his head in his hands. He didn't glance at Janey's approach.

Kim stepped around her workstation and whispered, "He ignored your comms just now." She glanced over her shoulder at Milano, concerned, and then back at Janey, her voice low. "He's in a bad way. Been sitting here for a few minutes. June found him in the private sauna. He won't speak to me. Won't speak to anyone and won't go to medical either."

"I don't think he's visited medical since—" Janey broke off.

"His wife's death there." Kim shook her head. Her customary hibiscus was tucked into her bun, its bright pink matching her lipstick and colorful blouse.

"I'll see what I can do," Janey said.

"I've been business as usual, hoping he'll come out of it," Kim said. "He doesn't seem to care that all the security staff see him like this." She waved to the bullpen behind the small lobby where the handful of agents worked at their consoles—those that weren't at their duty posts throughout the hotel-casino.

"I could offer some of my expensive stash," Orlando said. "Like last time."

Kim frowned. "He won't respond to my offers for anything to eat or drink."

Janey stepped closer to Kim. "Why didn't you call me the second June found him?"

"You have your hands full."

"Still. In fact, I'm going to call someone from medical—"

"Don't you dare," Milano said, his voice booming. He rose and strode toward her, a blue Turkish coat normally pristine and buttoned, undone, revealing a stained and wrinkled cream shirt as if he'd slept in his clothes. "You're Acting Chief McCallister again—if you're up to it, that is." He glared at her, grief weighing heavy in his gaze, skin pale and drawn. "I am sorry to hear about your mother."

Janey glanced at Orlando and then at Chief Milano. "My mother?" What did he know?

"Yes, I know you were on your way to see her, and then you got called onto a case. I—I just couldn't... If you want to see her, you can go if you want and assign another to the case. I don't care. You're in charge. Do what you want."

"I'd rather work the case, sir. Besides"—Janey lifted her chin—"my mother passed away this morning... at the same time... just as Prentice paged me. And there's a storm Earth-side. I can't get there anytime soon..." And Kim couldn't find you.

Was it this case that triggered Milano's breakdown or had he already been sliding downhill? The state of his clothes suggested he was already falling over into the deep end sometime last night. And he hadn't asked for help.

As if the wind had toppled him, he staggered back into the chair and stared at the floor. "I didn't know..."

Janey set her vacuum flask in front of him with a strong clack, triggering the heating mechanism. In thirty seconds, the potent tea would be hot. "Drink, sir. That's an order."

He lifted his head, his eyes bloodshot. "You're taking the promotion?"

"Temporarily. Until I close the case. Then—" She shrugged. She didn't need to pile on the fact that she might quit at the end of this case.

"May I suggest a massage, sir?" Orlando said. "It does wonders."

"And drink the tea, Milano," Janey said again. "Orders."

Milano stared at the vacuum flask for a second, then drank up. He peered up at Janey, surprised, his cheeks ruddy again, his eyes a little more alert, not so inner focused. "What is in this concoction?"

"My own special recipe," Janey said. "Feeling better?"

Milano stood, hand on Kim's desk for support. "McCallister, you need to talk to Schoeneman about the case and the possible lockdown. I haven't called him, but if Doc declares this a homicide..."

"I'm on it, Chief," Janey said and sighed inwardly. The worst part of being acting chief was running interference with the big boss. He was a handful, from what she'd seen and from what Milano had said about him—blowing hot, then cold, throwing his weight around with his sometimes-outlandish demands. Mercurial, powerful, he seemed to get what he wanted on charisma and by throwing his billions upon billions of credits around. Plus, he had what everyone wanted: precious metals from the asteroid belt.

Orlando wrapped an arm across Milano's shoulder. "I hear Sabrina is the best, down at the spa." He glanced at Janey. "I'll take him down there and make sure he gets settled."

"Sabrina?" Janey asked, lifting her eyebrows.

"She's a good masseuse," Orlando said.

Janey frowned.

"What?" Orlando said, helping Milano toward the door. "Jealous?"

Of course, she wasn't jealous. She'd gotten over the way he flirted with everyone—a few weeks ago, maybe a month.

"Meet me back in my office or in the—"

"—conference room. I know," he finished.

He'd been hers solidly for six months, and still, she was

jealous of any attention he gave another woman? That was dumb, irrational. But today was not a day for rational thinking, apparently.

Milano shook off Orlando's arm. "I can walk, young man. Go work the case with McCallister or your own. It's not my business anymore." He turned to Janey. "Tell Schoeneman."

"About the case, of course." She could do her job.

"No, I mean tell him that I'm finally taking that generous retirement package he offered me. And thank you. And that you're acting chief for the time being. Don't let him jerk you around." He headed for the door and then stopped, turning to her again. "Tell the troops thank you from me, good job, and all that."

"Will do, sir. When will you be leaving?"

"I don't know." He shook his head sadly. "I can barely decide what to do next."

"Take your time, sir. Grief obeys no master."

"Wise words from one so young."

"My mother had been dying for four years, sir. Everyone grieves differently." Her life had been marked by grief—first losing her eye as a teen, then her best friend five years ago. Then her mother falling ill.

He pursed his lips at her. "Not *sir* anymore, McCallister." With that, he turned toward the door and exited the security office with slow, plodding steps—the office he'd been overseeing for a decade. The only chief of security the hotel had ever known.

Orlando followed him and said pleasantly, "I'll accompany you if you don't mind. Then I'll work on my case. I have a hot lead."

"I do mind, but you do what you want. Sabrina is the best." Milano grumbled that last bit.

After that, they fell silent as they moved out of earshot.

Several security agents—June Acosta, Natalia Goldberg,

Miguel Liberosa, and Antonia Lane—stood around the front desk area whispering.

From the group, Antonia Lane spoke up. "What's going on with Chief? He wouldn't speak to us, acknowledge us? Is he sick? What can we do?" At five foot nine and a former championship college basketball player, Antonia carried her confidence and care for the team like a second skin. She'd been doing great in the investigative training and was due to take her investigator's exam next week.

Janey took a deep breath and stood taller. She could do this. Again. Second time in the last three months she was appointed acting chief. And second time her team shifted around to take up the slack.

"Antonia, I'm pulling you from casino duty." Janey nodded at the experienced security agent and took the time to make eye contact with the rest of the agents gathered around. "You're acting lead investigator. Just probationary. Until you pass your exam."

FIVE

"YES!" ANTONIA PUMPED A FIST IN THE AIR, THEN quickly subdued at Janey's serious gaze.

"I will be taking an active role, too. This case is strange." She needed to stay involved. Sitting behind a desk filing reports didn't suit her as it had Milano.

"Of course." Antonia held her gaze, no doubt wanting to convey her seriousness, her readiness. She pulled her shoulders back, a feral gleam in her eye, hungry for the hunt. "Whatever you need, Chief."

Janey turned to the rest of the team in the office. "Everyone else is on their regular shifts but may get pulled for extra work as the case progresses. Understood?"

June nodded, frowning. She liked her steady guard work at the spa and didn't like investigative work much. Natalia grinned. Built like a wrestler and from Brooklyn, New York, she was up for any challenge and had excelled at the investigative training—as had Antonia and Meilani. She knew she could rely on Clark and Jintao too, who were on their breaks now that the crime scene was secured.

"You can count on me, on all of us." Antonia peered at

each one in their huddle, waiting for and getting their nods, stepping into her leadership position like the natural she was. "What do you need?"

No one else said anything, but they shifted as if taking up more space. Things were changing around here.

Good question. "As Antonia shifts into her new role, I'll still set up the duty rosters, read reports, and pass them on to Schoeneman." They didn't need to know all the details. She was filling the space, paddling madly for some steady waters. "Antonia, you'll stay in the bullpen. No moving offices right now. Get up to speed on the Hampton Nel case. Work with Prentice and Stinson. Get me a list of possible suspects within the hour."

"Yes, sir." Antonia nodded and caught the eye of the others, eagerness in her gaze and strong posture like a champion racehorse at the starting gate. She'd done a fine job taking the lead on a theft case last month and could handle the lead investigator role well. Though how would she handle the stress of a murder case? Janey guessed just fine. Antonia thrived under pressure. She'd led her basketball team to the championships one year as lead scorer. She was familiar with high-pressure, high-scrutiny, and high stakes.

Something chimed. It was June's comm. She was due on shift at the spa. June stepped away to take it. Then Janey's comm dinged. It was Schoeneman. Word traveled fast.

"I'll be in my office if anyone needs me," Janey said.

"You're not going to take Milano's office?" Antonia asked.

"No, it's locked." She forgot to ask the chief about that, but she didn't want to trouble him with that line of questioning, not in his current state. Janey turned to Kim. "Can you look into it?"

"Of course."

Janey's comm dinged again.

"You going to take that?" Kim asked.

"In my office."

Across the hall, Janey unlocked her small office with an eye scan and let herself in. She sat behind her desk and stared at the faux hardwood surface. Then she took a deep breath and answered the comm.

"McCallister, here."

"McCallister, what's this I hear about another death on my station?" His voice boomed as if he were in a conference hall, resonant and grandiose.

"Didn't Milano notify you?" That slipped out before she remembered that Milano hadn't contacted Schoeneman about anything since the day before.

"No, that's what I don't like." Schoeneman's voice rose in volume and pitch, angry, at the edge of belligerent. Her temples pounded. Janey held her arm away from her, so the comm sound would soften. Didn't do much good. Schoeneman's volume increased, now with a kind of feral growl he probably used to scare his partners and investors. "Where is he? Why haven't I heard from him? Do I need to jet in and manage things myself?"

Janey had never heard Frederick Schoeneman so angry.

"No, sir, Milano made me acting chief. He's going through... He's grieving in his own way." Janey huffed out a breath and found her spine. "He accepts your generous retirement package, says thank you, and that I'm in charge for the time being."

Schoeneman growled unintelligible words.

"Sir?"

"I do not like the way things are being handled," he said. "I just got a call from one of the guests that her husband is dead. I do not need this right now. I never need this kind of news."

"Where? When?" The astrophysicist wasn't married as far

BETH BARANY

as his records stated. So there had to be a second death onboard.

Venus hells.

She sent the news to Antonia. The new lead acknowledged, asked for details. Janey didn't have any...yet.

"Put me on vid, McCallister, so I can see your face when I tell you how horribly you're doing your job."

The man jumped to mean fast like a tornado of dust devils barreling through the southwestern desert. Like the one preventing her from going home.

She didn't need this. Anger propelled her out of her chair. She stomped to the wallscreen murder board, cleared it of the rings of Saturn images she preferred when the wall wasn't in use, and opened a square for the vid channel.

Schoeneman's face filled the screen as if he was too close to the lens. He narrowed his eyes, making his normally classically handsome features—Roman nose, high cheekbones, strong jaw—look pinched, mean, and predatory. As if he was a hawk about to swoop down on an unsuspecting prairie dog. "Horrible, just horrible. If you can't do your job—"

"Mr. Schoeneman, sir. I—" Janey started, her face heating with anger.

"Now, you listen to me—"

Jupiter's balls. Of all the days... She huffed out a breath. "No, you listen to me. I don't need this job anymore. I can easily walk away. But you can't treat me like that, whether or not I work for you."

"I'll treat you however I like." His arrogant tone had her standing straighter, spreading her feet wider to steady herself, fingers itching for action. If she had to take him on...

"In that case—" Heat flushed her face, Janey reached to turn off the vid but stopped short. "You have no acting chief and no one to lead the team. And two deaths aboard."

"Two?" he asked, his voice suddenly soft. He glanced over

his shoulder worried as if at someone nearby. As if he didn't want anyone to hear.

Janey dropped her hand. He sounded genuinely confused and a little bit scared. What was going on with him?

"Yes, two." She crossed her arms and sent a thought message to Rhea to search for any news of Schoeneman in the media. A random thought, but any information on her boss could be useful in understanding how to work with this versatile and powerful personality, in her face, overtaking her work life.

Schoeneman shook his head and frowned, his voice softer. No facial micromovements to reveal a lie beneath his subdued gaze. It seemed like he was speaking the truth. "I am sorry for my outburst. It's just that...to receive a call from a guest and not from Milano..."

"I can understand how that could be upsetting," Janey said through gritted teeth.

"Fill me in. Please." His tone was respectful.

"Not much to tell," Janey said. "We got the call at 7 a.m. A Mr. Nel was found dead by the kitchen staff bringing him breakfast. She's been cleared. He was in perfect health. So far, it's only ruled a suspicious death by the ME. We may have to shut down station traffic if it turns out to be murder. I'll know soon." She'd better know soon. And now this second reported death.

"No, I'd rather that not happen," Schoeneman said, prim.

How could he be so naïve? He knew the protocol.

"Now two reported deaths, the first a suspicious death. If even one of them is ruled a homicide..."

Schoeneman wrinkled his nose as if he smelled some bad cheese. "Lisa said, 'suspicious death' and that Leo had been in perfect health, too."

"Their full names? Suite number?"

"Lisa and Leo Montaigne." He frowned, shook his head as

if sad over the loss of a friend. "Don't know their suite number."

"I'll get that from Housekeeping. What time did you get the call?" With discrete gestures outside of Schoeneman's view so he wouldn't see her multitasking, Janey waved into her wrist communicator with hand signs the details to Antonia and Kim and ordered Antonia to the scene to take statements and secure the premises.

She added: High-roller guest. Friend of owner. Treat with kid gloves until we know more.

"I just got the call," Schoeneman barked. "Right before I called you. Don't ask me, McCallister. You're acting chief now. Assign an investigator to the case."

"I have done. But, sir, I need details to do—"

"McCallister," Schoeneman interrupted her.

"Yes?"

"Delegate."

"I'm the most experienced investigator on board, I will not sit behind a desk. Not my style. Plus, Lane still needs more training. The others do, too."

"I really don't want to come to L'Étoile." Schoeneman frowned. "I just arrived on Luna Station for a board meeting, and I'm heading to the Near Asteroid Five station in the morning."

"I'll wrap up this case as quickly as I can."

"I want a report every hour."

Janey blew out a breath through a tight jaw. This administrative babysitting is what Milano did to manage Schoeneman. Now *she* had to. "I'll do my best, sir."

"Get that crackerjack hottie—"

Janey frowned at him.

"I mean Ms. Iona to file the reports. I wouldn't mind hearing from her. Tell her to file them via vid."

"She'll do what's most effective and efficient, sir. We have all the regular duty shifts to manage."

"Pull in that Orlando fellow. He's sweet on you. He'll do what you say. Besides, his case has stalled out." Schoeneman grinned as a feral cat did over its prey—all teeth, pleased at himself.

What did Schoeneman know about Orlando's progress on his top-secret Sol case? Orlando wouldn't even share details about it with her.

"I'll talk to him," Janey said as politely as she could.

"I'm counting on you to wrap up these two cases and rule them natural causes. I don't want my station shut down again. Enough of that. Murderers don't come to L'Étoile. People come to play, celebrate, and luxuriate. It's the Jewel of the Sky."

Schoeneman was spouting his own propaganda.

"I'll do my job, sir."

Schoeneman glared at someone off-camera, lifted an imperious finger as if he was telling someone to wait, then glanced back at her. "See that you do, Acting Chief McCallister." He closed the vid.

No pressure.

SIX

IT WAS TOO SOON TO CHECK IN ON ANTONIA. THE acting lead investigator didn't need her boss breathing down her neck. But had Janey prepared her well enough on how to handle a murder case? They'd already covered different scenarios in the recent trainings, and Antonia had done well in the mock investigations, diving into handling the outrageous scenarios Janey and Kim had created for the staff. Antonia had a cool head under pressure. The woman could handle it.

She turned her attention to the next step: Contact Doc. A knock sounded at her office door. The call would have to wait. Doc would let her know as soon as she made a determination on Nel's manner and cause of death.

"Open door," she commanded.

The door slid open, and in stepped Prentice, looking fresh, eager, and practically dancing from foot to foot as if she had some secret delight to share. "What can I do? Would you like some coffee and pastries?" She gestured with a tray in hand—a platter of all her favorite pastries and two cups of steaming coffee—perched at shoulder level like a Parisian waiter. All Prentice lacked was a bleached white apron and the classic imperious gaze of the centuries-old profession.

"Just coffee, thanks." Janey snagged a mug from the tray Prentice glided onto the desk. She inhaled and sipped, the familiar pungent aroma wrapping around her like her mother's comforter. A sigh escaped before she could stop it, the sadness bubbling to the surface.

Prentice rushed to the board. "May I?"

"May you what? Spit it out, Prentice."

That probably came out harsher than she intended because for a moment Prentice froze and blinked. But then the probie waved her hands describing gestures, her puppy-dog enthusiasm back in place.

"Start the murder board. I always loved this part of the investigation."

Janey sipped. "Seems to me you love all the parts."

"I do, Acting Chief."

"So, you heard."

"I did. When I got back to the bullpen."

"Has Lane started a timeline?" Janey asked.

"I don't know. I'll check." Prentice frowned a little pout and waved on the wallscreen. "No, she hasn't started one."

Antonia was probably up to her eyeballs in all the things.

Janey sipped some more. A star system swirled on one of the wallscreens in her small office—a nebula in the Triangulum system. Nebulas were nurseries of new stars. Maybe she should create a new start for herself. "Get her permission to start one and tag her in."

Prentice nodded and spoke her request into her comm. In less than a minute, Antonia replied with a "go for it." Prentice grinned, said thanks, and waved gestures in rapid succession over the wallscreen. She drew a horizontal timeline and then dictated, speech boxes taking her dictation.

"At 7:02 a.m., Ms. Mai Chen reports to security the mysterious death of Mr. Hampton Nel. At 7:09 a.m., Kim Iona sends Probationary Investigator Anahi Prentice to retrieve Investigator Janey McCallister from Hangar One. First walk-through of scene. At 7:15 a.m., initial walk-through and cursory examination of the victim, Mr. Nel Hampton, with then Lead Investigator Janey McCallister with Science Lab Technician Level Five Soren Stinson. At 7:40 am, the coroner, Doctor Wellesley Running Feather, arrives to pronounce and take body of the deceased to her morgue. Death speculated as suspicious as the victim was in good health and had no known health issues."

Prentice stepped back, tapping her chin. She glanced at Janey as if waiting for her approval.

"We still don't know if this was a suspicious death, let alone a homicide," Janey said. "And we have a second case."

"We do? I didn't hear the call come in."

Janey squinted at her. "How would you have heard it? The call went directly to Schoeneman who just called me."

Prentice stared at the board, her back to Janey, and said nothing.

"Anahi."

The young woman made a distracted noise and still didn't turn around.

Janey studied the young probie. The young woman acted like Janey wasn't there and peered at the thinly populated murder board as if it were the most fascinating thing in all the Sol.

"Anahi, how can you hear a call before anyone?" Janey repeated.

Prentice said nothing.

"Anahi, look at me. Do you have a scooper?"

"A what?" Prentice turned to her, her eyes wide as if in confusion or pretend innocence.

"I read your file and didn't see anything about enhancements, but I know they're easy to hide from the tests." With her ocular implant, Janey ran an all-frequencies scan. Her implant was able to scan from the visible and invisible light spectrum for any irregularities. Janey picked something up at the radio band—a frequency she didn't check often as not many communications happened on there anymore. Barely a wiggle, blips really, showed up like faint dots at the edge of the horizon.

"I see," Janey said softly.

Prentice held her gaze, didn't blink once. Then she looked away, sighed, deflated. "All these years and no one seemed to notice or care."

"Or pretend to not notice or care. Because it served them. I know you came up from the rough area in the Amazonia territory running errands for the mob."

"They liked me because I always evaded the sweeps. They never asked how." Prentice jiggled on her toes and stared at the wallscreen on the other side of Janey's office that revealed real-time unfiltered sunlight bouncing on the exterior of the hotel-casino space station.

The piped-in view helped ground her, remind her what she was about, where she was in the vast universe of it all. Just one person doing her job as best she knew how. Same as Anahi.

"Lo-fi sensors when you were twelve," Janey stated.

"Eleven and a half. I matured early," Prentice said without glancing at her. "Jumped at the chance."

Many teens went in for enhancements because it was fashionable—or necessary like it had been for Janey. Janey had had her challenges as a child, but at least she'd had a mother who doted on her. Anahi had had only the Jesuit orphanage. And here the young woman was, all bouncy and eager to learn. And eager to survive. Of course, she would hide her enhancement from everyone.

"You needed to? For safety?"

Prentice nodded.

"What else?"

"The whole radio bandwidth. I catch all transmissions." She spun toward Janey, her expression sober.

"How do you filter through all that?"

Prentice blinked, surprised. "You're not mad?"

"I have too much to deal with right now to be mad, but when this case is over—"

"Yes?" Prentice asked, worry warring with excitement in her gaze and in her whole body, the way she wiggled like a not-quite-full-grown dog.

"I may need to put a note in your permanent record."

"Oh." Prentice stilled. "Do you have to? I could be quite useful…"

Janey considered her for a moment. "As acting chief, that's part of my duty, but—"

"But what?" Prentice shifted from foot to foot, raced over to the tray for a pastry, and stuffed it in her mouth, washing it down with a big gulp of coffee.

"Prentice, stop for a second." Janey scrubbed her face. "Let's focus on the case."

"Yes, I know. The case is all." She grinned. "Does that mean I'm off the hook for my? …" She waved at the back of her head.

"We'll talk about it later. It means that we focus on the case."

"The case is all," Prentice said again. "Okay, good. Yes."

Janey hid a smile at the probie's enthusiasm. Hard to believe she was ever that young and quivering with excitement. Maybe not over cases, but certainly in her early days of teaching science to students not much younger than Prentice.

"What's next? And what about the other death?" Prentice asked.

"Good questions, all. We need to confirm the cause of death with Doc and check out this second scene with Lane and medical." Janey considered Prentice for a moment, then decided. "Let's go pay a visit to Mrs. Lisa Montaigne. Get the suite number."

"Yes, sir." Prentice waved into the Housekeeping roster on the walls screen. "Ah, Suite 806. There are Antonia's notes. Yup, she's on scene, pulling in the room's data, recording an initial interview. There're no silly names for the suites on this floor. I didn't realize there was another floor above the seventh. That wasn't on the floor plan."

"Many parts of the station aren't." Janey rubbed her temples. Anahi sure chattered a lot.

"But wouldn't the guests get lost?"

"It's on a need-to-know basis, the more exclusive you get. Guests like it. Part of the mystery, intrigue, and the shininess of the station."

Prentice looked confused for a moment, then smiled. "I can see the appeal. Jewel of the Sky, I get it."

"Let's go," Janey said. "Coordinate with Lane and get me Nel's movements and anyone he's encountered prior to his death. Lane's lead investigator."

"I heard. Makes sense. She's a good leader," Prentice said and set to waving into her holo, repeating Janey's orders.

"Also see if anyone had it in for him."

Prentice set up the parameters, then followed Janey out of the office, down the corridor, toward the elevators.

"Wait," Janey said, scanning Prentice's black uniform from head to toe and up again.

"What?"

"You're not dressed for this interview."

"What does it matter?"

"It matters. We need to blend in when we go to the front of the house."

Prentice fidgeted, pulling at her plain black collar. "I read that in the manual, but it was short on specifics."

"Do you have something... understated chic?" Janey asked. "Maybe in jewel green to set off your hair and eyes?

"I think so. At least I saw one programmed in the clothes-maker." Prentice froze, a look of alarm in her eyes—the first time Janey had seen that look on her since she met the young woman.

"You'll be fine," Janey said. "I'll meet you back here in ten minutes."

"Can you make it twenty, sir?" Prentice chewed her lip.

"Sure," Janey said and hustled to her quarters. She stood in the middle of the room, fuzzy-headed for a moment. She had her civilian clothes on, made more for comfort than chic. She switched into a jewel blue pantsuit with her favorite drapey matching jacket with hidden pockets, keeping on her protective undergarment and weapons.

Her comm vibrated against her wrist. It was Doc.

"What do you got, Doc?"

Doc sighed. "Not good. You need to come down here right away."

"On my way." About to exit her quarters, Janey commed off and pinged Prentice and Antonia. "Meet me at the lab."

"I'll be right down, but what about Mrs. Montaigne?" Prentice replied.

Antonia sent back the short message:

On the Nel and Montaigne scenes. Need time here. I'd like to stay. Sending for Soren since Doc's busy.

Janey replied with: That's fine. Good call.

To Prentice, she said, "Lane's handling that," and commed off.

They had their hands full.

SEVEN

Prentice met Janey at the entrance to Soren's lab. As they approached Soren's work area, he glanced up and waved them in, his eyes all bug-eyed from the equipment he was wearing. His 4-D glasses were tricked out from additional tech, wires, and membrane tacked on at odd, but no doubt useful, angles.

Janey waved back to him and led Prentice toward Doc's sanctum.

"I'm heading to the scene," Soren called after her. "Antonia requested."

"Thanks!" Janey said over her shoulder and kept going toward Doc's cleanroom and autopsy suite. They could only be accessed by passing through an aisle of shelves full of equipment, specimen storage, and half-made gadgets. Soren's stuff. Why Doc didn't have her own entrance, she had no idea.

Beside double swinging doors, Janey said, "We need to suit up."

"Why?" Prentice asked.

"Possible contaminants." Janey waved to the red light on above the door, and her gut clenched.

She led Prentice into the small locker room. As Janey stripped down to her skivvies, she commed Kim.

"Janey, how are you? What do you need?" Kim replied.

"Good as can be expected. Hey, will you check to make sure the environmental controls are working properly?

"Of course, Janey. What's up? Did you get a report from someone? I should have been notified, too."

"No, no report, just a hunch. Might be related to the case. Not sure."

"Will do," Kim said.

"Thanks." Janey commed off and suited up in a white skin-tight suit with a hood and face covering that circulated air and all one needed to survive in a cleanroom. She led Prentice, dressed similarly, into Doc's autopsy suite.

In her full clean suit, including mask, Doc nodded to Janey and said, "Your new apprentice?"

"Yes, Anahi Prentice, this is Doctor Wellesley Running Feather. Doc, meet Probationary Agent—"

"Yes," Doc interrupted. "Let's get to it." She waved to the body and pointed to the man's mouth. "See that slight discoloration around his lips?"

"No," Janey said.

"Zoom in," Doc said. "Use what you have, McCallister."

Janey snapped her gaze to Doc. "I haven't heard you so on edge before. What is it?"

"Start by looking closely," Doc replied, her voice tight.

Prentice stepped closer to the body and leaned over. "I don't see anything."

"That's because it's so faint as to be missed by most people." Doc peered at Prentice. "But I'm not most people."

"No, you're not," Janey said and blinked to zoom in with her ocular implant. "I'm at high res and it looks like a sort of bruise puckering the lips slightly. And there's something attached."

Doc opened Nel's mouth.

"A sort of film covering his mouth." Janey sucked in a breath. "A fine membrane." She eyed Doc. "Is this COD?" Cause of death.

"Yes. He suffocated to death—quickly enough to not realize it until the very last moment, yet slowly enough to be quite uncomfortable," Doc said. "I'll have Soren analyze the membrane. I wanted you to see it in context first."

Janey swore. "Not natural causes."

"In my thirty years in the profession," Doc said, "I've never seen anything like this. Nothing natural about it."

"Venus hells."

Her comm hummed against her wrist. She'd put it in silent mode and shunted all messages to her ocular implant screen. It was a message from Antonia asking for Prentice to help with the bag-and-tag since Soren was doing the initial body exam. Janey thought-commanded a yes, and soon. And document whatever you can.

"Yes, indeed, I'm ruling the manner of death a homicide," Doc said.

"I'm locking down the station," Janey said grimly and waved in the Code Red message. Kim would inform the rest of the security team, the hangar chief, and other department heads. And Schoeneman. He would not be happy. Such an understatement. She'd deal with him at her next check-in—which was two minutes overdue. She let out a small sigh, the weight of responsibility heavy on her shoulders.

"Who? How?" Prentice asked.

"That's your job to determine, Probationary Agent," Doc said.

"Right," Prentice said, her voice subdued.

"What else, Doc?" Janey asked. "Why are we in contamination suits?" She caught Prentice's worried gaze.

Doc pointed to Nel's open chest, at his lungs. "Green particulates on the outside of his lungs."

"The outside of his lungs! Not the inside? That's odd. What is it?" Janey asked.

"Don't know. Soren was analyzing it," Doc said. "Nothing on the inside of his lungs that shouldn't be there."

"Isn't that impossible?" Prentice asked.

"Nothing's impossible in my line of work," Doc said.

"But we didn't pick up anything in our sweep of the room," Janey said. "At least nothing that was signaled as dangerous."

"I'm not taking any chances," Doc said.

"So, asphyxiation was COD?" Prentice asked.

"Yes."

"Very evil and smart. Unless it was some kind of accident," Prentice said.

"Possible, but I doubt it. Identify, observe, and gather evidence," Janey said, one of her instructor's favorite mantras on the scientific method popping up. She glanced at Doc. "Thanks. We have another body on its way."

Hopefully, just a coincidence. Her gut clenched. Yah, probably not.

"Oh dear." Doc shook her head. "I had a feeling my vacation was over. Take care in the decontamination process. Set your suits aside for Soren to evaluate."

"We will," Janey said.

"Nice to meet you, Doctor Wellesley Running Feather," Prentice said.

"You can call me Doc, Prentice," Doc said.

"Doc." Prentice nodded and left for the locker room.

Janey followed but turned back to Doc when a thought

occurred to her. "Have you tested the air in this room recently?"

"No, but I imagine you can."

"Of course. I'm just wondering if what caused Nel's death is airborne. Is it random or targeted? Why is there a second death? Are they related?"

"Good questions, McCallister. Go find out," Doc said.

Janey nodded and reached the door to the locker room.

"I'm sorry to hear about your mother, Janey," Doc said softly, gruffly. "I didn't say that earlier. Should have."

"Thanks, Doc." Janey made for the decontamination chamber to strip, take a quick sonic shower, and dress.

Janey was exiting the locker room with Prentice when Orlando commed.

"Hey."

"Where are you?" Orlando asked.

"We're in the lab. About to check in with Soren." She headed to his work area. He wasn't there. That's right. He was on scene as an assistant coroner.

On Soren's desk, beside his four-dee-glasses, was a handwritten note with her name on it. That was sweet. Most people didn't leave paper notes. It said: No answers yet. Never seen anything like it.

"Scratch that. Soren doesn't have anything for us yet. We're heading to Suite 806," Janey said. "We caught a second case. Mysterious death."

"I'll meet you there."

"Dressed for it?"

"Always," Orlando said with a purr to his voice.

Prentice glanced away, but not before Janey caught her smile.

Janey swiveled, her back to Prentice for privacy. "I mean it, Orlando. These are guests. On second thought, I don't want you there. She might feel ganged up on if she has more people there. Especially after Antonia has already been there, too."

"Okay. Where do you want me then? You need all hands. I heard about the station lockdown order. Homicide, I gather."

"Unfortunately. You're helping me? Is Milano settled? And I thought you had a hot lead."

"I got what I needed...for now. And Milano is in the capable hands of Derik working his back and Cecily his feet. He's out like a kitten."

"Good. He needs a break. Fill me in on your case."

"Now?"

"Yes, as Prentice and I head up to the front of the house. I'm acting chief now, I need to know what all my security staff are doing, even ones on loan and working their own cases." And sleeping in her bed.

She'd kept out of his case until now, but things had to change for the foreseeable future.

Orlando blew out a breath. "I'd rather compile my thoughts and present them to you in a quiet environment. If you don't mind—boss, Acting Chief."

"Okay, then. My office, one hour."

"Yes, ma'am," Orlando said with a smile in his voice and commed off.

Eight and a half minutes later, Janey was in front of Mrs. Lisa Montaigne, in her well-appointed ninth-floor suite. Mrs. Montaigne sipped from a glass of bubbly in the middle of the main dining room, surrounded by plush furniture and a low coffee table. Everyone grieved in their own way. She was an overly pretty blonde-haired woman with the indeterminate look of the extremely wealthy middle-age. A petite woman, she wore an off-the-shoulder classic black evening gown with a choker of rare pearls.

And she'd been crying. Her makeup was perfectly in place

except for a smudge of mascara under one eye. She shredded a tissue with manicured fingers.

At Janey's side, Prentice was for once not fidgeting, quiet and still.

"Please tell us what happened, Mrs. Montaigne," Janey said.

"As I told the other investigator"—Lisa dabbed her eyes— "I don't know what happened. I got out of my shower, dressed, and Leo was slumped over in bed, the day's financial news reports from headquarters across his lap. He liked them on hardcopy..." Lisa waved toward the bedroom, sniffed back tears, then rubbed the back of an empty chair in rose brocade. The chair sat in a semi-circle with other comfy chairs and a love seat of the same rich pattern. The kind of fabric that demanded you caress it for a hand massage, just as Lisa was doing. Probably for comfort.

Janey corralled her attention back to scanning the scene. The sitting area was situated so whoever lounged there had a prime view of the starscape. But at this hour, the window was shaded against the bright direct sunlight.

"Was he ill or did he have any medical conditions?"

"No, no. I told your young agent all that." Lisa turned away and dabbed her eyes, shoulders shaking with silent sobs. "They took the body already..."

"I'll need to see the bedroom."

Lisa shrugged in response and turned away from Janey to sip from her glass.

"I am so sorry, but we need to ask these questions. To help you, we need to examine what happened from multiple perspectives."

Janey had scanned Antonia's notes and images on the way here. Soren's, too. They'd gone down to Doc as they were coming up. In a silky-looking deep blue nightshirt, in death,

Leo was positioned as Lisa said—slumped in bed, pages strewn across his lap.

Lisa turned back to Janey, her face returned to a mask of haughty calm, hardly a smudge of her mascara. "I'm not sure what all your questions can do. They can't bring him back."

"No, they can't," Janey replied. Then after a moment, she said, "Tell me about the purpose of your visit to L'Étoile."

Lisa nodded as if to acknowledge that this was an acceptable question. "We usually come every year, but we had to skip last year due to a… well, that doesn't matter. We came to enjoy the latest show and to have business meetings as we always do. Leo's office set up tons of meetings, usually at the show…"

Lisa was still talking about the nightly show in the casino. Janey had blanked. How much had she missed? Her implant screen said eight seconds.

"We were going to brunch with the Hamachis," Lisa finished. "I need to cancel the reservation." She glanced away again, dabbing her eyes. "Or they can keep it. I don't care."

"We càn notify them. What time was the reservation for?"

"Now." Lisa sniffed.

Janey nodded to Prentice, who got the message and stepped away to call the Phoenix Restaurant and let the Hamachis know. Maybe she'd missed nothing Lisa Montaigne said. She'd check with Prentice later. Why hadn't Antonia handled the cancellation? Maybe Lisa hadn't said anything about it. "And what time did you call Mr. Schoeneman?"

Lisa waved her tissue dismissively. "I told the other woman. Why are all of you so tall?" She huffed. "Oh, what does it matter, Miss?"

"Chief McCallister, ma'am," Janey said. "Won't you sit down? Can I get housekeeping to deliver you something? Tea perhaps?"

"Yes, thank you. The Phoenix house black tea blend.

Simply the best. If we"—she choked—"can't have their brunch, at least I can have their tea. The room won't make it for us." Lisa teared up and dabbed her eyes.

The kitchen suite food crafter didn't have fancier items. Those were reserved for the Phoenix Restaurant as part of the deal of having the restaurant on the station.

Janey glanced at Prentice. The probie nodded again and moved away, down the hall, deeper into the hotel suite to put in the request for tea.

"Mr. Schoeneman wanted me to check in on you personally."

"That's kind of Frederick." Lisa sat on one of the brocade chairs, tore at the tissue, and dabbed her eyes.

"I'll get the report from my staff, I just wanted to hear it first-hand," Janey spoke softly and approached Lisa, perching at the edge of the chair. "You understand?"

"I don't, but I suppose you are just doing your job." She peered at Janey. "I want to leave, but the dockmaster said I can't. That we're temporarily unable to leave. He wouldn't say anything else."

"All the jets are off-station at this moment." One of the excuses they told guests when a lockdown was executed due to any grave problems on board like a murderer running around loose.

Lisa shrugged. "I'll request a jet from the Stantion head-quarters." Her husband's company. Janey had scanned the couple's hotel record on their way to the suite.

"I'm afraid no jets are allowed to dock at this time."

Odd that she would want to leave so soon and make no mention of her husband's body, funeral arrangements, or the like.

"Unacceptable." Lisa stood, her back rigid, her mouth pursed. "Frederick will hear about this."

"He already knows, and he's given me complete authority

in these matters, ma'am." Janey stood too, towering over the older woman.

Lisa Montaigne harrumphed and headed toward the depths of the suite, mumbling something about the indignity of relying on emergency pods like economy class guests.

"Ma'am, we're not done here. I need to hear what happened..." Janey raised her voice. "I'd like to look around."

"Knock yourself out." She waved a dainty hand over her shoulder and disappeared into a room—probably the woman's bedroom. "Lock the door when you leave, Acting Chief."

EIGHT

JANEY CONSIDERED STORMING AFTER HER TO ASK her harder questions like did her husband have any enemies, and who would want him dead, but she had no evidence that her husband's death was anything more than by natural causes — as medical indicated with they first arrived. Soren agreed, with the caveat that Doc would let the team know soon.

Janey glanced about the suite. Nothing was out of place, but she couldn't be too careful. She turned to Prentice. "Bag and tag any anomalies, the paper screens, and any other devices you find. Image the area before you do. And scan for prints."

"Understood."

"Also, do a sweep of the room for particulates, all frequencies and wavelengths. I'll do the same, and then we'll compare it with what Antonia gathered." Janey didn't have to run a third sweep, but she needed to feel useful, and she wanted to nose around.

"Yes, sir. Should I cancel the tea?"

"No, let housekeeping deliver. She probably needs it."

"We're treating this as a crime scene," Prentice said. "Is it?"

"We have no evidence of that." Yet. "But after the morning we've had, we can't be too careful."

Their sweep revealed nothing out of the ordinary and nothing popped. Even the small kitchen area was neat and clean, the food crafter clean and barely used.

Janey went down the hall to the bedroom where Mr. Montaigne died. It was a large room dominated by a king-sized bed, with dark blue silk slacks, a matching silk suit coat thrown on a chair, black polished shoes stowed under the chair, and a thick plush bathrobe crosswise on the clothes. A man's room. The silky blue embroidered bedspread had been turned down, presumably to remove the body. Janey scanned with her wrist comm and her ocular implant, but nothing of note showed at the particulate's scale.

On the larger scale, she took in half a dozen thin paper screens strewn across the bedspread. The thin screens appeared ordinary for a financier, full of tables, charts, and grids that hovered above the near-transparent surface as holograms. Leo could interact with them, manipulate them to run projections, she imagined.

From Switzerland and based in Zurich, Leo Montaigne was an investor who owned the company Stantion Capital, involved in the banking and finance sector. As far as she could make out, the sheets contained information about the financial markets, currency exchanges, and commodities like coffee, rice, wheat, and soy. Was their presence relevant to what happened? Her team would know more once they examined them.

She itched to snoop in Lori's bedroom—something was bothering her. In the hotel record for the couple, there was no mention of Lisa's job title. Lisa seemed too ambitious to not work, and something about the woman made her itchy, right between the shoulder blades, where it was hard to reach. Maybe she was the sort of wealthy businessman's wife who organized parties and supported charities. Or maybe she worked in her husband's firm. Her team could follow those threads. Yet here she was.

Janey went to the next bedroom and knocked on the door.

After a moment, Lisa answered, irritated, her eyes bleary, wearing a silky pink sparkly dressing gown. "Yes?"

"Are you visiting L'Étoile for work or pleasure?"

Lisa sniffed, closed her dressing gown around her trim petite frame, and slurred her words slightly. "A bit of both." She regarded Janey as if from a distance. Her pupils were enlarged, making her eyes appear almost black. Perhaps she'd taken a mood drug.

"Thank you," Janey said. "We'll follow up if we have any further questions."

To that, Lisa shut the door.

Back in the living room area, Janey watched Prentice wave into her comm, a crease in her forehead. Then Prentice glanced up, a little startled to see Janey. "Just filing the report with Antonia."

"Good," Janey said. "Let's go."

Back in her tiny office, Janey integrated her notes to the file Antonia started. Details were populating the murder board. Prentice worked beside her doing the same in companionable silence. Janey stepped back to examine the timelines for one murder and one suspicious death.

"Nothing odd from our readings of the room," Prentice mused. "And Soren notes at first review that Mr. Leo Montaigne seems to have died from natural causes. He and Antonia didn't report that same sugary smell that we noticed in Mr. Hampton Nel's suite. Where is Antonia, by the way?" Prentice asked. She spun as if Antonia was in the tiny office with them. She wiggled her shoulders and headed toward the door. "I wonder what Doc has found on Mr. Montaigne."

"She'll let us know when she finds something." Not *if*. "Where are you off to?"

"Maybe I can help Antonia. I just need to *do* something, you know?"

"I know." Janey waited, but Prentice didn't leave. She hid her smile and waited. Then it came, another question from Anahi. The young woman had an insatiable thirst for knowledge.

Prentice marched back to the board. "When did you put the station on lockdown? I didn't hear you issue that command."

"When we were with Doc. Via my holo, one-touch protocol. Outside the range of your scoopers, evidently."

Prentice nodded and added that detail to the timeline.

"The two deaths are a little over one hour apart, one level apart. What similarities do you see?"

"Both deaths occurred on the station." Prentice chewed on her lips and fiddled with her uniform collar. "Both happened in the morning. Both victims are middle-aged men, and both were supposedly in perfect health."

Janey lifted an eyebrow.

"Right," Prentice said. "What else? I'll see if they crossed paths, knew each other—here, on the home-world, or somewhere else." She glanced at her wrist comm, the holo image up. "Right. That's what Antonia is asking me to do."

"Good," Janey said. Antonia was up to speed. "See if they had any friends, colleagues, or acquaintances in common. Or enemies. Start with the station and then beyond. Concentric search pattern."

"Chief, yes, sir. That's what Antonia says, too." Prentice grinned and headed for the door.

Janey sat at her desk and stared at her tabletop comms,

then waved to open the large holo screen. The opaque screen shimmered to life, and Janey sighed. Antonia was stepping into the lead investigator role nicely, and Janey had to deal with the duties of her new position. She rolled her shoulders, not liking the constricting weight of that as if she was squeezing herself into an ill-fitting coat.

The door snicked open. "Are you going? ..." Worry laced Prentice's voice.

Janey glanced at the probie in the threshold. "Going where?"

Prentice waved about indicating the corridor and beyond and frowned as if she wasn't sure of something.

"You okay, Anahi?"

"Of course. I just want to know..."

"Me too," Janey said under her breath.

"Sir?"

The probie had wanted to shadow her, presumably to learn. Janey cleared her throat. "I'm checking in with Kim and the rest of the staff on other administrative details like staff rotations, coordinating with the other security departments, and tracking reports." She grimaced at the last duty— not her forte. A sigh slipped out. She'd done the job temporarily a few months ago. She'd be fine. "I'm acting chief, remember? I need to get up to speed on those duties. Again."

"Kim can handle it."

"Prentice, you're running the show now?" Janey said mildly, banking down the irritation.

"No, sir. It's just that...I like learning directly from you. Shadowing you. Tagging along, you know, the like."

"You're doing just fine."

"I know, it's just that there's so much to learn." Prentice left and headed across the corridor for the bullpen.

"Yup." Janey locked up her office and headed for the bullpen, too.

The learning never stopped in this job—a plus for keeping it.

She froze in the middle of the security office lobby. A pros and cons list for staying an investigator on L'Étoile flashed on her ocular implant screen, her personal assistant Rhea tracking her thoughts.

"Acting Chief." Antonia entered the security office, breezed past her to the bullpen, and sat at her workstation. "I'll have Montaigne and Nel's prelims for you shortly. The list of suspects as you asked."

"Thanks, Antonia. Good job," Janey said and aimed herself toward Kim—the reason she came into the busy security office.

Kim manned three comms and three wide displays, a look of concentration in her scrunched-up brow. She spotted Janey, nodded, and ended her conversations efficiently one after the other.

"You caught me in one of my octopus moments." Kim smiled wryly.

"Octopus?"

"Using all my channels almost simultaneously," Kim said. "What can I do for you, Acting Chief?"

"Janey is fine, Kim, please. I'm getting enough of that formality from everyone else."

Kim nodded. "You got it, sweetie."

Janey huffed out a breath.

Kim slipped around her monitors, handing her her vacuum flask. "You came here for this?"

Janey took it. Hadn't she left her vacuum flask in her quarters? "No, I came here to find out why I couldn't get into Milano's office. What have you found?"

"Well, remember that bug that was glitching the station when you first arrived last year?"

"Of course. It caused havoc to my implant and the comm systems."

"Well, it's back."

"How could it be back? I thought we solved it."

"We did. It's not back exactly, but its cousin."

"How? What's it affecting?"

"So far, it's only keeping us locked out of Milano's office. And I don't know where it's coming from."

"Could be something he installed," Janey said. "He could have planted it so we couldn't get access to his office."

"If so, I can't tell that yet. He's still in his massage. I didn't want to disturb him." Kim drummed her stylus on the desk. "Not sure what he's protecting as I have access to all his files from here. Was there something specific you needed from his office?"

"No. Just wondered why it was locked. Why now?"

"No coincidences, eh?"

"Right."

"What else, boss?" Kim grinned when Janey frowned.

"You mean, once I get past this awkward in-charge stage?"

"Again," Kim said.

"Again." She'd been acting chief for a few months during and after the last big case, when everything had crumbled horribly for Milano. "Will you check in with Milano after his salon treatment? And keep close tabs on him. I'm worried about him."

"Me, too. Will do." Kim's fingers flew over one of her several wall screens, flittering as nimble as a hummingbird.

"Are you sure nothing else is being affected by this tech bug?" Janey asked.

"Correct. Nothing else." Kim gave her a look like she wanted to know more but held back.

"What about environmental? You checked with the engineers?"

"The engineers are running a deep diagnostic right now," Kim said, "but their preliminary scans show that there is nothing and has been nothing unusual at all. No unusual chemicals that they could measure. They're sure—triple-checked."

"The biologic scrubbers have been cleaned recently?"

"Just last week." Kim moved closer to her, into a huddle. "The Redstone twins have both contacted me, irate about the lockdown."

"What are they telling guests?" The housekeeping twins, Peter and Paula Redstone, managed everything for the front of the house—housekeeping, front desk check-in, concierge—and were the main liaison with security for everything except kitchen. Kitchen had their own security staff.

Kim read from one of her monitors. "Paula is telling guests," Kim read, "'unexpected repairs on the hangars.' And that 'it would be unsafe to dock at this time. We'll be up and running as soon as possible. Hangars are off-limits to all but personnel for safety reasons.'"

"That's fine. Aren't they supposed to clear such statements with us first?"

"They copy from what I send. Procedure."

"So glad you're handling these communications."

"It's my job."

"And you do it well. The staff department heads have been briefed on the shutdown?"

"Of course, boss." Kim flashed a smile, having too much fun covering the standard admin details that she knew Janey tolerated. "I had security staff hand-delivering the message personally to all department heads. Just in case the comm system is glitchy there, too." Kim firmed her mouth.

"What is it?"

"Guess? Señora Chef Prima Donna. She's complaining that her staff can't come back with the fresh produce they left for." Chef Gina Gutiérrez owned and ran the Phoenix, the hotel-casino's premier six-star restaurant.

"They boarded the jet I was supposed to take to go home. Well, she'll just have to wait."

"If we don't close these cases soon..." Kim left that sentence hanging.

"I know. Boy, do I know. Schoeneman will have all our heads." She glanced over at the bullpen. It was sparsely populated. Her day staff were all at their posts, except for Prentice and Antonia. Some working when they should have been resting like Jintao and Clark. "But if he wants justice served, he needs to let us do our jobs. Which we are." She checked the time on her wrist comm. "Speaking of, I owe him my hourly report."

"It's late," Kim said, sympathy in her voice. "I heard rumors that the board was going to maybe pressure him out...cut him off..."

"Maybe that's what he was behaving so strangely with me," Janey said. "Wait, how did you hear that?"

Kim fiddled with the pink hibiscus in her dark hair, delaying.

Janey's comm vibrated. She flashed up the holo screen and checked the messages. "Venus hells."

"What?" Kim settled back behind her monitors.

"Doc said this second victim died the same way as the first. Nearly undetected asphyxiation by way of the hard-to-detect mystery membrane. No need to come down." Janey peered at Kim. "Why wouldn't she talk to me like she usually does? Why send just a message?"

"Could something be wrong?" Kim waved on her central desk screen, checking. "The comm systems seem to be working normally."

Janey acknowledged Doc's message and asked if everything was okay.

The message quickly came back: Didn't mean to cause alarm, just didn't want to disturb. Janey read that aloud.

"See? She's just being considerate of your time. All the balls you're juggling."

Janey squinted at Kim. "You announced my new position?"

"Yep, to all staff." Kim glanced up from her multi-screens. "What? They needed to know. Smooth transition and all that."

"Prentice is right. You could do my job."

"Then who would do mine? Besides, I like my job," Kim said brightly—a bit too brightly.

"I know. I liked mine and would like to get back to it," Janey said. "Schoeneman needs to find a new permanent chief of security."

Kim looked pained.

"I said something wrong."

"No, it's just that I don't only like my work, I love it," Kim said without looking up, her fingers moving across the three monitors like an accomplished musician.

"I know. Sorry. This place is your entire life," Janey said. "You haven't had a vacation off-station in—well, ever since I've been here. I've never asked you about that."

"I've taken vacations, but just about everyone I care about is here." Kim shrugged and was about to say something else, but her comm pinged, the tone used for the security switchboard.

"Onboard Security, how can I help you?" Kim's tone was efficient yet warm.

She paled. "Thanks for letting me know, Jintao. I'll let the chief know. Secure the scene and—"

She paused, listening. "One moment." Kim opened her mouth to speak, but Janey jumped in.

"Another death?" Janey asked.

Kim nodded, frowned. "Suite 854. A Mr. Hwang. No known causes. Collapsed in the kitchen."

Jupiter's balls.

A third death in as many hours.

What the Venus Hells was going on?

"Have the acting medical chief meet me there and send Antonia. Doc, too," Janey said and rushed out of the office. Then she rushed back in. "And Prentice, too. I'm on my way."

Janey heard Kim say, "Call medical but have them hold on transporting the body. Chief McCallister and the team will be there in three minutes."

Halfway to the elevator banks, Janey's comm pinged with Schoeneman's bass tone as Prentice caught up to her at a jog.

She kept going and opened the channel. "Sir."

"Sitrep." Situation report. His voice echoed as if he was a huge space. Maybe a space jet hangar.

"Two homicides, sir. Station in lockdown." Which he knew. "We're on our way to another sudden, mysterious death." Third in as many hours, she wanted to add, but he could do the math.

Schoeneman swore in a few languages—some she recognized, others she didn't. "A third? Who is it? I'm coming."

"Please, sir, don't. Your jet could be just the opportunity the killer or killers are looking for to get off-station."

"I want a list of suspects now." Schoeneman commed off without waiting for a reply from her on who the guest was or without telling her what he planned to do. His prerogative. It was his station. But it was frustrating, nonetheless.

Prentice was quiet, not looking at her as they boarded and rode the elevator to the eighth floor. Again.

Just as the door opened, Prentice spoke, subdued, "For the first two victims, do you think it could be targeted biologics that caused asphyxiation somehow?"

"There's no evidence for that. But the thought did occur. What made you think of it?" Janey stepped out of the elevator.

Stationed at the elevator door, Clark greeted Janey with a quiet, "Chief."

"Where's Jintao?" Janey asked.

"In there with medical, securing the scene with Antonia. And Soren. Meilani is there, too, but she—"

"Couldn't break cover," Janey finished, nodded her thanks before heading toward the suite.

"Speculating what could connect them is all, sir," Prentice said, continuing her train of thought.

"We know nothing about the third victim, so withhold judgment until we know more." Janey gave her a stern gaze. "We follow the evidence."

"Of course, Chief."

"But good creative thinking." Janey strode to the suite door, but not before catching the grin on Prentice's face.

In front of a soundproofed shimmery curtain covering the suite door, Meilani Shawhan greeted Janey. "Chief."

A petite woman, Meilani had been a gymnast in high school. She fit well the undercover role as private security in a sleek black pantsuit with a tailored long jacket, diamond choker around her neck, and diamond studs in her ears. She'd been hired by a third party for the Hwangs. Janey remembered from the duty roster she'd drawn up a few days before—a lifetime ago.

"Report," Janey said.

"Antonia and Jintao were the first on scene. I called them

in. I couldn't break cover." Shawhan shrugged. "They're in there now with Acting Medical Chief Horsely and Soren, as assistant coroner." Of course, Doc had her hands full with two bodies and would send Soren, again.

"Stay here until we clear the scene and Antonia gets your statement," Janey said.

"Yes, sir. Sorry to hear about your mother."

"Thank you, Meilani." Janey nodded, then went farther into the suite, Prentice at her side.

She took in the scene. The large suite was an open floor plan. Off to the left was the kitchen where the medical team huddled with Soren. The bedrooms were farther to the left. In front of them, a long glass-topped dining table. To the right was a step-down sitting area arrayed in plush warm beiges and browns with sky-blue and spring-green accents. Across the room, a floor-to-ceiling window dominated the space, though an opaque filter muted the sunlight and displayed a nature panoramic scene. As if viewed from a neighboring mountain top, sharp mountain peaks jutted into a blue sky and puffy white cumulus clouds lumbered. Quite hypnotic.

Murmuring drew her attention back to the sitting area. A short, trim woman with long, straight black hair faced away from all of them toward the window, wrapped in a silky black robe. Mrs. Hwang, she presumed. Antonia spoke to the petite woman in a low voice, trying to keep a neutral expression but compassion leaked through. Janey couldn't make out the words, but she could guess they were words of sympathy. Hopefully, her lead investigator was asking all the essential questions, too.

Janey spun away and headed for the kitchen. Soren examined Mr. Hwang's prone body on the kitchen floor, running a scanner over him. She didn't have a good view of him but could see his thick white hair and delicate sky-blue silk slippers on his feet. Mr. Hwang had crumpled facing the food crafter, making a cup of green tea. From a few feet away in the hall, Jintao observed, a somber look on his face, checking his holo from time to time, probably taking readings.

Soren straightened from examining the body and turned to Acting Medical Chief Alison Horsely to confer in low voices. Then they noticed Janey.

Soren spoke first, grim, "No obvious signs of injury or illness. I don't have the right equipment to see deep into his throat. So, Doc will have to determine the manner and cause of death."

Alison jumped in, reading from her wrist comm's holo screen. "He had a clean bill of health before arriving, no pre-existing conditions."

Janey nodded. What else was there to say?

"We can announce that his cause of death is unknown at this point," Soren said.

Alison closed her holo. "Janey, I suppose congrats are in order for your promotion—Acting Security Chief."

"Like your situation, though, Alison. Not so easy."

"True," Alison said, pocketing a scanner. Steady in a crisis, Alison had taken over three months ago in the same difficult circumstances that had brought Janey into her first acting chief promotion. "Ready for us to transport the body?"

"Not my call," Janey said, and she called out to Antonia who was in conversation still with Mrs. Hwang.

Antonia joined them in the small kitchen. "Yes, Chief?"

The acting medical chief didn't miss a beat and asked Antonia, "Are you ready for us to transport the body?"

Antonia glanced at the body, gulped, then surveyed the room, a pained expression flitting across her face. She took a breath, her gaze on the small woman.

"It's a lot, I know," Janey said in a low voice. "Let's review what you know."

"Thanks, boss." Antonia blew out a breath and spread her feet a little wider as if to steady herself. "According to his wife, Mr. Hwang stepped out to the kitchenette to prepare tea just ten minutes before now. She remained in the bedroom longer. When she arrived, he was on the floor in the kitchen, without a pulse. Then she called her security guard, Meilani, who called us. Preliminary scans of the space haven't picked up anything unusual, though we haven't searched everywhere."

"Same as the other crime scenes," Janey added.

"I'd place time of death then at approximately nine a.m." Soren glanced back at the body, then turned back to Janey and gave a grim smile.

"Could Mr. Hwang have died the same way as the other two victims?" Jintao asked, tentative. "Though how that is possible I have no idea."

"That's what we need to determine." Janey nodded, then addressed Soren. "There must be a way to see down his throat now."

Soren brushed his air out of his eyes, considering. "Horsely, your medical case, maybe there's something in there I can use to enhance my tools."

In a few minutes, Soren had tweaked his scanner and bent to study the body. Another minute later, he stood, concern in his gaze. "My scans can read a barrier in the throat, not normally part of the human body, of unknown origin and chemical makeup. With these tools, that's all I can pick up."

"Same with the other two victims," Antonia said in a hushed and horrified voice.

"That's three too many." Horsely pursed her lips.

"Not natural causes," Soren said. After a beat, he added confused, "Who could cause this?"

"And how?" Jintao chimed in.

"That's what we need to find out," Janey said to Antonia. "You need to find out."

Antonia nodded, a determined set to her shoulders. "Homicide, boss?" She glanced about the room again. "We all took readings from the suite."

Jintao nodded. Alison and Soren, too.

"Like always," Alison said. "I'll send it to you."

"To Soren and Doc, too," Antonia said. "We need to do a multivariate analysis with all this data."

"Good call," Janey said.

"I bet Schoeneman is not happy about all of this," Alison added.

"That's putting it mildly."

He wanted suspects. So did she. She had no one under suspicion yet, only a whole station of guests and staff to question. That was too many. She needed to narrow down her suspect pool.

Antonia turned to the medical chief. "I'm ready for you and your team to take the body to Doc."

"Do you mind if I accompany the body?" Prentice asked.

Janey lifted her eyebrows.

"I want to see all the processes and procedures from the adjoining departments. I might see something new that will help us." Prentice bounced from toe to toe. Then stilled.

"Sure. Meet us—"

"In the bullpen. Will do, sir." Prentice practically skipped out of the hotel suite, following the medical staff guiding the hover stretcher.

Horsely brought up the rear, shaking her head at her holo, probably studying the other two slim case files.

"I'll finish the scan of the suite with Jintao, then start the report and come back for another round of questions, if the evidence warrants it," Antonia said. "She's in shock. I gathered what I could." Her lead investigator glanced at the petite women in the middle of the sitting area, gazing out at the changing landscape on the curtain screens.

"Yes, your instincts are good, Antonia," Janey said, distracted by an idea that flew in then out. She rubbed her palms up and down her face. Stars, she was tired all of a sudden. Maybe a nap was in order. She could hand off her job to Antonia's capable but inexperienced hands and punch out of this job.

"You okay, Chief?" Jintao asked, his voice sounding far away as if her spirit were a balloon floating far away from the ground.

Antonia put a gentle hand on Janey's shoulder. Her agent's grounding touch brought her soul back to her body. Her vision went from bright and blurry to dark and focused. A bit disorienting, yet she could feel her feet now.

She could do this.

"Yes, fine," Janey said. And with that, Jintao and Antonia moved toward the kitchen and the bedrooms respectively, and Janey was alone with Mrs. Hwang. Antonia threw a look of concern over her shoulder at her, but Janey waved her off and turned her attention to the interview she needed to conduct. Another perspective would be valuable. She reviewed Antonia's notes from the interview with Mrs. Hwang. Only times and actions, no more. Yes, she needed more.

In the center of the sitting area with its cream-colored furniture, the petite woman with long, straight black hair stared at the window coverings as if she was in a trance. Not moving, seemingly barely breathing.

"May I ask you a few questions, Mrs. Hwang?" Janey stepped down into the seating area, taking care to make some noise. "I know this is a really difficult time for you."

Mrs. Hwang turned around. Janey could finally get a good look at her. She wore a long-sleeved black kimono, lace at its cuffs and edges. Around her waist holding the black kimono closed was a thick cloth belt knotted intricately. Tear tracks made vertical lines down Mrs. Hwang's cheeks, marring the smooth white powder coating her face and neck. Resembling a porcelain doll, she was younger than Janey expected, though probably no more than Janey's age and a good twenty or thirty years younger than Oscar Hwang. Mrs. Hwang studied Janey with big eyes lined with black, her eyebrows horizontal black slashes. Her lips were painted a deep cherry red and matched the painted edges of her eyes.

"I am not Mrs. Hwang." She spoke in a surprisingly low rich alto, for someone so dainty looking. "I just let them think that."

"Then who are you?" Janey asked.

NINE

"WON'T YOU SIT? CAN I OFFER YOU SOMETHING?" The not-Mrs. Hwang said, the perfect hostess, deftly avoiding her question. "Tea perhaps. I know we have some in the kitchen. It's quite adequate." The petite woman spun toward the kitchen, taking the few steps with grace and a kind of floating lightness, her long black hair swaying with her movements.

"No, thank you. I think we ought to talk."

The young woman spun, studying Janey as if she were weighing her options.

"Please, sit." Janey indicated the wide brown brocade comfort chair across from the matching settee.

The not-Mrs. Hwang returned to the sitting area and sank into the chair Janey indicated, lifting her long hair out of the way with a practiced, graceful flick of the wrist. Janey took the settee.

"I don't know if I introduced myself," Janey said. "I'm Investigator, I mean Acting Chief Janey McCallister."

"I'm Nasturtium—like the flower." The woman straightened, pulling her shoulders back slightly as if taking up more space, even in her grief.

Janey waited but the woman added no more.

"No last name?" Janey prompted.

"No, ma'am, Acting Chief." She ducked her head in a submissive gesture, but that had to be more out of habit or an act. There was nothing subjugated about this person. Not a woman who bowed easily to others' whims.

"Okay, Nasturtium. I'd like to ask you some questions." Into her comm, Janey waved to access the file Antonia had already started. "I see that Mr. Hwang traveled alone to L'Étoile." Janey glanced up. "I don't see a check-in record for anyone by the name of Nasturtium." Antonia couldn't have noted that since she hadn't received that information. And most likely hadn't asked for it, having her hands full with the third victim. "What is your connection to the deceased?"

Nasturtium sat perfectly still, not blinking, not even appearing to breathe.

"Did you travel under an alias? How did you arrive?"

When Nasturtium made no reply, hardly seemed to move, Janey reached out to touch the woman gently on arm. "Are you all right?"

Nasturtium jerked back. "I'm fine. The shock you know." She sighed, slumped a little. "Do you know anything about grief, Acting Chief?" Her eyes widened, new tears threatening at the edges.

Maybe grief pressed as heavy on Nasturtium as it was on Janey, a heavy blanket, muffling the noises from the world outside and from feeling much of anything within.

Janey pushed out a breath to create a space to speak. "As a matter of fact, I do."

Then she shut up. Sometimes the best way to encourage someone to talk was to let the emptiness stretch so long that the person felt obligated to fill it.

Sometimes.

Nasturtium didn't rush to fill the silence. Instead, she stared at the window shade. Huge cumulus clouds marched across its light blue backdrop, displaying what looked like a summer day on the prairie. The room smelled of delicate gardenias. Or perhaps that was Nasturtium's perfume.

As if Janey had a spring under her, she popped up to search the suite, even though her team had done their job. She needed to move. Her own grief was heavy enough. She didn't need to sit so deeply in another's.

Janey took her time examining the sitting, dining, and kitchen area and spotted nothing out of the ordinary. She made it down the hallway to the bedrooms—this suite had only two—before Nasturtium called out, "Please don't go down there. That's private."

Her voice held a plea so different than her calm demeanor. Janey hesitated for only a millisecond but forged ahead. The three bedrooms were each neat and orderly, all clothes either folder or tidied away. The two bathrooms were the same, and all toiletries were ranged neatly on the counter in half-zipped containers. Her scans picked up nothing unusual, matching her teams' data. Janey returned to the main room and stood in the small kitchen, visualizing Mr. Hwang on the kitchen floor.

"How did he die?" Nasturtium asked.

"Our medical examiner will have the official reply soon, but it appears that he suffocated." Again, Janey sat across from the young woman who was perched at the edge of the chair, staring off into the middle distance.

"How?" Her voice was soft, mechanical almost.

"We don't know yet," Janey replied. "It happened very quickly. He would have hardly suffered."

Nasturtium let out a little sigh. She seemed sad, not guilty. But appearances could be deceiving.

Janey needed to switch gears and connect with Nasturtium to get her to open up. Maybe she'd reveal a motivation or her guilt or drop some other detail that could aid her. Janey needed more clues. They had no real suspects yet. And she needed to find out who did this and stop them before anyone else got hurt.

Into the quiet, she spoke, "My mother died this morning." At the simple words, Janey's tears threatened to clog her throat, the heaviness of grief an oppressive cloak.

"I am so sorry."

Janey waited a moment until the tightness in her throat passed. "Thank you. She was sick for a long time."

"That must have been hard."

Janey nodded. She could be home, helping Teresa and the others. Yet here she was working.

Was this her place? What was her place?

"Why are you here—working, Chief McCallister? You could be home with loved ones."

Janey glanced up, surprised. How could Nasturtium know her thoughts? She stared at the plush beige rug accented with tiny blue sparkles. "I owe it to the dead and their loved ones to bring them answers. Pursue justice and to bring light to the darkness."

Nasturtium hummed a comforting sound.

"I know too much about grief," Janey said. "When my best friend was murdered, I'd been the one to find her. I hadn't been an investigator then, but I persisted and found the answers when the official investigators had seemingly given up. I owe it to my best friend to find out who killed her. And I owed it to you. I will find out who killed Oscar and do my best to bring them to justice."

She peered up at Nasturtium, who watched her intently as if Janey deserved all the care in the world. An attentive, beautiful, graceful woman, almost as if she was well trained in the fine art of attending to the secret hearts of others. She got Janey to reveal things about herself. Focusing on the case brought her light, too. Then something clicked into place.

"Are you a contracted mistress, Nasturtium?"

The woman nodded, not acting surprised at Janey's question. "Since I was twenty. We used to be known as kisaeng."

"I haven't heard—"

"That's the Korean term. Maybe you've heard of geishas or oirans."

"Geishas, yes." Nasturtium was dressed like one. "What name did you use to register at Bijoux de L'Étoile?"

"Why? Do you suspect me of something?"

"Should I?"

"The doctors, the other investigators, you were all so secretive. Oscar was in perfect health. He was fine early this morning when we had sex," Nasturtium said with an open sob, holding her gaze with Janey's, no embarrassment in her sadness or her frank talk.

"His death does appear to be a homicide. Like two others on this station."

"Murder? You didn't say that." Nasturtium peered at Janey. "Two others, too?"

"All this morning. Do you happen to know anything about those?"

"Why would I? I've been here all morning."

"Do you know a Hampton Nel?"

Nasturtium shook her head, no.

"How about Leo Montaigne?"

Nasturtium brushed away her black hair that had fallen into her face. "Should I?"

"These were two men found dead this morning. Same as Oscar."

"I'm sorry that I can't help you more." But she didn't sound sorry. She sounded resigned.

Janey leaned forward. "What is your real name?"

"Why? So, you can track my movements?"

"No, we can already do that."

"This hotel is supposed to be privacy-assured." Nasturtium cocked her head like a bird, not angry just curious.

"It is. The monitoring is for your safety." Into her comm, Janey called up a facial recognition search. Antonia would have gotten to it soon, but Janey could get to it now. The benefit of teamwork.

In a moment, she had a series of stills of Nasturtium in her white powder face, sporting a bright red floral kimono, and Mr. Hwang, in a matching kimono. The images showed them eating at the Phoenix restaurant in the casino, crossing the Mediterranean-themed, spacious lobby, and relaxing at the high rollers' tables with Nasturtium gambling and Mr. Hwang watching. She shunted all the images to the case file with a note for the team to analyze.

Janey showed the images to Nasturtium. The woman eyed them impassively and then turned away to stare at the window shade again. In the foreground, spring green grasses rippled while white cotton candy clouds scudded above, a strip of bright blue sky in the background.

"I loved him," Nasturtium finally said. "I could never hurt him. I didn't kill him." Her voice was earnest, soft, and no deception was displayed in her tone or in her face.

"He wanted out of the contract?"

"Oh no. I mean, yes, but it's not what you think. He was talking about marriage."

Janey checked Oscar Hwang's file. "I see here that there is already a Mrs. Hwang back home in Seoul."

"On paper only. He hasn't seen her in years. *Hadn't* seen her." Nasturtium gulped. "It was a money marriage, for their families' vast industrial fortunes. They don't even have children. After the honeymoon, I don't think they spent another night together. Even that night was only ceremonial. Oscar was a traditionalist for his family, in appearances only." Nasturtium spun toward Janey and spoke with fervor. "Oscar and I have been together for eleven years. With me, he was true."

Janey guessed the math—Nasturtium's age, Oscar's. "Ever since you became a contracted mistress," she stated rather than asked.

"Very good, Acting Chief."

"I still don't know how you came aboard. But we will find out," Janey said. "Don't leave. Your security guard works for us."

"I am a person of interest," Nasturtium said mildly.

"I see you're familiar with our terminology. Yes, you are our number one suspect in the death of Oscar Hwang." Until they had someone better.

A look of shock flittered across her face and was gone in less than a tenth of a second, but Janey caught it.

"Are you taking me in for questioning?" Nasturtium said.

"Soon. Seems like this has happened to you before." Janey gestured to encompass herself and the challenging situation.

"There's been a few misunderstandings," Nasturtium said in a whisper, but Janey heard her clearly.

"We'll dig into your previous 'misunderstandings.'" Janey headed for the door, then stopped and turned around. "Unless you want to confess."

"I've done nothing wrong." Nasturtium lifted her chin.

"Don't leave your suite," Janey repeated and left.

They'd bring Nasturtium in for questioning when they had more to go on than a suspicious guest with no hotel record and no record of her travel onboard.

TEN

BACK IN HER OFFICE, JANEY REFILLED HER COFFEE, set her room tone to quiet melodic jazz, and waved open the three timelines on her wallscreen. Then she pivoted, landed in the corridor, heading for the bullpen. A wave of grief passed her and left her feeling empty. She stopped. She didn't want to interact with people right now. Her team would contact her if they needed anything, and they were working.

For a second time in as many minutes, she was back in her office. She stared at the timeline on her wall screen. She could work, and she needed to report in to Schoeneman in about thirty minutes. They needed to find their murderer. Was it one person or several? Was the problem environmental or human-made?

She needed answers.

Back to work, it was. The emptiness was still there, but so was something else. Her insatiable drive for justice, for the truth of what really happened to those who could no longer speak for themselves.

All three of the victims had been found at different loca-

tions in their suites. Nothing significant there. She called up
the building designs for all three suites anyway, but the floor
plans didn't have the details she was looking for.

"Call Antonia," Janey said to her wall screen. Antonia's
face showed in a circle. She was at her station in the bullpen.

"Boss?"

"I need you to go check the crime scenes and look for any
vents above the dining table."

"Looking for an airborne poison?"

"Possibly. These are unusual homicides. We're looking for
unusual clues. Think outside the box."

"Yes, boss. I can do that," Antonia said, determination in
her voice. She pivoted to wave into an adjacent screen.

What had Orlando been doing in the environmental
control room? A sinking feeling landed in her gut. She didn't
want him to be involved, or worse, responsible. But the
timing, at least with the first death, was too coincidental. She
didn't want to suspect him about anything either. She loved
him. But his past...

Venus hells.

"Boss?" Antonia prompted, calling Janey back from her
musings.

"When you're done checking the scenes, talk to the environmental engineers and see if there are any glitches. Kim
said there wasn't, but I want you to go there and see for
yourself."

"On it." Antonia commed off, and Janey paced her small
office. She should be the one running around the station. She
could, she reminded herself, but she also had good people
working for her, and she needed to let them do their jobs.

She could lend her experience and skills to the task at
hand.

All three victims had the odd, dangerous membrane in

their mouths. The first two, Doc had said they died from asphyxiation, the membrane cutting off their oxygen. Most likely, the third victim had as well. Doc said she'd never seen such a membrane before and had no idea what it was made of. They were all waiting on Soren to complete his analysis.

What if another death happened?

Was this an unknown, undetectable airborne contaminant?

Would more guests turn up dead? Would they have to evacuate the station? She hoped it wouldn't come to that.

Janey had nothing to go on for how the membrane developed to kill three middle-aged men. Where had it come from? How had it developed? And why these three men only? She'd have to wait for further analysis from others more specialized than her.

She sighed and glared at the screen, then took a mechanical sip of cold, bitter coffee. When lifespans were on average one hundred and twenty to one hundred and fifty years for many people, these men had been in the prime of their lives. All three victims were what counted for middle-aged, ranging from sixty-five years old for Nel to seventy-five years old for Hwang.

Besides where and how they died and their ages, that was where their similarities ended.

The three men were of different ethnicities and lived in different parts of the earth. She checked their fields of work. A pan-African national, based in Southern Africa, Nel was an astrophysicist and a professor. Montaigne was based in Zurich and was in the financial services industry. Hwang's registered address was in Seoul, Reunited Korea. Listed as semi-retired, he still had controlling interests in the Hwang companies, but their names didn't tell her anything about their industries. She waved through into a few of them. She spotted rice agricultural interests in Middle Africa, the manufacturing of rockets and space stations in Lunar and Earth orbits, and precious metals mining in the asteroid belt.

Hwang had been one of the wealthiest men in the Sol. Who inherited all that wealth? Surely not Nasturtium—her main person of interest—her only suspect, so far, plastered large across the top of the wall screen. She added Mrs. Lisa Montaigne for good measure, not a suspect yet, but someone she needed to question further. Rather, her acting lead investigator, Antonia Lane, needed to question further, once they had more leads…more evidence.

They had no hard evidence on Nasturtium connecting her to the murder of her lover, and Nasturtium knew that. But the lack of information on the contracted companion and how she came aboard were too mysterious to ignore. As well as illegal. Yet Nasturtium hadn't invoked her standard privacy rights: the right to see what information L'Étoile had on her and the right to have her data be erased once she left —the latter for a fee.

Maybe she didn't know her rights or think she had a right to her personal data. No, that couldn't be it. Nasturtium was smart and knew Janey had no evidence on her. She wasn't pressing her advantage. But why?

Maybe Nasturtium knew that security could legally expel her from the station, as it appeared she snuck on and therefore had no legal claim to be here. Janey would expel her under normal circumstances, but these weren't normal times, And the station was on lockdown. No one was going anywhere.

She needed to dig into everyone's background, but without clear suspects beyond Nasturtium, she had no right to dig beyond the public records. For that, she needed probable cause. Guests who came to Bijoux de L'Étoile Casino Hotel space station paid handsomely for their right to privacy while at the hotel—as well as in their daily lives.

Unless extenuating circumstances, like those that affected the health and safety of the station and its inhabitants, she had no right to search them—overtly. If she could prove a real and present danger to the station, then she'd have carte blanche to question everyone and dig behind firewalls.

If she could prove that there was an airborne pathogen... Bugging Soren wouldn't make him work any faster. He was the best at what he did.

Nevertheless, she was the chief.

She commed Soren via the vid screen.

"What?" Soren barked, then saw who it was. "Sorry, Janey. Chief." He shook his head. "I don't have anything for you yet."

"I need to know if anyone else could die."

"I don't think so."

"Why didn't you tell me that sooner?"

"Because I'm not sure."

"About what?"

"So much. Believe me, I'm working as fast as I can."

"Tell me what you have so far." Janey huffed out a breath and let the familiar lab with its humming and quiet ticking away calm her.

Soren frowned. "I doubt you'd understand."

"Soren, I am responsible for the security of nearly three thousand souls," Janey said. "I need to know if anyone else could die. Do I need to evacuate or not?"

Soren paled. "Understood, Chief. Okay, there are proteins in that membrane made from a biological material engineered in a lab."

"The relevance of that?"

"The proteins only interact with certain other proteins."

"Spell it out, Soren."

"As if this—whatever formed the membrane and suffocated the victims—was targeted to people with specific genetics."

"Targeted." Janey wanted to sit down, but her chair was across the room behind her desk. "What genetics specifically?"

"Biomarkers in the cell—"

"Okay, we surmised death wasn't by natural causes. Now you're saying that these men were targeted."

"Yes. That's why I think it's highly unlikely more people will die if they haven't already."

"We'll run a search on our end," Janey said, grim. "Keep me posted."

Soren nodded and shut off the vid.

Janey ran a quick bioscan. Everyone wore biotrackers, either as part of their bracelet comms or around their neck as part of their necklace idents. All two thousand seven hundred souls on board—nine hundred guests and eighteen hundred staff—were accounted for. It had been over forty minutes since the last death was reported. If they could get through the next twenty minutes with no sudden and suspicious deaths, would that mean they were safe from an outbreak? She had to hope that Soren was right about these three deaths being targeted. Somehow for some mysterious reason.

Why these three men? How were they connected?

A search box chimed in the upper left-hand corner of the murder board, pulling her attention away from Soren's revelations.

With a flick of her wrist, she opened one of her team's completed search results.

Excellent. On the screen, a relationship map bloomed, a web of lines connecting the three dead hotel guests. Antonia must have modified it to include Mr. Hwang on her way down to Doc's with the body. Good initiative of her acting lead investigator.

Now she could examine how, if at all, the victims' lives intertwined. Maybe there she'd find a suspect on board and find a motive for the death of Nel, Montaigne, and Hwang.

The web of lines was quite a tangle. Lines connected associates, business partners, and family members. Below the dense web, she found a list of the relationships and a numerical value after each pair of names. At the top of the list were the relationships with the most connections.

What she saw at the number one position surprised her. Hampton Nel was directly connected to Lisa Montaigne. Their first victim's sister was the second victim's wife. That was strange. No one was listed on Nel's next of kin information. Lisa hadn't mentioned her brother being on board.

Now she had a reason to question Lisa.

The second strongest connection surprised her, too. While interesting, she didn't know how it was relevant. Yet, more information was always better than less.

Hwang had a much younger sister, Ji-woo Hwang, who was listed as working for one of Schoeneman's agricultural subsidiaries in one of the Central American farm corporate states. Her current location was unknown, and she hadn't had a fixed address in over six months. From there the relationships dropped off in significance: loose business relationships three steps removed or more. Friends of friends knowing friends of friends.

What was also surprising was that the three men didn't appear to have crossed paths—in the public record at least. That didn't fit. Hampton Nel should have crossed paths with Leo Montaigne since Nel's sister was married to him.

She examined Nel's movements, last place of work, and recent travel. Antonia and Prentice had done a thorough job. Nevertheless, the records were thin. Nel traveled a lot for research, it seemed. Over the last six months, he'd been holed up in the Hubble array, on neighboring science space stations, or at other observatories on Earth. He'd most recently been to the Sol Academy of Science station in cis-lunar space. He had a cottage in the Gaborone Granton, but he seemed to not have been there in months, what with all his travel. Perhaps he was on a leave of absence from teaching. She added a note for the team to verify that fact.

Prentice charged into her office without knocking, breathless. "It *is* a triple homicide," were the first words out of her mouth.

"Doc's confirmed the same cause of death for Oscar Hwang?" Janey said.

Prentice nodded, catching her breath. "She has. Exact same, and—" She interrupted herself when she saw what Janey had been looking at on the murder board. "Oh, the results. I saw the ping on my comm, but then forgot it, with all the excitement—"

"Prentice, slow down. Take a breath."

Prentice nodded, approached the murder board, and studied the relationship web and the ranking list. "Would you like to bring in Mrs. Montaigne?"

"Not yet." Janey wanted to do it herself but did also need to give Antonia experience.

"What do you want me to do?"

"I want you to talk to the Redstones and show them this photo." Janey called up Nasturtium's white-powered face with bright red lipstick from the surveillance data.

Prentice opened her mouth to ask more questions.

"Go, the clock's ticking. Be discreet. She's a person of interest and was my main suspect until I saw this list. Maybe still is. Let Antonia know what you're doing."

"Yes, sir." Prentice scooped the data onto her holo and hurried out, no word about needing to work side-by-side with Janey. Probie was spreading her wings.

Janey sent a request to Antonia to dig deeper into Lisa

Montaigne's social connections and see whatever was out there readily accessible. Time to check the Montaigne's financial records and see if Lisa Montaigne had a financial motive to kill her husband. But that still didn't answer about the other two. Or maybe Hampton Nel had been her target and that was why she hadn't mentioned he was on board?

ELEVEN

According to the information Antonia had already compiled, upon Leo's death, it appeared that all the company holdings would go to a trust run by a trustee, and not to his wife. Lisa was to receive a generous allowance. There were no children and no mention of heirs. So, nothing to gain financially by killing him.

Next, she studied Nel's financial records. He didn't have any savings as he lived in a Granton where all his needs had been taken care of. He didn't have a will on file, and no next of kin, but he did have lots of research on string theory, virtual particles, quasars, and black holes. So intellectual property. His university, who'd paid for his stay on L'Étoile, would probably want his papers and research on L'Étoile and would get it unless someone contested it. Janey would have the team follow up with that.

Who could have committed these murders? And why? She needed a motive. On a hunch, Janey opened a private file, off the station's servers, and opened a black book from a previous case. She ran a cross-check between the names in the book—all suspected black-market vendors dealing in war—with the names flagged in the three murders. No immediate results. All that meant was that her three victims weren't black-market arms dealers or connected to them. That was a small comfort.

How could you get those membranes deep inside three victims' throats? There'd been no sign of a struggle, no evidence of any other person in the suites, other than who should be there. Who had the ability to break into these three suites, undetected and leaving no trace of themselves?

An extraordinary thief.

She tightened her jaw. She knew one of those. Orlando. But she really didn't want to go there. What would he have to gain?

Then the person would need to have advanced biomedical experience to install the nearly invisible membranes that suffocated three men. In addition to the who, there was the how. Soren came to mind. Though he practically lived in his lab, she couldn't dismiss him out of hand. She gritted her teeth and made a note to review his movements at the time of the murders.

And right on cue, Antonia sent her a list of staff whereabouts at the time of the three victims' deaths. Besides Soren, there was only a handful of others with the appropriate medical training: the medical staff, of course, a few people down at the spa, and Sal who ran hydroponics. Sal had several advanced degrees in bio-modulation. A few of the engineers in the machine shop had food science degrees.

Yet, every one of the staff had a clear alibi, according to their tracking system. Even Soren. She was glad. She didn't like suspecting her friends.

Sal would be a good consultant on the case.

Janey commed her. When Sal answered, Janey explained she needed to talk to her about an unusual case and could they meet somewhere private.

"My staff are out to an early lunch. Come to hydroponics, Janey."

"Great, I'll be there in fifteen minutes. I need to look into a few things."

One fact was niggling at her: Oscar Hwang's younger sister, Ji-woo Hwang. She opened a new search, and what she discovered chilled her. The sister was listed as a missing person and had a Sol Unified Planets open case file on her, too. The young woman had been employed by a coffee consortium in Central America owned by Frederick Schoeneman, and then there weren't any more details about her. In fact, there were no more records of her anywhere after her disappearance.

Janey couldn't open the missing person's file on Ji-woo Hwang. Of course, she couldn't. The file was locked with a Sol Unified Planets Police Investigative Services security code. Orlando's jurisdiction. He could unlock the file.

Had she stumbled into the middle of a human trafficking ring? The same one Orlando had been investigating about seven months ago?

Her heartbeat too loud in her ears, Janey called up a picture of Hwang's younger sister, Ji-woo, and placed it alongside a woman she met on-station from an earlier case. This woman, Amelia, had a new ID now and lived in an unknown location to be far from the reach of the mysterious people who ran the human trafficking ring she'd fallen into. The two other women she knew directly or were suspected to be caught up in the ring: her best friend Christine, who'd been murdered five years previous, and another woman, also in connection of a previous case on L'Étoile, who was presumed missing.

All pretty, and all in their twenties.

She called hydroponics. "Sal, I need to postpone our

lunch, but I'd still like to come by later today. Does that work?"

Sal assured her she'd take a break anytime for the interview. Janey thanked her, closed the call, and commed Orlando. This young woman could be a lead he was already following or one he didn't know about. She had to consult with him now.

She let the call ping repeatedly. Nothing.

Orlando didn't answer. She closed the channel and paced. Antonia had set a search query looking for commonalities of the three victims' financials. Hopefully, something out of the ordinary would reveal itself, but there was nothing so far.

She commed Orlando again. Still, no answer.

He'd want to know about Hwang's younger sister. Maybe her disappearance was connected to his case. Wouldn't be the first time.

The team hadn't sent in the report on the hallway vids, so she ran the analysis for outside each of the victims' suites to see if there had been anybody in or out. Running the cameras at four-times speed for the previous twelve hours before the deaths sent up no red flags. Nel hadn't left his suite at all. The Montaigne couple returned from probably dinner and gambling at fifteen minutes after midnight. She'd already seen Oscar and Nasturtium's movements from the day before. They returned to their suite at two in the morning.

That analysis done and flagged for review, she commed Orlando for the third time.

Still no reply.

It was the second time he'd disappeared on her today.

Her chest tightened.

The staff station map showed he was in his quarters. They needed to talk. And now.

At Orlando's door, she knocked, then pinged him through her comm, then knocked again.

Why didn't he answer?

He couldn't be sleeping, could he? And even if he was, he'd normally wake and answer. Maybe something was wrong.

She needed to do something. She wanted to storm off, but that wouldn't solve anything.

Maybe he was in there—as the biosensors showed. Maybe he was in danger.

Time to resort to drastic measures. She used her security override code on his door's panel lock in the wall. The door still didn't open.

Orlando had skills and maybe had blocked her master security code. She'd contemplate why later as she was one of the few who had those codes.

What if he was sick or worse? ... She hated the paper-work, but she didn't see any other way. From her belt holster, she pulled her laser-sighted pistol and shot the panel lock. That did the trick. The door slid open.

Orlando wasn't there, but his wrist comm was on his bedside table. That was why the biosensors thought he was there. Why had he left his wrist comm behind? And how had he done so without triggering the bio-meter alarm?

Janey set her jaw—she didn't want to suspect him of some kind of illegal activity, but that was where her mind went—and called Kim. When she answered, Janey said, "I need you to do something for me. It's personal, not case related."

"What is it?" No hesitation. Thank the stars for Kim Iona.

"Track down Orlando."

"As acting chief, you can do that."

"I am, by calling you. What do you have?"

"No, I mean you can do the search yourself."

"I did, but I need you to verify it for me."

"I see. He's in his quarters."

"He's not. That's where I am. Search for him on the cams, would you? You can do it faster than I can." She wanted to run hard and fast, but that would solve nothing.

"Hold on. I need to switch to privacy mode," Kim said.

"Okay."

Janey waited as Kim put up a privacy screen on her workstation. Staff understood. It happened from time to time. Since Kim manned the front desk, she didn't have an office door she could close.

Panic mounted. Was something wrong? Was he up to no good? She pushed away her panic to gather the facts.

Orlando's room was neat, clothes folded on chairs, paper screens blanked out and tools ranged in open boxes. His table was cleared. He wasn't packed, though no doubt he had a go-bag stashed like she did. She opened the closet and there it was on the floor. His clothes hung neatly, all fancy wear encased in protective covering, his shoes and polished boots ranged and squared.

She closed the closet and crossed to the bathroom. Towels were folded and placed on the drying rack. Comb and brush on the counter. She spotted something out of place: a small perfume bottle next to the soap—a woman's brand. She uncapped it and smelled it, sighed involuntarily, her body relaxing despite the seriousness of her spying. It was Orlando's familiar and comforting scent, mildly woodsy, hinting at something wild and mysterious and evocative of him. Why was a male cologne inside a perfume bottle branded to women?

Kim came back on the comm, sounding worried. "Janey, I don't see him anywhere."

"He's good at staying out of view." Janey chewed her lip.

"Want me to set up a scan to ping you when or if the cams spot him?"

"That would be spying," Janey said. "He wouldn't like that."

"It's too late for that. Plus, he probably wouldn't like that you broke into his room."

"How did you know that?"

"When you shorted the panel lock—what? by shooting it? —that got logged. Right after you used your security code override."

"Are you spying on me?" she huffed. "Sorry, don't know why I said that."

"You know we track those things. Janey, you're stressed and—"

She rubbed the bridge of her nose. "And what?"

"I want to help you." Kim paused. "What do you need?"

"I need Orlando's files on his case because there may be a connection to the murders—or at least one of them. But it's just a hunch. I have no evidence."

"I don't have access to Orlando's files."

"I didn't think you would. That's why I need to talk to him. It's urgent."

"I'm sorry, sweetie."

"Not your fault."

Where could she find him? What if he didn't want to be found? What if he was involved somehow? She couldn't, shouldn't go there. Why? Because they were sleeping together? They had promised each other love and the truth. But things changed. A year ago, she'd met him on a theft case on L'Étoile while he was undercover, deceiving her and her boss. Through her doggedness, she'd uncovered his true identity as a Sol Special Police spy, and they agreed to work together to solve the ensuing murder case.

Their joined focus and charged attraction seemed to bring out the best in both of them. He'd gotten his high-level arrest, and she'd closed her first murder case on L'Étoile and won the respect of her new team. But then he'd left with his collar, and she hardly heard from him until he returned to L'Étoile months later for another top-secret case. Once again, their cases seemed to overlap. By the successful conclusion of their connected cases, they'd formed a stronger, deeper bond. She trusted him. She'd taken him home to Mom and the aunties. The vacation had been lovely. They'd exchanged words of love. He'd gotten himself stationed on L'Étoile for his top-secret work. Their relationship felt secure, mature, a dance of binary stars.

"Acting Chief, I need to go."

"Don't call me that."

"Bye." Kim closed the comm.

Weird. What would make Kim so formal? Milano was no longer in charge. Maybe there was other staff that Kim had to be more professional with than she was with Janey, but she couldn't think of who.

Janey needed to get her act together. Her stomach grumbled. She could work and eat, and on the way to the commissary, she could search for Orlando. Though if he wanted to stay out of sight, there probably wasn't anything she could do about it.

What a time for him to go rogue.

She sent a priority request to maintenance to fix Orlando's door and left his quarters. As she took the curving corridor to the other side of the staff level on the way to the commissary, she checked the gym, the library, and the small staff shop. No Orlando.

Short of doing a door-to-door search—Janey swayed at the entrance of the commissary. The room fuzzed.

"You okay, Chief?" Someone grabbed her elbow and guided her to a table and hovered over her while she sat.

"I'm fine. Just need to eat," she managed to say. She was due to call Schoeneman but not on an empty stomach.

"I'll get it for you."

She eyed who was speaking to her. It was someone on the kitchen staff. "Thanks, the daily special is fine."

Grateful for the help, she ate whatever was put in front of her and studied Lisa Montaigne's connections or lack thereof. People, thankfully, left her alone.

Lisa was married to Leo Montaigne twenty years previous and didn't work—as far as the records showed. Lots of charity volunteering as she'd already seen. They had no children, foster, adopted, or otherwise.

Odd that she couldn't find any evidence of Leo Montaigne and Hampton Nel meeting, seeing as they were brothers-in-law. She didn't find any records on the Montaigne wedding. Surely, Hampton would have been there. Yet the ultra-rich could pay for extensive privacy screens and deeply scrubbed their public personas.

Janey scanned Lisa's charity work. Lots of photomontages there, as Lisa posed for the media doing good deeds. Nothing stood out until she came to how Lisa traveled to Central America to help children affected by flooding, in the same area/region of the Schoeneman's agricultural subsidiaries in one of the Central American farm corporate states. Same place Mr. Hwang's sister had worked at briefly. The connection didn't flag earlier in the relationship search because the timing was off by five years.

Not much to go on. Plus, it was only circumstantial. And how did Lisa's travels to the Central American region where Mr. Hwang's missing sister had worked connect to the case? Loose threads that would come apart as soon as she pulled, no doubt. But she had to pull—it could be a starting place. And it was another reason to question Lisa Montaigne. As soon as she was done with lunch.

It was time to put more pressure on Nasturtium, too.

While she ate, she ran another facial search of Nasturtium, this time without the white powder, and sent that through the police agencies and the Sol Unified criminal database.

She should have done that sooner or made sure her team did it. She should have made sure they did it first thing, but now that she had lunch in her, she could think more clearly, more methodically.

When she glanced up for a moment, the staffer who'd helped her when she'd arrived at the commissary took that as an opening and came over to congratulate her on her promotion. They wanted to chit-chat and ask after her well-being and offer her condolences about her mother.

It was too much. She said her thanks as hastily as she could and hustled back to her office. She was overdue to report to Schoeneman. Orlando should show soon and would hopefully come clean to her. Or she'd call every department on the station to hunt him down.

That reminded her. She called in a repair team to fix Orlando's panel lock. The tech who answered said they'd get to it soon, and that the job was already in their queue. They couldn't spare anyone at the moment. The whole tech team was repairing and doing maintenance in the water recycling system.

"What's wrong with it?"

"Nothing's wrong. Just routine maintenance a little early."

"Why?"

"I'm not sure."

"Check. I'll wait."

"Yes, Acting Chief."

Janey paced her small office.

Two long minutes later, the tech came back on the comm. "Apparently, the saline levels were off by a point-two variance. Really nothing to worry about, but we need one hundred percent compliance or Mr. Schoeneman goes ballistic. Know what I mean?"

"I do. Thanks." Janey clicked off.

Could be nothing. Could be something.

She commed Soren. When he picked up, she asked, "Do you have a source yet on the membrane used to suffocate the victims? I haven't heard from you in a while. I have no solid leads. I need something."

"Hey, McCallister, Acting Chief. I think...well—that is— it's just..."

"What's going on? You aren't usually this evasive."

"I'm in the middle of a really delicate procedure. Can I comm you back? I should have the answers you seek soon."

"How soon?"

"Don't know. Bye."

That was strange. In all the time she'd worked with Soren, he'd never acted so cagey.

First Kim, now Soren.

Not good.

TWELVE

JANEY BLEW OUT A BREATH. COULDN'T BE HELPED. She had to deal with Schoeneman.

In case she was interrupted, she set up the privacy shield and commed Schoeneman a few minutes early. He didn't reply, but his automated system dumped her into a call-back queue.

Fine. She'd wait. Frustrated, she stared at the murder board on the wallscreen. Rhea pinged her on her ocular implant the news on Schoeneman. Like Kim had said, his board was pressuring him out and wanted major changes in the stockholder rules to benefit themselves. No wonder the man was as jumpy as a desert flea.

One of the team's searches pinged, and with a swipe of the air, she opened the search results.

They were the results from the facial recognition search on Nasturtium in the Sol offenders database. A much younger version of her face scrolled up. The young woman had been booked and released on a few counts of indecent exposure in a few conservative locales, but her name for each booking was different. She'd been booked as Rose in

Decatur, Iowa Territory, as Dahlia in Sydney, Australia Protectora, and as Carnation in the Central American Coban Territory.

Janey sucked in a breath at that last location in Central America—a major coffee-growing region—and checked the dates. The booking coincided with Hwang's sister's disappearance, only days after, in fact. The records showed that Hwang-Soo Corp, Mr. Hwang's main corporate holdings, paid Nasturtium's booking and release fees each time.

A possible connection to Hwang's sister's disappearance. Maybe Nasturtium and Oscar had been searching for her.

Her comm pinged, the bass tone signifying Schoeneman.

Janey stepped into the privacy booth surrounding her desk. "Sir, I have a list of suspects. About to conduct my next round of interviews. Is this channel secure?"

"Of course. Send me your list."

"I'd prefer not to, not until we have something definitive," Janey said. "I need to approach with caution—"

"No, not you. Assign someone else to conduct the interviews," Schoeneman blasted. "You need to be managing the investigation, not doing the investigating."

"I have done. I told you, Antonia Lane," Janey said. "But I'm sure you want the best on this. She hasn't passed her qualifying exams yet."

"No excuse. Lane's tough. Champion scorer and all that. She'll get experienced. What about that red-headed crackerjack, Prentier, we just hired? She was top in all her scores."

"Prentice. She's still a probie. Lacks field experience."

"You're not making this easy, McCallister."

"What do you mean? We're working as a team. I have everything in hand." Janey blew out a breath. No, talking to you is making my job harder, she wanted to say, but she held back. No reason to prolong the conversation.

"Fine. I'm just testing you. You understand. I want an

arrest in one hour and my hotel out of lockdown. Understood?" He commed off.

"I'll do my best, sir," Janey said to dead air and plunked back into her desk chair.

She rubbed her choker. This pressure was what Milano had shielded her from. She could really do without it. But talking to Schoeneman came with the job.

The door swooshed open, and in stalked Orlando. He swept the small office, looking for her, but his gaze passed through her. He'd only see the wall behind her desk. The privacy shield hid her from view, invisible to people with normal vision.

He schooled his expression to glacial and turned toward the door, about to leave. He was pissed.

Janey dropped the screen. "Orlando. What's wrong?"

He turned toward her, his eyes widening a hair, his only sign of surprise.

"Did you break into my room?" he said as if they were strangers and he was interrogating her.

"Yes, I was looking for you. I pinged you three times."

"I was busy."

"Doing what?" She crossed her arms on her chest.

"My case."

"I thought you were compiling notes for me. Which is it?" she said quietly.

"We need to talk." He stalked the short distance to her like a dangerous cat ready to pounce.

"We are talking."

Orlando flicked a glance at the murder board.

Janey gestured to blank it, and the wallscreen switched to a default setting—a waterfall encompassing the four-foot length of the screen. Not that there was anything about him there. She was being foolish, reactionary. Maybe a little but guilty. She *had* busted his door.

Orlando gazed back at her, his eyes slits, predatory, watchful. Janey forced her hands to remain at her sides and not cross them at her chest to protect herself from his cold anger.

When he didn't speak, she jumped in to fill the awkward silence. "What's going on? Why did I have to use my gun on your door panel?"

"What are you doing breaking in and snooping around my room?" He leaned back from her and slipped a hand into a pants pocket, the epitome of cool and casual.

"I was worried for you. When you didn't answer—" She finally folded her arms. "I wanted to find you. Find out what was going on."

"What is going on?"

"I asked you first." Janey glared at him, not budging.

He said nothing, held her gaze, perhaps weighing what to say and what to hold back. He had color on his cheeks, his breath coming a little faster. He was not cool and collected anymore.

She exploded. "I've had enough of your secrets. I call. You don't answer. Twice today. Of all days." Sadness crashed on her. She spun away from him and stared at the wall's fuzzy white frothy image.

"Janey." He sounded close—she felt the heat of his body— but he didn't touch her. He must have come around her desk, and she hadn't heard him.

"I have two jobs to do. Managing you shouldn't be a third." She turned to face him, angry heat in her chest. She was overloaded. It was all too much. "What's going—"

He held up a hand at her lips. "I'll tell you everything, but first I have to show you something."

"What?" She didn't feel charitable. "What's going on? I have a missing person's link to one of my cases. Maybe connected to your case. I couldn't open the file on her, and I couldn't find you anywhere. Where are you snooping around? I'm not going to find another dead body, am I?"

"What?" Orlando stepped back as if he'd been slapped. "You're accusing me? How could you think that?"

"I don't know what to think," Janey said. "I know that you have the skills to get into locked places unseen. I still don't know exactly how you do that. Maybe into other places on the station too." He'd snuck into a guest's suite to steal his precious jewel, her first big case on the station over a year ago.

"Janey. Stop. Just stop." He moved closer to her, into her personal space. He didn't touch her, only stood there, eyeing her with concern.

"I can't. I have to wrap up this case for Schoeneman in the next hour. I have suspects. No clear evidence, though. No idea what the membrane is. Soren is acting cagey. Kim, too. Where were you?" She didn't like the plaintive sound of her voice but there it was.

"What do you need?" He leaned in, his voice soft, soothing, his gaze, open, real. No manipulation.

She blinked. He was on her side. He was one of the good guys. She had to believe that.

"I need to know what you're working on and how or if it connects to Hwang's younger sister. I need help cracking my case. I need you to answer when I call, dammit."

"I'm here now." Orlando inched forward and opened his arms to give her a hug.

Janey shook her head and backed away. "Start with where you were, Valdez."

"Last names, McCallister, huh?"

She glared at him.

He scratched his chin.

She fidgeted with her choker.

He blew out a breath. "Water filtration."

"Where? Not the air filter system?"

He shook his head, no. "You remember the tunnels we found in the last big case?"

Janey nodded. How could she forget? Unmapped tunnels behind the station walls where they'd been trapped for hours by station saboteurs.

"Well"—he glanced at her—"I found a way in to check the water filtration. Necessary for my case." He didn't say how it related to his case, nor any details about the case.

"Where precisely? And how does this relate to my case or yours?"

"That's what I wanted to show you."

"Why?"

"Because it's hard to map."

"No, I mean why are you mucking about in the environmental controls room and in water filtration. What does that have to do with your case?"

"It's complicated."

"You can do better than that."

Janey's comm pinged. It was Prentice.

"I have to take this." Janey opened the comm. "McCallister here, go."

"Acting Chief, we determined that Nasturtium came up through the StarEl under the name Gloria Weiss." The StarEl was the space elevator used by staff saving money on the roundtrips and miners on their way to the asteroid belt.

Janey sucked in a breath. "White Morning Glory. Another flower name. Thanks. Anything else?"

"Just that she arrived two days before Mr. Hwang did, and as far as the Redstones can tell, she stayed in a staff dorm room with other housekeeping staff."

"Have you confirmed that?"

"No, not yet."

"Go do that, then."

"What will you do? Have you talked to Mrs. Montaigne yet? Can I be there when you do?" She was more eager than insolent. "Antonia said to check with you."

"Prentice, just confirm Gloria—or Nasturtium's—movements in as much detail as you can. That's all. We need to know why she didn't travel with Mr. Hwang, and why she was under an alias. What was she up to? Why all the secrecy?"

"So, talk to the roommates?"

"Yes, you know what to do. Also, see if she is related to any of them. How did she manage to stay there without anyone noticing?"

"By myself?"

"Yes, you're on a roll. Go. Clock's ticking."

"Thanks, boss!" Prentice closed the comm.

"God, was I ever that green?" Janey asked.

"Not since I've known you. You've always had it together." Orlando eyed her intently and whispered, "No crack in the armor."

Janey stepped around him and headed for the door, out of his seductive aura. "I have plenty of cracks. Especially today." She lifted her chin. "Orlando, show me the water filtration. And tell me how it relates to this case."

THIRTEEN

In the service elevator, Orlando pressed for the top floor, the Observatory.

"We're not going to hydroponics?" Janey asked. Hydroponics, where the water system was controlled, was on the lowest level.

"Nope."

"I saw you in environmental controls this morning." She blurted out the words, hating that she felt like she'd been spying on him. At least she managed to keep her voice quiet. She had a right to track him down.

Orlando gave her a funny look. "You were spying on me?"

"No. Yes? No." She sighed. "I needed to speak to you." She waited, but he didn't fill in the blanks. "When are you going to tell me what's going on?"

"I will soon." After a beat, he asked, "How are you?"

"Not good. But the show must go on."

"We need to get away—"

Janey closed her eyes. "Not this again."

"I mean it this time," Orlando said. "I'm close to closing my case. That's what I was doing in environmental. I can feel

133

it. And you have your funeral leave… I could go with you. Lend moral support. Celebrate your mom."

Janey held her tongue, when she wanted to lash out at how he'd left this morning when she most needed him. The memory of waving him off flashed. She had told him to go. She resisted leaning against the elevator wall and crossed her arms instead, staring at the door until it came to a stop. She had to hold it together a bit longer.

Orlando reached for her, but she escaped his grasp by stepping into the narrow corridor. The Star Gazer, a small observatory garden known only to a few, was down at one end. She and Orlando had their first rendezvous there. Seemed so long ago.

The other way led to a stairwell.

Orlando brushed past her, heading in that direction. He stopped in front of a section of the wall that looked like every other section of grey rectangular panels. They were about five feet from the door leading to the stairwell.

"Why are we stopping here? Is there a tunnel?" Janey asked. "I thought my team mapped all of them. I don't remember one on this level."

"They didn't miss anything." Orlando waved out a sequence on his back-up wrist comm, and a holo image danced. A moment later, a panel slid open to reveal iridescent tubules that carried water, waste, and power from place to place throughout the hotel-casino.

A low humming filled the corridor.

"What is that sound?" She frowned. "What am I looking at?"

"Don't worry. I had it sealed off. That hum is the pressure differential."

"Some kind of sonic cloaked barrier?"

Orlando pulled out a stylus and pointed it at one of the thin tubules. "See how this one is bluer than the others?"

He shined the light on the other tubules, ten in all.

Janey blinked, checking their light spectrums. Under normal light, that tubule did indeed look markedly bluer. She turned to him. He looked fuzzy. She blinked to adjust her ocular implant. He appeared normal again. "But what does this prove? And why the need for so much secrecy?"

"I'll tell you—"

"And you took off your wrist ident for this and are wearing a non-standard one. Why?"

Orlando nodded to her wrist comm. "Can you turn that off completely?"

"If I do, Kim will have the whole security team hunting for me."

"Mierda. I should have thought of that," Orlando said. "Can Schoeneman track you? Does he have access to the station tracking system?"

"No, I don't think so," Janey said. "What's this about? You're avoiding the issue."

"I'm not. Just being extra cautious. All will become clear soon, I hope." He lifted an eyebrow. "So? About the tracking system?"

"Only Kim and I have access to our tools for tracking on board."

"Sure?" Orlando asked.

"Milano knows about it, had access, or maybe still does. He locked me and Kim out of his office. We think. Not sure."

He looked thoughtful. "We may need to verify that."

"I still don't get it. What is going on?"

"Can you misdirect your ID signal or have Kim misdirect it?"

"Probably. You mean falsify the record?"

"Yes."

"But we're here already."

"I know. I wasn't thinking it through. Please. Just have

Kim direct your ident to be somewhere else like a few floors down."

"You're not going to reveal all until I do this?"

"Correct." He looked grim.

Janey commed Kim.

Kim answered. "So sorry about earlier. I'll explain when you get back down here."

"You are tracking me?" Janey asked. "Then you know where I am."

"Top floor," Kim said. "And with Orlando by the swing of your endorphins."

"You're monitoring my vitals, too?" Her voice raised in pitch to a near-squeak.

"For your protection, I told you," Kim said. "Too many strange things going on. Are you okay? Your heart rate is elevated, too."

Janey swore.

"Yes, just a precaution, Janey," Kim said in an even, neutral tone. "I don't want anything to happen to you. I made a few modifications to your wrist comm."

"I didn't know."

"But we discussed it."

"When? You know what? Doesn't matter right now," Janey said. "Orlando wants to mask my location."

"Why don't I put you two in the Star Gazer turret room?" Kim said. "Not many people know about that place. If it ever came down to it, you two could be each other's alibi."

"We already are, but that's believable. Are you going to tell me what was going on earlier when you hung up on me?"

Orlando beckoned to her.

"Yes, hold on," Kim said. "Another call is coming on."

"Convenient. You'll fill me in later?"

"Of course. That's what I was going to say," Kim said with a smile in her voice and commed off.

Orlando moved a few feet farther toward the door and uncovered another panel, this one by hand with a pocket screwdriver. The iridescent tubules were connected into a white box.

He pointed to one of the tubules. "The black one, its connector is stripped. Like someone without the right tools tried to open it."

"And didn't succeed," Janey started. "What does this have to do with my case? Your case?"

"Hold on." He unscrewed the next panel to the right of the open one.

"What is that?" Janey stared at a clear box. Inside the box, opaque liquids swirled, creating a mesmerizing pattern.

"Look at it in ultraviolet."

Janey switched to that electromagnetic frequency. "I see black swirling in with blue-ish liquids." She switched back to normal vision and glanced at him. "What am I looking at?"

"Somebody injected the air filtration system with this mixture."

"From here? Orlando, I am so lost." Janey scrubbed her face. "Not water filtration? What does this have to do with anything, your cases or mine? What is all this? And how would you even know to look here? Why were you searching here?"

"Do you trust me?"

Janey checked her heart and her gut. Something was off, but she didn't think it was Orlando. It was probably her. "Despite things not adding up here"—she quirked her head at him—"I do trust you."

As soon as the words left her mouth, her heart sped up. She felt the truth, but her mind immediately scolded her for trusting him without all her questions answered.

"Good." He held her gaze for a long moment. "I know you may not believe this, and I don't have all the evidence...but hear me out." He waited until she nodded, then continued, "I think Schoeneman sabotaged his own station. Probably to collect on the insurance. He's hemorrhaging money in his asteroid mining operations and been squeezing his agricultural operations dry."

"What? How do you know?" Janey scowled.

"I can read between the lines.

The empty grey corridor seemed colder than usual, all of a sudden as if someone had turned down the thermostat ten degrees. She rubbed her arms. "But how could he sabotage L'Étoile? He's not even here."

"He doesn't need to be here to manipulate environmental controls. The Zurich headquarters could. On his command."

"But why would he? What would he have to gain?" She eyed him.

"I told you. The insurance payout." Orlando paced the short width of the corridor, not meeting her gaze.

"Where did you even get that idea?"

"I had Soren analyze this black content—"

"So that's why he's been so cagey," Janey said. "He should have just told me what he was up to. He was supposed to be working on the membrane."

"That's just it. He was. And it's my fault he didn't tell you. I wanted to be sure..." Orlando had the decency to look guilty. Then he brightened and continued. "There's a component in the membrane that when analyzed comes from this black stuff and shows up as an organic component."

Anger flared in her chest, and her vision narrowed. She swallowed against dizziness. "I take it back. I don't trust you. You've gone around my back again, having Soren do work for you without my approval. You're sabotaging my case. Soren telling you things about my case before he tells me. He hasn't told me." She clenched and unclenched her fists.

"No. We're helping—"

"Kim, too? You're having her work for you too behind my back?" Her voice rose again.

"No!" He lifted his hands. "Whoa. You're overreacting."

"No, I'm reacting normally when betrayed." Janey headed for the door, then realized she was going in the wrong direction and turned around for the elevator at the end of the hall. "Seal those up."

"Don't you want to hear the rest?"

"Orlando, you treat this station like your personal playground and what does that make me? A sucker! Turn around."

"What?"

"You're under arrest."

"On what charge?"

"Station sabotage."

"I didn't do anything. I thought you trusted me."

"How can I do my job with you jumping over the chain of command? I was a fool for trusting you." And for sleeping with you. "You're a guest on this station, at the aegis of the security department. And will remain so—in holding."

Orlando stared at her. "It's me, Janey, me, *mi corazon*."

"Turn around." Her body was shaking. She'd been such a fool.

"The panels."

"Fix them," she said through clenched teeth. She didn't understand how she could have been so blinded by his charm and looks for all these months. So, what if they'd talked about love and commitment back on Earth.

He bent to replace the panels, screwed back on one panel, and glanced back at her. Then he lifted the second one in place. It slipped in his grip. She bent to help him.

He shoved her, not hard, but enough to knock her off balance.

He dashed for the stairwell.

"Stop, Orlando!" she shouted. "Venus Hells."

Orlando pushed through the door to the staff stairwell. She raced after him, comming Kim. "Send a team to the staff stairwell between eighth and ninth levels, then lock all doors. Perp coming down. It's Orlando."

"Yes, Chief," Kim said, evenly. "Keeping the channel open."

"Thanks," was all Janey could manage.

She saved her breath and clattered after Orlando. He was already down to the next landing. He tried the door. It was locked. He ran his wrist comm over it and pushed the door open. It opened. Damn master thief. He probably had a master key to open any lock.

Janey put on a burst of speed, jumped down three steps, and rushed the door.

It didn't budge.

Janey used her wrist ident to unlock the door. That didn't work. Orlando must have jammed the lock. Maybe even changed the master lock code. She wouldn't put it past him.

"Kim," she said a bit winded. "Unlock the service stairwell door to level eight."

"He's jammed it with some kind of code," Kim said, "but —one second, and...okay. Got it."

The door clicked, and Janey shoved it open to the guest hallway. No one was there. Guest hotel suites were located on either side, and there was a sweet lavender perfume wafting on a light breeze. Ferns perched on the wall swayed.

Janey stopped, stumped. "Kim, he has a wrist comm on. Can you hack into it? It's not standard issue. He used it to unlock the stairwell door."

"I can't, Janey. Not without more time," Kim said. "Janey, are you thinking straight? Something else may be going on."

"Get on it, Kim. Please. Orlando has just moved to our number one suspect."

FOURTEEN

JANEY RUSHED DOWN THE EMPTY HALLWAY. "KIM, can you check the guest rooms for Orlando? I'll check the hallway vids."

"Yes, hold on. And I'll send staff to converge on your location."

"Fine." Janey waved on the wall screen to examine the hallway videos for anything at all. Footage scrolled. In the few seconds before Janey entered the hallway, Orlando had stepped into the hall, then disappeared.

His cloaking device. It was flawless. She couldn't see him at all. He was probably still in the hallway.

"Orlando!" she called. "Come back in. We can talk about it. Running only makes you look guilty."

Yet why would he show her the inside of the panels if he was guilty of planting the black stuff? She'd never would have found it if he hadn't shown it to her, but he was still hiding something from her.

Janey watched the screen as she talked, hoping for some anomalous reading or blip. Nothing. She scanned the hallway, flipping through wavelengths with her ocular implant as she went. There. Something that didn't show up in the vid at the far end of the corridor, at the wall.

Then it was gone. She blinked to zoom in with her ocular implant. There it was—a shimmer or a blur. It disappeared again. She dashed in that direction.

She reached out, in case he was still there, and touched air. At waist level, there was a panel like the ones he'd shown her on the level above.

She didn't have a tool to open it, so she scanned using various frequencies to see through to the other side of the panels. The area wasn't full of tubules for the water, energy, and air systems. Instead, it was empty. Some kind of passageway.

Her heart pattered with excitement. She called up the map for the tunnels. Yes, directly on the other side of this wall was a tunnel that led downward to the lowest level, right to the station's escape pods.

From the elevator, Goldberg, Clark, and Cho approached her.

"Chief, where do you want us?" Goldberg asked.

"Does anyone have a screwdriver?"

Cho handed her one, quizzically.

"Thanks. I want you to head down to the machine shop, aft entrance," Janey said. "But don't go in, and don't let anyone past."

"But no one uses that area," Clark said.

Janey lifted an eyebrow.

"Right, good place for someone to hide, Chief." He nodded.

"Get going," Janey said.

A chorus of "Yes, Chief" followed, and they hustled off toward the staff elevator.

Janey went to work and used the screwdriver to take off the panel.

She called out, just as they were approaching the elevator. "One of you replace this panel, please, once I'm through."

"Where are you going?" Goldberg asked, concern in her voice.

"In."

Goldberg trotted back and watched her go headfirst into a tunnel space a little wider than the diameter of her body. A tight fit, but it would widen out soon, Janey knew. With a snick, Goldberg replaced the panel.

Janey commed Kim. "I'm in one of the tunnels on the eighth level. You'll lose my signal soon."

"I still see you," Kim said. "What do you need?"

"Orlando is either heading for an escape pod or the weapons turret."

"I have eyes on both places. So far nothing."

"Thanks. I'm heading for the escape pods. I sent the team to the aft entrance of the machine shop. They don't know—"

"About the weapons turret."

"Right. I told them to guard that corridor. Do you see anything down there?"

"Checking," Kim said.

Janey gave her a moment.

"No, but if he's cloaked..."

"I know. I couldn't even see him until I ran through the entire spectrum."

"What frequency was that?"

"Oh, right, checking, I flipped through them so fast," Janey said, and then she was quiet as she studied the buffer on her internal screen. Most data was immediately buffered into her personal AI stored in quarters. But the most recent data was accessible—the last ten minutes usually. She found the frequencies, two of them, and sent them to Kim.

"Two frequencies?"

"Odd, I know."

"I'll run them over the vids and see what we get," Kim said, and Janey imagined that she was already reviewing the video feeds.

"If I don't check-in or you don't see me pop back onto the screens in twenty minutes, then send help."

"The three I just sent you?"

"Everyone."

"Got it, Janey. Good luck."

"I need more than luck. I need a miracle. If Orlando doesn't want to be found—"

"Then there's no finding him," Kim said grimly.

"Mierda." Janey commed off.

The tunnel was horizontal for six feet, then would slope downward sharply. She crawled on all fours. She took her time, adjusting her ocular implant as she went for any signs of Orlando. But that meant she was blind some of the time.

The tunnel was dusty, dry, and smelled of metal.

If Orlando had come this way, there was no sign of him.

At the end of the horizontal length, Janey stopped. The forty-five-degree slope ended about fifteen feet below. A slide. Janey adjusted herself, so she could go feet first. She tipped herself at the edge and shoved off.

Halfway down the tunnel, something jarred her to a stop. Something at her feet, an invisible barrier. She reached down to feel it and waved on the light beam on her wrist comm to reveal a piece of dull grey metal. She glanced about.

There. A panel was missing from the tunnel above her.

Some kind of crawl space. She reached to pull herself up. Arms grabbed hers and hoisted her the rest of the way. The tiny space was lit by some source she couldn't see. Probably a small lamp.

"Orlando! What—" She struggled to get out of his grip, but he held tight.

"Shh," he said. "Stop. This place is tiny and unfinished. You'll hit your head on the rough edges and cut yourself."

She stopped struggling. By the light of a small camping lamp, the spiky edges of the graphene beam walls cast ominous shadows. The edges hadn't been smoothed down, nor the walls painted. Either the builders had forgotten about the place or hadn't cared. The cubby hole smelled of faint grease and stale dust.

"I got it," she said. "Let go of me."

"Promise you won't go anywhere?" He spoke with calm, but his expression was stern on the edge of dangerous, his nose and cheekbones sharpened by shadow.

"Where could I go?" Janey asked. "Down the tunnel to the escape pods?"

"Yes." He stared at her, worried.

"I'm not going anywhere. I tracked you here, remember?" Her stomach tightened with dread or maybe the anticipation of going somewhere else, anywhere else.

"Good, because you really need to hear my side of the story."

Janey glared at Orlando. "Finally. If you hadn't run, if you'd only told me in the first place—"

"Janey, please." He patted the air as if that would calm her. "You didn't even give me a chance. Geez." He sighed a big sigh, exasperated with her.

The feeling was mutual. She crossed her arms. The space crowded in on them. A faint hum came from somewhere beyond the walls. Some heating ducts could be nearby.

"Just stop with the coulda, woulda, shoulda," he continued. "What is done is done." He watched her, wary. Understandably so.

She waited.

"Janey, please listen..."

"I'm listening."

"With your judgment filters up."

"Do you blame me?" she said. "I feel used by you, Orlando. I don't know what is real. I don't know who you are. I can't trust you. I wish I could." She sighed and stared at the exit hatch at their feet. "I thought we had something. I thought we were a good team. Maybe more."

"We are."

"No, we're not. I was just fooling myself. I'm just another good time to you on your way to closing another case. I see that now."

"What? How can you say that?" Orlando gulped, holding back a stronger emotion. "After all the time we've spent together. After all we've shared...and said."

"But you can't deny that your work is your life above your relationships."

"You're the same way, Janey."

"Am not. I have—had family." She sighed. "I have to take you in. You know that. Just messing with the systems you were in is an arresting offense. Only authorized personnel can be in there."

He shook his head. "Janey, my work is dangerous. I didn't want to involve you until I had something. I have something. Let me explain it to you."

"I'm not stopping you. What are you waiting for?"

He nodded. "It's a long story."

"I'm not going anywhere," she said. "Thanks to you."

"Thanks." He smiled wryly.

"Don't thank me yet. I haven't heard what you have to say."

FIFTEEN

"THERE'S THAT JUDGMENTAL GAZE AGAIN," Orlando said.

"Evaluating. Deal with it." Janey scrubbed her face. "By the way, you have only a few more minutes before Kim starts the search for me. So, talk."

Orlando nodded. "I've had Valkyrie working on anomalies and scenarios about the lost women for years."

Valkyrie was the name he gave to his personal AI. Janey nodded. She knew he used Valkyrie in this way. She'd done the same with big cases she couldn't crack.

She waited.

Orlando met her gaze and held it. "What I'm about to tell you, I shouldn't. My boss did not okay it."

She nodded to show she understood. He was taking a huge risk. For her.

"All signs pointed to Schoeneman and this station, but I can't reveal all my cards as this is still an open and highly sensitive investigation." He frowned and gave a look that said, even to you, *mi corazon.*

"I know. This work..." All these secrets to uncover.

"When I was finally assigned here, I was able to get more data and monitor more systems."

Something fell into place.

"Including our secret vid system," Janey said.

"Yes, and more. Valkyrie grabs all systems discreetly."

"That's so illegal." She narrowed her gaze at him. "Are you the source of the computer virus that hit the comm and other systems when I first got here sixteen months ago?"

"I'm afraid so," But he didn't look contrite, just determined, mission-driven. He didn't do what he did for the glory or the pay. He did it to get to the truth.

Janey relaxed her shoulders as that realization sunk in past her fatigue.

"I installed sniffers in the radio wave frequency to monitor the guest roster, betting patterns, movement around the station, that sort of thing."

"Those would be the most undetectable, but why all those things?"

"I told you...All signs pointed to Schoeneman and this station."

"What signs?" Janey hugged herself more tightly and shivered, hot and cold waves running through her in quick succession. "Kim never found your sniffers."

"She found the few I meant for her to find." He looked at her concerned. "Are you cold? You're in delayed shock. From your mom."

She shook her head. "Continue." It didn't matter what she was going through in the moment. Besides, it would pass, and she would have plenty of time to grieve once this case was over.

"Among other things, I was looking for a pattern of use, of people coming and going, anything that would point me in the direction of the ring leaders of the human trafficking ring."

"What other things?" Janey hugged herself tighter, the shakes coming from deep in her body. Even though she had her protective insulating layer on beneath her clothes, for some reason, it wasn't enough.

Orlando paused and reached out to her but didn't touch. "You sure you're okay?"

"I am far from okay," she admitted. "Go on. You have two minutes to get to the point." Her teeth chattered. She clamped her jaw shut.

"Or what? No, don't answer that. Sorry. That was uncalled for." He waved at the holo screen of his non-standard wrist comm. "The data has been pointing to someone tampering with the environmental controls, so I was checking it out for a closer look. I found signs of sabotage, but I don't know what it means. There was some kind of additive in minute quantities in cracks of the panels. The blue-black stuff I showed you."

She said nothing, her mind blank but absorbing. Numb again.

He peered at her, watching, evaluating. Then he spoke again. "I was able to scrape off a tiny quantity this morning in environmental controls and was having Soren analyze it when you called him."

"You were there with Soren when I was breaking into your quarters." Janey rubbed her arms, then stuck her fingers under her armpits.

"No, I was with him after that. I was snooping around when you shot the lock off my door," he said dryly. "You are cold."

"Just continue. I'll be—" Janey said but didn't want to finish. Who knew what she'd be? "What did Soren find?"

"He says it's a kind of algae that doesn't show up in the bio-scans in the environmental filters. The algae react only in certain conditions. He was narrowing that down for me. He wanted more samples. My tracking led me to the panels I showed you."

"Why those panels?"

He shrugged. "Like I showed you, my sniffers show they'd been tampered with. It's easy to be undetected if you're determined enough."

"And you have the right gear to be cloaked."

"Exactly," Orlando said. "Even if you're not. There's a monitoring gap in your vid system."

"There is?"

"Yes, a blind spot that anyone with skills like mine can circumvent."

"Really?" Janey shivered and noted the glitch on her holo screen for Kim and her team to follow up on. "Never mind. That's for later. What is this algae stuff? What does it react to?"

"Soren says it's a sort of designer algae, keyed to a particular person's genetics, and it acted as poison on them, forming that membrane, and killing them with deadly accuracy."

"Keyed to who?" Her insides turned cold. The skills needed to create such a poison.

He showed her his holo screen.

Janey stared at the genome laid out both in visual and code formats. "This just says that point one percent of the population would be tagged by this. Three people died."

"That's what I was going to bring to you. Which of the murdered guests does this genome match?"

"Not sure." She waved into the case files and swore. "Those details aren't on my comm. They're not kept in the regular personnel files. I'll need to get them from medical or their medical records on the planet. I can't contact them from here. There's no comm signal."

Her heart pounded. Clues, at last. "Maybe all three men

were the targets. Or maybe only one. Or two. And the others were diversions. But who? And why?" Anger flared in her chest, and thankfully, the shakes stopped. "Orlando, why didn't you come to me right away with this genome information?"

"Does that mean you believe me?"

"I may have acted in haste, attempting to arrest you for station sabotage, but still. You should have looped me in right away."

"Yes, I should have." He looked contrite for about a millisecond, then grinned. "Is that an apology?"

"I'm not sure. I need to sec all the data you've collected."

"It's a massive amount. Sifting through it would drastically slow down your investigation. I'd be happy to get you the summary report."

"My team can handle it. We need the genome data to start." She eyed the hole below them and the slide. "I thought that's what you were going to do."

"I wanted to show you first what I discovered. Privately. Outside of all prying eyes and ears and sniffers."

"You're exasperating." She rubbed her hands together to warm them up.

"Likewise." He smiled.

She cracked a small smile despite her best efforts. It felt odd, with all the sadness floating through her today and the stress. "How do we get out of here?"

"Why? So, you can arrest me?"

"I won't. But if you had come only peacefully before…"

"Instincts, I'm afraid, *mi corazon*. Being locked up once was enough."

"When you were young and foolish?"

"I am still young but no longer foolish."

"You'll have to tell me about it sometime," she said.

"If you don't arrest me first," he said with a straight face.

"Don't test me, Orlando."

"I would never."

She snorted. "Maybe I did act in haste."

He wisely kept silent.

Then she said, "Shall we take the slide?"

"After you, Madame."

SIXTEEN

ORLANDO WENT AHEAD, REMOVING THE BARRIER on the slide as he did, so they could slide down to the lowest level. Arms over his head as if he were at a child's play yard, he let himself drop down the forty-five-degree angle slope and yelled, "Janey, come on! It's fun!" as if they weren't in crisis mode, solving difficult and high-stakes cases.

Before she could second-guess him and develop a full-blown rant, Janey sat and shoved off, terrified and liberated at the same time. She didn't have to do anything in this moment. She couldn't. The tube smelled tangy metallic.

And then in ten seconds of a straight descent in the near dark, they arrived.

Orlando hopped to his feet, graceful and lithe, and fiddled with his off-book wrist comm. Janey let herself slow to a complete stop before she stood at a grey corridor outside the escape pod landing at the base of the station. She didn't trust herself to be so cavalier with her body. Too many disorienting factors were swirling in her right now, making reality tumble inside of her. She didn't need to aid the discombobulation anything further by pretending she was a carefree child. She'd never be a carefree child again.

Nothing fancy in the décor. Utilitarian hatch doors leading to small crafts. In the station history, there'd never been cause to use them, thank the stars, yet maintenance teams kept them in good working order—as all space stations had to.

Janey turned to Orlando. A spurt of anger sped through her and loosened her tongue, heating her body. "I should arrest you just for delaying me in my case."

He snapped his head up. "You need me." He kept his tone level, but he'd wanted to meet her anger with his and banked it at the last moment.

"I hate to admit it, but I do." She puffed out a breath, deflated. "What are we doing here?"

The corridor was empty as expected. No guest or staff would come to the escape pods unless they had to.

"Nothing, it was just fun." He flashed his charming smile.

"Okay, I won't arrest you." She snorted and shook her head, forgiving him a little more. Damn charm. True that he was a spy working for a government agency. True that he wasn't supposed to tell her everything. But still, it was frustrating. "You do not play well with others, Orlando."

He lifted an eyebrow at her. "Thank you."

Incorrigible.

Time to get back to the case. She commed Kim. "I have Orlando. Please call off the search. Instead, please have Mrs. Lisa Montaigne and Nasturtium brought into separate interrogation rooms. Remind the team to give them their rights' warnings." Wouldn't want to violate their Basic Sol rights of representation, protection, and court use.

"Of course. Yes'm, Chief. Is he in handcuffs?" Kim asked with entirely too much cheer and curiosity. "No, don't answer that. You okay?"

"Yes. I'll fill you in soon. McCallister out."

Janey headed for the guest express elevator that would take them to the main lobby.

"Why not take the staff turbo?" Orlando asked. "Aren't we headed to the interrogation rooms?"

"I want to check on something." Janey stepped into the elevator. "Let them stew and wonder what they're doing there."

"They might lawyer up." Orlando joined her.

"That's a chance I'm willing to take. If the evidence pans out, it won't matter for one of them, and the other will only be inconvenienced in the interest of solving the murder."

The chrome elevator with black accents and mirrored walls felt too closed in. Soft tinkling music played, and a lavender perfume filled the space.

Janey backed into a corner, shivering. Damn. Not this again. She wasn't cold, but her body acted like it was. She couldn't stop shivering. Orlando edged closer to her.

"Something is wrong, *mi corazon*."

She shook her head.

"We need to get you to Medical." He wrapped his arms around her.

For a second, she relented and let herself be enfolded by his heat and woodsy scent. She relaxed for a breath, relishing the connection. Then she wriggled loose. "No, Orlando. The case, we have to close it."

"This isn't the way to interrogation."

"It is," Janey said.

"No, we're headed to the lobby."

"I know."

"Nothing you say makes sense right now, *mi corazon*," Orlando said, his voice close to her ear, reaching for her. "We need two weeks in the salt baths of Agua Caliente. And no work."

For a second, she shivered, and blackness descended, then it cleared in a flash as if nothing was wrong. Warmth flooded back into her body. She was in Orlando's arms. His heat felt delicious, surrounding her.

The doors opened. A guest stepped in, then stopped when he saw them. "Oh, I'm sorry. *Mi esculpa*," the man said with a Spanish accent and backed out.

Orlando nodded to him, grabbed Janey's hand, and led her out of the elevator to the round, spacious lobby. A brilliant chandelier dominated the high-ceilinged domed space, spilling out a warm sunlight-like effect of mid-morning. Olive trees with the small dark green leaves dotted the edges of the lobby, and mosaics peeked through their branches, hints of yellow and green swirls revealed as the branches rustled in the breeze. There were no viewscreens of Earth or the stars, so the design made you think that around the next curve you'd see the Mediterranean Sea. Piped-in sounds of the waves lapping on the shore completed the illusion.

Two men sauntered into the casino, letting out the cheery and overbright clang and dings of the slot machines at its entrance.

Orlando led her toward noise.

"My lead...the case," Janey protested weakly.

He whispered in her ear. "You need a wee break."

"It can wait five minutes," she said as they crossed the threshold into the bright casino.

He made a beeline for the bar.

SkyBar. Her favorite part of the station.

They wove through slot machines—all that tinkling and clanking, blinking and rainbow lasers dancing. She let out a breath once they were past the blasted machines.

At midday, the casino had only scattered gamblers at the poker and blackjack tables and a few at the high-roller tables farther in. The holo band wouldn't start their nightly show until later. Musicians from around the Sol would pipe in with a live singer. They had a six-octave range diva from Kuala Lumpur at the moment. Janey had enjoyed their show when Mom visited last week. Mom had even gotten dressed up fancy, pearls, heels, and makeup. Mom had been here, only seven days ago. Felt like a lifetime and like a moment ago. Never to see Mom again, never to talk to her again.

Janey picked up the pace to the bar, rushing through the high-ceilinged area as large as a football field. And yet with strategic lighting and dark wood gambling tables and a dark carpet, the area had an intimate lounge feel. A bouncy, melodic dance tune wafted along with the scent of sweet alcohol.

Off to their right, the enormous wallscreen was dimmed so the light of the Sun wouldn't dominate the casino. Instead, a soft starfield appeared to move as you walked through the casino, the way the night sky follows you in a nighttime stroll under the stars.

At the bar that extended into the casino, Janey sat and accepted the cool drink Orlando handed her moments later. She hadn't seen Faizah, the bartender, come over. Orlando slipped a protective arm around her, and she sighed and stared at the wide window of stars above them.

SkyBar got its name not only from its location on L'Étoile but also from the widescreen directly above the back wall of the bar and ceiling. Since the station was tethered to Earth by its elevator, StarEl, the starfield changed with the planet's rotation. Plus, the wall and ceiling screens could be tuned to anything—the station's powerful telescopes, cameras that faced outward to the cosmos, or from any recording the casino's entertainment director desired.

On the ceiling screen viewer this afternoon, the Andromeda Cluster was on display. Earth's closest galaxy.

Maybe she could sign up for a long-haul gig and head out there. And never come back.

"Drink," Orlando said.

She sniffed it. "But it's alcohol. I'm on duty." Faizah, in her long dreads braided with sparkly rainbow ribbons, was down at the other end of the bar, sneaking concerned looks at her while she mixed a drink for the two men who'd walked in ahead of them.

"You're not working another second if you can't focus." Orlando squeezed her in a sideways hug, and a bit of liquid sloshed over onto her hand. Without thinking, she licked it. The warm heat jolted her. A Champagne Sparkler, her favorite drink, a little bitter and a little sweet. He was paying attention. He did care about the little things.

She sat up and glanced at Orlando.

He was watching her carefully, brown eyes full of concern and focus, penetrating her as if to jumpstart her mind. He stood flush against her, his arm still across her shoulders. "You wanted to come to this level for a reason, Janey. What was it?"

She blinked. "I can't remember." She closed her eyes for a moment, then opened them, blinking to run through the spectrum as she gazed at Andromeda.

Psychedelic spinning colors, then glowing vibrating reds and oranges, then flat colors, and finally, nothing. She palmed her eyes with one hand.

"I need the membrane results from Soren," Janey said with a sigh before dropping her hand and straightening. She needed to get herself checked out. She needed to get herself in gear. She did feel a little better, though. "What is it, and where did it come from?"

"He's still working on it. He needed more of a sample," Orlando said. "So, I got it for him."

"Then he should have gotten it," Janey said. "He's authorized for that part of the station. He can go wherever he likes. Besides, Doc has two more victims with the same manner of death."

"He wanted to stay in the lab and work with those samples, so I went instead. It had been my discovery after all," he whispered in her ear over the upbeat loud music. "What are we doing here? You have a hunch, I know it."

"Orlando, he could have asked a machine shop engineer to go. Why you? And why is my team going behind my back?" Janey waved a hand. "Forget it. I remember why I wanted to come here."

"Why?"

"Someone in the kitchen I wanted to talk to."

"Who?"

"Gina."

Orlando shook his head. "Oh boy."

"Her training in food chemistry—"

"I don't think you're up to a confrontation with the chef."

"Watch me." Janey stood and nodded to the bartender. Faizah nodded back and opened the bar flap.

Janey set her drink on the bar and pushed through into the storage room that connected SkyBar to the massive kitchen behind it. She stopped halfway through the cool room full of shelves, replete with bottles of condiments, dried spices, and boxes upon boxes of exotic culinary delights from around the world. She scanned the shelves.

There it was. Her AI had reminded her where she'd seen it before. The random fact finally tumbled loose from one of the times she'd last been in the storeroom.

Satisfied, she continued to the end of the storage room. At the door leading to the kitchen, she stopped and turned to Orlando. "I'll do the talking."

"I'll just stand there and look pretty."

Janey shrugged. "Or intimidating."

BETH BARANY

He glared. "I can do that." Then he smiled, ruining the effect.

The kitchen was busy with dinner prep. Staff was used to her and Orlando by now, and none of the kitchen's own security team challenged her as they had over a year ago when she'd newly arrived. She wove her way to Gina's office toward the back.

Janey knocked and let herself in, Orlando at her side.

"To what do I owe the pleasure?" Gina glanced up from handwriting into a book, perched at her counter-high worktable.

"Chef Gutierrez." Janey nodded.

"Chief McCallister," Gina said. "I'm in the middle of recipe planning, so…"

"I just have a question for you about blue-black algae I saw in the storeroom. Halfway up in a plain box, center of the room. Origin, Guatemala, Central America."

"What about it?" Gina looked quizzical.

Orlando jumped in. "Do you have any of it missing?"

Janey glared at him. He didn't look contrite.

Gina said nothing and clicked on her sleek keyboard projected on the table, presumably checking their stocking records. "No. All accounted for. Why? Is this related to why my staff can't get back on-station?" Gina leaned against the wall, crossed her arms, and gave Janey a challenging look.

"Yes," Janey said.

Gina came around from her desk, ignored Orlando, and stood beside Janey, peering down at her from her height of six feet one in spikey heels. Gina lifted Janey's chin and moved her head from side to side.

"You do not look good, McCallister. I'll get your tisane for you, *ahora mismo, immediatamente.*" Gina spoke Spanish when she was concerned for a friend, and now that Janey was one,

160

the chef liked to mother-hen her. Janey tolerated it, to an extent.

Janey pulled her head back. "Gutierrez, I'm fine."

"You are not fine," Gina said and clicked her wrist comm. "Danielle, make me one vervain tisane to-go for the security chief. The usual extras. On the double."

"Yes, Chef."

Gina crossed her arms again and glared at Orlando. "You are causing her heartache on top of her demanding case and family situation."

"I didn't mean to," Orlando said quietly.

"Enough mothering from you, Gina." Janey gulped at the sudden grief welling up. She shoved it down.

"You came here for something. You could have just called for the information you needed or sent one of your staff," Gina said. "You're acting chief now. And you need all the mothering you can get."

Janey held the gaze of the world-class chef. "You're right."

Danielle slipped into the office, gave Janey a vacuum flask, and slipped back out with a nod to Gina.

"Thank you, Gina," Janey said and sipped. Sighed. Heat ran through her body, zinging and zipping in all the right places. "This. I came for this."

In all the running around, she'd misplaced the other vacuum flask.

"When can my staff get back on-station? I was counting on their produce for some dishes I was planning to create tonight."

"I hope to have an arrest in—" Janey checked the time and swore. "I need to notify Schoeneman in ten minutes."

"What are you wasting time with me for?" Gina said in a mock stern tone, but her gaze held only kindness.

Janey nodded and lifted the tea. "Thanks for this, again."

"Anytime, *mi hermana*," she said. "The algae are all

accounted for, but I'll have my staff double-check and let you know."

"Thank you." She turned for the door, then turned back when an idea struck her. "Who else could have some?"

Gina glanced up, searching her mind. "Aquatics, gardening, hydroponics. You checked all those, I presume."

"I assumed yours are the freshest, what with the high turnover, so I checked with you first," Janey said. "We're checking the other locations, too."

Gina nodded, went behind her desk again, and scribbled in her recipe book, effectively dismissing them.

Janey wove her way through the kitchen, the storeroom, and out from behind the bar, all the way back through the forest of well-attended slot machines, through the busy lobby, and to the staff elevator. She felt disembodied but calm. Must be the tea. Things would connect again in a moment. They had to.

SEVENTEEN

JANEY HEADED FOR THE STAFF ELEVATOR.

"You okay?" Orlando whispered.

"One foot in front of the other." She waved into her holo screen, studying what she had on the case. Without looking at Orlando, she spoke, "Can you send me the algae type, the genome, and anything else ready to go?"

They stepped into the elevator. Orlando danced his fingers through the air in front of his holo screen, then looked up, "Done. Medical for you."

Janey ignored him and commed Prentice. "Status?"

"In the hallway outside the interrogation rooms, Chief."

"And?"

"Lisa and Nasturtium both came quietly and without a fuss. Surprised me."

Janey made a noncommittal noise. "Stay there. We'll be there soon." Janey commed off and huffed out a breath. To Orlando, she said, "I have to call Schoeneman, get the algae verified, narrow down the genome, and figure out who is the target. That will narrow down which of these two women is the perpetrator."

They exited the elevator into the security staff service corridor.

"Divide and conquer," Orlando said. "I'll go back up to the ninth level and get what Soren needs."

"Report back to me from Soren's lab. I need that information as soon as—"

"Possible. I know." Orlando leaned in for a kiss, surprising Janey, though she didn't know why. She kissed him back. Then with a smirk, he jogged back to the service elevator.

Janey strode to her office, stepped in, set her vacuum flask on the desk, and studied the murder board.

She called Medical and spoke as soon as the comm was picked up.

"Horsely, will you send me the medical records for the three murder victims? I just sent you their identities. I specifically need their genome."

"Yes, sir. If you're calling for Medical Chief Horsely, she isn't in. She's in the lab with Doc."

"Thanks. I expect to hear from her as soon as she has something."

"Oh, she didn't tell you?"

"Tell me what? What's the message?"

Janey's comm vibrated on her wrist, the holo screen flashing open, lighting up too bright. Janey blinked to narrow the visual spectrum. A high-pitch whistle drowned out anything the medical assistant was saying. The sound stopped, and Janey was looking at pinpricks, no, tiny holes on the ceiling tiles.

"Chief, are you alright?" It was Antonia Lane hovering over her, helping her to her feet.

"Where did you come from?" Janey swore. "How long was I out?"

"About five seconds," she said. "I heard a cry. Let myself in."

"Good initiative, Lane." Janey rubbed her pounding temples, where giants in clogs danced a rager.

The door whooshed open, and in strode Chief Medical Officer Horsely, Orlando right behind her.

"How did everyone get here so fast?" Janey said, a little wobbly on her feet. Her office felt tiny, wallscreens show starscapes. Her stomach protested. She wasn't floating in the blackness of space. Her temples pounded more, and her sight seemed tinged with red.

Horsely waved her medical holo over her and frowned at it. "We were already on our way when Anthony commed me." Her medic. "Come on, this way." Horsely nudged her by the elbow across the hall to the conference and into the smaller break room, out of sight of staff milling about the coffee and pastry station. "I need to check you out. I don't like what I'm seeing." She tsked. "Your blood pressure... And Mr. Valdez told me you're having memory lapses, blackouts, and the chills."

"But the case," Janey protested, but she let Horsely lead her to the bed-couch.

Horsely nudged her to take a seat. "Other people can put two and two together for you temporarily. We don't need the chief and acting chief down for the count. Who will make the hard calls? We need you up, so stay down for a few minutes."

"Yes, ma'am."

Horsely grumbled about stubborn patients and continued to wave her medical comm over Janey.

Orlando crowded into the small room.

"You don't need to be here," Janey said.

"Yes, I do," he said and crossed his arms.

Alison gave Orlando a stern look. "My patient said, 'out.'"

Orlando flashed Janey a concerned look, and Janey shooed

him away with a tilt of her head. She couldn't talk at that moment because Horsely had her opening and closing her mouth. As Horsely scanned her, humming and nodding over the scan details, Janey commed Antonia.

"Yes, Chief?"

"I need you to compare genomes against a substance Soren has been analyzing."

"On it." Antonia continued when Janey didn't say anything for a few long minutes, "Anything else, boss?"

"Yes, follow up with medical for the murder victims' records. I was in the middle of that when I, well, when—Just follow up on that and—"

"Are you okay, Chief?"

"No. Horsely is checking me out right now. I need you to—"

"Don't worry about the case, sir. I have it in hand."

"You do? What would you do next, Antonia?" Janey closed her eyes against the pounding at her temples.

"Study the murder board, your case notes, look for loose threads to pull, and—"

Antonia paused. So, Janey opened her eyes and stared at her holo screen. "What else?"

Antonia said softly, "What do you recommend next?"

"Get the team together to get clear on the timeline and the evidence. We need a solid case."

"On it." Antonia's normal confidence was back. "The suspects, want me to take a crack at them."

"No, we need more. And I want to do it."

Her comm intoned with Schoeneman's tone. "I have to take this. Alison, clear out, please."

Schoeneman's tone insisted again.

Horsely held a compressor to Janey's neck.

Janey felt a jolt down her spine. "What was that for?"

"A mild sedative to calm your nervous system. It's over-stimulated. What have you been drinking or eating?"

"Just Gina's tisane."

"Where is it?"

"On my desk."

"You need rest, a vacation, family bereavement leave, not running around under all this pressure." Horsely frowned.

"I'm trying to catch a murderer," Janey said.

"I know, Chief," Horsely said. "But health first." Then she left the small breakroom.

Janey opened the comm channel. "McCallister here."

"What was taking you so long? I told you to delegate, Acting Chief McCallister."

"My job, sir."

"Report."

"Two people in interrogation."

"No arrests? I said—"

"I know what you said, sir. I'm doing my best."

"Of course. I expect nothing less. I'll be there in thirty minutes. En route, already."

"It's not safe, sir."

"It's my station. I'll run things as I please."

Janey frowned. "What if that's what the killer wants?"

"Don't be ridiculous! I am no target."

"You may be. Your station may be. Like last time."

"Not going to happen. Others tried it and failed."

"There is no need for you to come, sir. I highly advise against it for so many reasons. You've already been kidnapped once—"

"I have a private security team with me. I'll be fine."

Janey snapped her mouth shut, at a loss for further objections.

"McCallister, don't bother meeting me at Arrivals. I know you have your hands full."

"I do indeed," Janey said. "I'm lodging a formal report stating that I don't recommend you board L'Étoile."

"Fine. I'll delete it."

"I'm not filing it with you but with the Sol Space Authority."

"Going above my head..." Schoeneman said, cool and controlling. "Not a good idea."

"You hired me to do a job, and you're not making it easy. You're also making yourself a convenient target."

"Do you have any evidence of that?"

"No," Janey said reluctantly.

"Then upon what basis—"

"A gut check, sir."

"Thank you for telling me that, Investigator...uh...Acting Chief, but I'm not sure how much we can trust your gut, what with all the pressure you're under."

"I'm happy to tender my resignation, sir, if you don't believe in me, won't let me do my job, and then proceed to insult me repeatedly."

"Oh, shake it off, McCallister," Schoeneman chuckled. "You're doing fine. I didn't realize you were such a light-weight. So sensitive."

"And I didn't realize you cared so little about your own safety," Janey said, steaming, but not ready to go for the jugular.

What would that serve? She really didn't need this job anyway. But she would complete this case because she couldn't let it go. She had to finish what she started. Nel and the others deserved justice, like anyone else, like everyone else.

EIGHTEEN

SCHOENEMAN COMMED OFF WITHOUT A GOODBYE. Janey stood, and a dizzy spell washed over her. She just needed a minute to gather her thoughts. Maybe more than a minute. She lay down on the bed, closed her eyes, and shielded her ocular implant. Her visual field went dark.

Moments later, a knock on the door brought her to sitting, her heart pattering. She'd moved too fast. "Yes?"

She couldn't see. All was black. The door opened and closed. Someone padded closer, quiet as a cat. She inhaled, not afraid. A musky male with a touch of woodsy cologne. Orlando.

"*Mi corazon,*" he murmured close to her.

Her ocular implant. She blinked, adjusting it to normal vision.

Worry lines bracketed his mouth. Tension pulsed in his neck.

"Orlando. What is it?"

"Schoeneman is docking."

"Already?" She stood on stockinged feet, grateful for

feeling steady, and checked the time. "I was out thirty minutes. Why didn't anyone wake me?"

"Doctor's orders. She wanted us to leave you alone as long as possible."

"Interrogation room?"

"The ladies are still there. Stewing." He gave a feral grin, showing teeth.

She glanced at him sideways. "Did you take off my boots?"

"You looked uncomfortable."

"I really didn't want Schoeneman on-station," Janey said. "That complicates things, a lot. The killer could make a run for it, even though hangar security knows their job."

Orlando sobered and glanced at his holo comm, his real one. "I know."

"What is it?"

"While you were napping, the team found the genomic match, and Soren thinks he figured out how the membrane worked."

Janey swore and shoved her feet into her boots. "Both clues are huge. You should have woken me."

"I told you—" Orlando reached out to steady her, but she waved him off and rushed out of the conference room, across the hall, and back to her office. He followed her in, nonplussed by her brush-off. Thankfully, he was used to her moods by now. Maybe he was a keeper, after all. She shoved relationship matters out of her mind. After that power nap, it was time to get back to the case. A new certainty flooded her system. They were getting closer to their killer.

In front of the murder board wallscreen, Prentice was tapping away. The young agent looked up at Janey, concern in her eyes. "Chief, are you alright? Antonia wanted Meilani and me to update things." Beside her, Meilani nodded, somber. She was out of her fancy duds from when she was doing private security for Mr. Hwang and Nasturtium and back in back-office grey coveralls and practical boots. Prentice continued, "She's with Soren, I think. Antonia, I mean. I thought it easiest here in the quiet. Fewer distractions. If you want, I can work back in the bullpen. I know you've been going through a lot lately—"

"Anahi, slow down. That's fine. I'm better. What you got?"

"I think, *we* think"—Prentice nodded at Meilani and waved around to include the team—"Mr. Leo Montaigne was the intended target, and Mr. Hwang and Mr. Nel were unfortunate, horrible accidents. We think." She chewed her lip.

"Good thing we have Lisa Montaigne in custody," Meilani said. "But does Nasturtium need to be there?"

"She did board illegally," Prentice said.

"That's right. She can stew a bit longer," Janey said. "Tell me how you came to the conclusion that Leo Montaigne was the intended victim."

She stared at the three long double helixes spinning majestically. DNA carries genetic instructions for the development, functioning, growth and reproduction of all known organisms and many viruses.

Venus hells. Who could pull off such a detailed attack? It was quite brilliant and sneaky, really.

"See," Prentice said, shifting from foot to foot, "here are Hwang's, Nel's, and Montaigne's genomes."

"Go on," Janey prompted.

"Right, so the mutated algae—oh yeah, that's what Soren said it is—a genetically altered algae—very clever—the black goop Investigator Valdez found in the environmental systems. Not sure how?" Prentice took a breath.

Orlando jumped in. "Soren said the algae have been genetically altered for Montaigne's genome."

"Traces of that algae were also discovered in the

membrane that formed in the victim's mouths," Prentice said. "That's how you knew to look for algae?"

Orlando took a breath and glanced at Janey. "It's a long story."

Prentice looked between Janey and Orlando. "I guess not one for me."

"I'll continue, yes?" Meilani said. "Unfortunately, Hwang and Nel's genomes are a seventy percent match to the engineered algae."

Prentice said with a banked excitement, "What are the odds that they would be on-station at the same time?"

"Unlucky coincidence?" Meilani asked.

"I think so," Prentice said. "And Montaigne's genome is a ninety-nine-point-seven percent match."

"The intended victim," Janey said.

Prentice and Meilani nodded.

"Motive?" Janey asked.

"I'm stumped." Prentice leaned against Janey's desk.

"Lust, love, loathing, or loot," Meilani said.

"Good. You've remembered your training," Janey said. "Now we just need to figure out which one."

Everyone looked at her, nodding.

"I have an idea." Janey opened the cross-check she had running in the background on the murder victims and their possible connections to Bakaj's black book of villains from an earlier case.

Strange that her AI hadn't let her know of its results yet. The list was finite. The program should have been done by now, and she should have been notified hours ago, but what with her memory gaps, who knew. Maybe the ping had come in when she'd been out of it, so she hadn't seen them.

She opened the search program, and there they were—the cross-check results, clear as day, waiting for her like data does. The results had her sucking in her breath. Orlando came over and made a considering sound.

"What? You knew?" Janey asked.

"I speculated," Orlando said.

"What is it?" Prentice asked.

"Mr. Montaigne is listed in Bakaj's black book of war profiteers, listed as a black-market gun runner and materials supplier," Janey said.

"Not looking good for Lisa Montaigne," Meilani said.

"If she knew about it," Prentice said.

"We'll ask her that," Janey said, nodding at Orlando.

"What does this last symbol mean?" Prentice asked, pointing to a symbol that Janey hadn't been able to make heads or tails of.

"I'm not sure it matters," Janey said. "We have enough to question Lisa."

"I'm good with codes and ciphers. And Meilani is better than me," Prentice said. "Can we have a crack at it?"

"Sure." Janey stepped back. "Have at it. But keep this file, and your notes, where it is—off the main system."

"Yes, Chief," Prentice and Meilani said in unison.

Together the two security agents took their place in front of a copy of Bakaj's black book on the board and started whispering over semaphores, polyalphabetic ciphers, and frequency analysis. Way over Janey's head. She'd spent hours on the symbols and foreign language code in Bakaj's little black book, and she still couldn't crack all of them.

Orlando turned to Janey. "Shall we go to interrogation?"

"I'm not ready. I need more. Otherwise, Lisa will lawyer up. I need more leverage." Janey stared at one of her wallscreens—the one of Saturn's pebbled rings, slowly dancing around the gas giant.

"Montaigne was a bad guy," Orlando said. "Maybe his wife killed him. Maybe she had too much of his illegal gun-running. Maybe he had a whole harem of young women on the side—"

"All speculation," Janey said. "His murder was so detailed, planned, very smartly done, with a hard-to-trace murder weapon, that algae, and with an obscure delivery method, which I'm still not clear on."

"Why are you playing the devil's advocate?" Orlando asked.

"Just getting prepared."

"Soren can explain it better than I can," Orlando said. "Maybe Mrs. Montaigne's super smart and wanted to plan the perfect crime. She must have a good reason."

"Doesn't seem likely." On another part of the wallscreen, Janey opened Mrs. Montaigne's bio. "She has no history or background in chemistry, biology, or engineering that I could find. Just involved with lots of charities…"

"She's good at networking," Orlando countered. "She could have an accomplice. Spouses are most often killed by the other spouse."

"She could have an accomplice."

"Nasturtium?"

"But Nasturtium would have known then that Oscar would be at risk…" Janey shook her head. "No, that doesn't add up. But it's something to run at her. She is a cool one. I still don't like Nasturtium for it. She's hiding something, but I don't think she's a murderer. We have no evidence linking her."

"Wouldn't be the first time two women teamed up to kill their husbands," Orlando said. "I've seen it far too much."

"You have?"

"Among other things." Orlando stared at the board, but it didn't seem like he was really looking at it.

"If I may?" Meilani jumped in.

"Go ahead," Janey said.

"I've been with Nasturtium and Oscar, Mr. Hwang, for a few days," Meilani said, "and I didn't hear an unkind word between them. They were both full of gentle loving kindness toward each other. He doted on her, and she adored him. It was sweet really. She seemed genuinely sad about his death and had been looking forward to a new future with him as his wife."

"But maybe she assisted Lisa?" Prentice added earnestly. "I know you implied that…"

"And you said it. But what evidence do we have?" Janey pressed.

"Or there could be a different accomplice," Meilani added.

"But who?" Prentice shifted from foot to foot.

"Where does the evidence lead?" Janey asked, more as a reminder to her team.

"Maybe someone related to the missing person's case—" Orlando mused.

"Right, Hwang's missing sister," Janey said. "Maybe she had a lover who is exacting revenge. But we haven't found Montaigne's connection to your…case." Janey didn't want to share specifics of Orlando's case around her team. She wasn't supposed to know anything about it and hadn't been officially read in.

"I know," Orlando said, pensive, and he waved up a privacy screen and stepped closer to her, including her. "Those men are squirrely," he started up. "I haven't been able to pin down any direct evidence…only circumstantial. And they're all too rich to bring to court with only circumstantial evidence." Orlando opened his holo and showed her Hwang's missing sister, Ji-woo's, file. Janey skimmed the report.

Oscar had reported his young sister, Ji-woo, missing two days after she missed a regular weekly check-in. The young woman was last seen in Coban, Guatemala, working at the headquarters of Kavé Holdings. Coworkers saw her leave work at nineteen hundred hours and head for transport. No one remembered seeing her after leaving the perimeter of the building cameras. There was a lot of traffic all around the building, being in the center of the corporate coffee head-quarters district. The area was heavily watched and guarded. There were private cars scooping people up all the time and a tram system nearby taking people out of the center to their high-rise residences. Neighbors reported not seeing her that evening.

"She just disappeared?"

"Like many of the women I've tracked. Into thin air."

"So sad," Janey said. "Why was her file sealed?"

"Any files tagged with Kavé Holdings are subject to search and seizure by the corporate lawyers—if they know about it. It's routine for our files to have the best security. Otherwise, our cases would collapse practically before they have begun."

"Makes sense. But how does this all connect?"

"I think I know how," Prentice said, eyes wide, a guilty look plastered on her face. Her enhancements were powerful if she was able to listen in past the privacy barrier. "I couldn't help overhearing about Hwang's sister's plight. I assume that's your beat, Investigator Orlando, these missing women from good families. Sorry, I'm able to listen in…"

"You're a force to reckon with, Anahi," Orlando said.

Prentice blushed. "I want to help. That's the only reason I listened. I swear, I'll say nothing. Sol Security Police are tough." She gulped and fidgeted, glancing at the floor. Perhaps she'd had direct experience with just how tough the Sol Security Police were.

"I know. You keep this information off any system, you understand?" Orlando said, sternly, more serious than Janey had ever heard him be.

"Understood, sir," Prentice said contritely. "That life…" She shook her head, a bleak look in her eyes.

"Just so you know, women we investigate come from all kinds of families."

"Understood." Prentice nodded.

"We've deciphered the markings in Bakaj's black book," Meilani announced.

Janey stepped out of Orlando's privacy screen. "Show us."

Meilani indicated the screen with a pointer. "This string of symbols means 'nest maker.' I see in your notes that you thought it meant 'bread machine' or 'bread staker.'"

"Neither of which made sense. But neither does 'nest maker,'" Janey said.

Orlando gave a look like she should get it.

"What?" Janey asked.

"I've seen it before," Orlando said. "It was a common expression."

"It is? Where?" Janey asked.

"Everywhere."

"Ji-woo was my age about when she disappeared," Prentice said. "Making nest. Like a bird. For eggs."

"Right, of course." Janey shook her head. "Stolen, kidnapped, lured into being some rich man's baby maker." She sighed. "But why? There are legal channels for being a surrogate."

"Because they can," Orlando said.

"Do we have evidence of Montaigne involved in illegal surrogates besides a code in a secret black book?" Janey asked.

Orlando said nothing.

Prentice shook her head.

Meilani shrugged. "I didn't see anything like that in our deep dive. But we can only go so far into Sol Security database."

"I think we have enough," Janey said. "We have an idea why Montaigne would have been killed... Revenge perhaps for his illegal trade of women or their babies. We know he was targeted specifically with the genetically modified algae. Though how the algae created the membrane, I still don't understand. We have a possible motive."

"What about opportunity?" Prentice asked.

"She's on board with her husband," Meilani added.

"Circumstantial, but a start." Janey nodded. "What about means? Lisa doesn't seem to have the knowledge of biology or chemistry to pull off this sophisticated crime."

"She could have hired help," Prentice said. "But we have no evidence of that." Her shoulders drooped.

"But we have some solid information to question her with now," Janey said. "Let's see what she knows."

"And what she reveals"—Meilani grinned—"by what she doesn't say."

"Indeed," Janey said, nodding, approving. Her team was getting it.

"It's always the wife," Orlando said.

"Really?" Prentice glanced at Orlando.

He nodded, then shrugged. "Often."

"Prentice," Janey said, "I need you to dig deeper into Mr. Montaigne's files, financials, any whisper of his underground dealings."

"Chief, we already did. Found nothing of significance." Meilani called up the files.

"Even with all the privacy locks off?" Janey asked.

"Yes, it's as if someone scrubbed his files," Prentice added.

"Maybe a failsafe kicked in after he died," Orlando said. "I've seen that."

"Who could have scrubbed his files?" Meilani asked.

"The killer, most likely," Janey said. "Follow the disappearing money. Coordinate with Antonia on tracking down who could have done that."

"I'll work with Antonia," Meilani said. "I want to get to the bottom of this."

"Thanks, Meilani," Janey said. "Be sure you work with Kim, too. She knows tech systems like nobody's business."

Meilani nodded and got to work, waving in messages to her holo.

"I'd really like to watch the interrogation," Prentice said.

Janey eyed her, considering. "Okay."

Her comm hummed against her skin. It was a message from Kim that Schoeneman was in her office.

Venus hells.

She needed an arrest, she needed to keep Schoeneman away from her suspects, and she needed to look a murderer in the eye and ask, "Why?"

"We need to go," Janey said. "Interrogation room now."

NINETEEN

Outside the door to Interrogation Room One, Janey stopped. "Prentice, observation room."

Prentice nodded, a little chagrined, but she banked that and headed for the next door down.

"You okay to do this?" Orlando said quietly.

"I'm fine," she replied. The grey corridor halls were soothing, and no piped-in music distracted. The faint smell of lemony antiseptic of the recent passage of the cleaning bots lingered.

Orlando touched her arm. "I got your back."

"I know, thanks." Janey smiled gratefully. "But I'm bending the rules, letting you participate—you being under my command and all."

As an investigator of the Sol Special Security Police, Orlando had jurisdiction over crimes against humanity and cross-border crimes and could only act on capital crimes once an arrest was made.

"Of course," Orlando said, serious, courteous, getting into character, she supposed.

They headed into the room.

In a black and white tennis outfit, hair coiffed perfectly, legs crossed, Lisa Montaigne examined her perfect manicure as Janey across the table sat in front of her. Prentice must have interrupted the woman's workout in her suite. Orlando leaned against the back corner. Janey shook her head at him. He got the message and sat beside her.

Long and narrow with white-grey walls, the interrogation room wasn't built for comfort or to impress anyone on style. The air was neutral like a clean room. No hum or buzz to distract. Lisa took her time with her detailed examination of the room. Then she landed a lazy, self-important gaze on them. To Janey, Lisa pursed her lips and narrowed her eyes, ever so slightly, then went neutral. But Janey caught the flicker of movement clear as day.

"For the record," Janey said, "Acting Chief Janey McCallister and Sol Special Security Police Investigator Orlando Valdez are speaking to Lisa Montaigne about the death of Leo Montaigne, her husband."

Lisa eyed Orlando up and down, clearly not impressed. Finally, she spoke in a patronizing tone, "You've had your fun. I need to arrange for my husband's funeral. I must go now." She sniffed again and went back to examining her nails. But she didn't head for the door. A bit of good news.

"Mrs. Montaigne, we think your husband was targeted," Janey began.

"Of course, he was," Lisa said, her tone cool. "He's dead, isn't he? Poor bastard." She paled and cupped her eyes with her palms for a long moment as if the grief was all too much to bear. Or maybe the idea that he was targeted.

"Perhaps you're not understanding me," Janey said. "Let me explain. There were two other deaths this morning, but your husband was the intended target."

She snapped her gaze to Janey, haughty again, calm restored. "Whatever for? Leo is a—he was a good man." She touched up her perfect eye makeup, designed to make her look sophisticated.

"No, he wasn't," Orlando said. "He was involved in black-market gun-running, warmongering, and human trafficking,"

"What are you talking about?" Lisa stood. "I really must go. I've been nice enough to wait for you, and now you insult me—"

"Sit down, Mrs. Montaigne," Janey said.

"You have nothing to hold me with. I want my lawyer now." Finally, she asked for her lawyer. Maybe the seriousness of the situation finally pressed upon her.

"Fine," Janey said. "You'll get your call. Sit. Please."

Lisa held herself rigid as if she was about to pick a fight. After a long moment, she sat. "Fine, but I'm not saying another word until my lawyer pipes in. She's probably eating dinner or having a martini in her gorgeous penthouse with a Manhattan view to die for." She sighed as if transported to good memories. "I want my call now."

Janey waved a command to unlock the table call functions. "Go ahead. Make your call." She had to let Lisa place her call per the Basic Sol rights of representation, protection, and court use.

Lisa made the call, and they all heard a melodic ring tone. An automated answering service picked up, and Lisa left a curt message for her lawyer to call her back tout de suite, a Geraldine Tonga. In the last few seconds, she said something in rapid French that Janey didn't catch. The room recording would have caught it though. They'd find out what Lisa said soon enough.

"You are indeed in deep shit," Orlando said.

Right, he spoke French.

He leaned forward. "Now, where were we? Of course, you don't have to say anything, but we have evidence that your husband was involved in the human trafficking ring I've been tracking for years."

He sat back, a satisfied ease about him, the cat who ate the canary and all.

"What?" Lisa's nostrils flared. The skin tightened around her eyes. Either she didn't like the topic, she knew more than she let on, or she was hiding something else. "Who the hell are you anyway?"

"We told you," Orlando said in a neutral tone, "I'm Sol Special Security Police Investigator Orlando Valdez."

Lisa sputtered something about Frederick bailing her out, then crossed her arms and clammed up.

Janey needed more information. So, she went fishing. "I think you found out what your husband was doing on one of his many trips away without you, and outraged, as a good Sol citizen you are, you arranged to have him killed." Janey paused and let her sarcastic remark sink in. Lisa glared at her, fiddling with her sparkly diamond tennis bracelet. She continued, "It's horrible to be profiting from war and from the misfortune of others—especially from misleading and exploiting young women and preying on their desires for a better life."

Lisa's eyes widened, her pupils dilating. She firmed her jaw, possibly against the words that wanted to tumble out.

"That's right," Janey continued. "It's horrible. You know many people. You probably reached out to one of your connections at a university or lab that could manufacture the perfect untraceable weapon, a near-perfect match to your husband's genetic code. You probably brought the substance on board, harmless algae that passed the scans—no problem. Then, if my speculations are correct, you paid a certain someone to sneak on board through back channels and feed the algae into our environmental system, so it could work its way into the air ducts to find your husband, killing two additional people in the process—innocent, decent people minding their own business. With full lives and people who cared about them." Nel must have people who cared for him. Like Lisa Montaigne, his sister.

Janey leaned back in the chair and waited.

The older woman seated across from her shifted in her chair. A large bead of sweat collected at her hairline. "You have no evidence," she said. "Otherwise, I'd be under arrest. This is ridiculous."

"We can hold you here another twenty hours with probable cause," Janey said and waved on the table comm. "Go ahead and call her again. We'll give you some privacy."

Janey motioned with her head to Orlando and headed out of the room, him following right behind.

They entered the viewing room next door. Prentice was staring intently through the mirrored window. She whispered when she saw Janey, "She's calling. Do you—"

Janey nodded, raising a hand to stop Prentice's next words. She pointed to the window and indicated to watch. She turned off the audio. The lawyer wouldn't want them to be listening. But watching was needed. Mrs. Montaigne spoke rapidly, her back to the window. Cagey woman. Janey swore under her breath and turned on the audio.

"—and get me the jet pronto. I'm tired of this game." She slumped her shoulders. "No, just do it. I don't care if the station isn't accepting space jets. Call Frederick. Get it done and get here. Merde." Another pause. "Of course, I'm innocent. The cocky investigator has nothing on me. Her man candy, however, may be too close for comfort." She snorted. "No, Geraldine, I did not have my husband killed. Why would I? He was my meal ticket. Besides, I loved him, in my fashion." She was quiet for a moment and then glanced over her shoulder at the opaque window. She knew Janey was in the observation room.

Lisa sighed. "I tell you, they have nothing on me. I'm squeaky clean, you know that. Stop grilling me. You of all people. Yes, I miss him, I guess." She shrugged and sat, staring at the screen. "No, I don't want to turn on the vid. Just get here ASAP." She laughed a forced fake laugh. "Leo had his moments. What can I say? We'd been married a long time." Another long-suffering sigh. "Gerry, I'm tired. Be a dear and do as I ask. No more questions. Yes, goodbye."

Lisa waved the table and closed the comm. She tried other features, but the table screen had gone dark. Janey locked her out.

"I can't tell if she's guilty or innocent," Prentice said.

"She's a slippery one," Janey said. "I thought my story was plausible, but she's right, I have no direct evidence."

"Always circumstantial…" Orlando said, looking pensive. "She thinks I'm on to something. That's good. Which part triggered her?"

"Oh, oh! I have this!" Prentice said. "That you have evidence that he was involved in a human trafficking ring. The evidence is the black book, right?"

Janey elbowed Orlando. "What if she runs the ring?"

He said the same thing at the same time and grinned. Looked like he wanted to kiss her right there. But he didn't.

"What evidence do you need exactly, Orlando? You've never talked about that," Janey asked.

"Women willing to name their captors," he said and lifted a finger. "Everyone's been too scared to do that openly. We only have deep background, but no one wants to go on the record."

"That sucks but is totally understandable," Janey said.

"Evidence of money changing hands," he added, lifting another finger. "But they're excellent at hiding the money trail."

"What does that leave you with?" Prentice asked.

"Confessions, taped clandestine conversations, and snitches who know the inside world." Tapping the rest of his fingers. "I thought I had one of those, but—" He shook his head. He'd lost one of his informants recently, but Janey didn't know the details.

"I have an idea," Janey said. "But it means involving Schoeneman."

"You can't," Orlando said.

"Why not?"

"Because I think he's in charge of the human trafficking ring."

Janey sucked in a breath. "Schoeneman?! You never told me that! But I guessed… you never confirmed."

"I know." Orlando frowned. "But you can't show your hand to him."

"I know this is a tangent," Prentice said. "But what about Nasturtium? If she was the one to plant the algae, why did she? That would have been a huge price to pay to help Mrs. Montaigne. Why would she do it? She lost her love. If she knew that Mrs. Montaigne allegedly murdered her husband, maybe she'd be willing to help us get a confession."

Janey blinked. "All speculation. I was just running with a theory. But great idea, Prentice."

The probie beamed.

"You conduct the interview."

"Really? What about Antonia? She's lead."

"I've decided. Let's go." Janey turned to Orlando. "What about you?"

"I need to do a few things."

"What?"

"I can't tell you."

She frowned at him.

"It's for your own safety." He put a hand on her cheek. "Trust me."

She stared into his dark brown eyes. "I want to."

"I'm one of the good guys. I've always been," he said with resolve, holding her gaze. "Despite appearances. Remember that." Then he left.

Janey shook her head. "Let's go, probie."

She couldn't control Orlando. She had to trust him. She had to trust he was on her side, so she could close this case.

TWENTY

JANEY UNLOCKED INTERROGATION ROOM TWO AND
entered, Prentice on her heels. The inexperienced agent
glanced at Janey, a question in her eyes. Janey gave her a nod
of confidence. Prentice gave herself a little shake and took the
center chair. Janey leaned on the wall, off to one side. It was
time for the probie to prove herself, and the young woman
knew it. Based on everything Janey had seen in the last
month and especially today, she had every faith that Prentice
could step up.

This interrogation room was identical to the other one.
Nasturtium had her hands folded in her lap, her eyes closed.
She was breathing deeply. Was the woman asleep? Smudged
tear tracks marred the young woman's powder-white cheeks.

Prentice drummed her fingers on the table.

Nasturtium opened her eyes and watched Prentice
without expression. She glanced at Janey. "Chief."

"Ms. Nasturtium, I'm Security Agent, Investigator in
Training, Anahi Prentice," Prentice said and paused a beat.
Nasturtium finally nodded slowly as if in a daze, and Prentice continued, "Were you aware that your *namarado* was

killed as a way to get to another man, a sort of targeted accident?"

Nasturtium's eyes widened. "What do you mean?"

"Leo Montaigne was the intended target," Prentice said, "but your dear *namarado*, Mr. Oscar Hwang, was a seventy-nine percent genetic match to the genetically altered algae that killed Mr. Montaigne."

Nasturtium covered her mouth, and tears welled up in her eyes. She seemed genuinely shocked.

Prentice leaned forward. "We think you helped plant the algae on the station and killed your *namorado*, and Mr. Montaigne, and one other man, Mr. Nel, a gentle scientist."

"No! How? What? This can't be happening." Nasturtium shook her head. Then she blew out a breath and sat back. "You have nothing on me."

Prentice opened her mouth and then closed it. Janey jumped in. "You're right, we don't. But we'd like your help in getting evidence. Or—" Janey left that hanging.

"I will not help you," Nasturtium said.

"Why not?" Prentice asked. "Mrs. Montaigne killed your *namarado*—"

"Stop calling him that. He wasn't only my lover. We were life partners. Besides, what we had was private. You can call him Oscar or Mr. Hwang or whatever else you want, but not that."

"Does it upset you that your true love was killed by a woman who is more conniving and secretive than the Swiss bunker vaults?" Prentice said. "Who manipulated you? Who killed your happily ever after?"

Janey put her hand on the probie's shoulder before she went further overboard. Prentice sat back, breathing hard.

"Oscar's death changed everything." Nasturtium stared at the table. "She killed him…"

"Who? Lisa Montaigne?" Janey asked softly.

Nasturtium nodded.

"Help us catch her," Janey said.

"How? There's no evidence. If I was caught, I was to say I acted alone. There's no paper, no digital crumbs connecting us. She made sure of that."

"How did she transport the algae?" Prentice jumped in. "How did she get it past the biologics sensors at boarding? Did you wear it or something?"

Nasturtium blinked. "Wear it?"

"What did you do? How did you make the genetically programed algae? How did you get it into the air system?" Prentice leaned forward, about to go on the attack with more unresearched questions.

Janey moved beside her. Prentice sat back and looked at Janey, out of her depth. Janey nodded. "Let's switch places."

Prentice relinquished her spot, and Janey took her place. "Nasturtium, please sit. We can protect you."

"How?"

"What do you want?" Janey asked.

Nasturtium considered Janey and then sat back in the metal chair. "Do you have the authority to cut me a deal with the prosecution?"

"I can put in a good word, especially if you cooperate and help us catch Mrs. Montaigne."

Nasturtium shook her head. "None of this was supposed to happen."

"Leo Montaigne wasn't supposed to die?"

"Oscar wasn't supposed to die," Nasturtium said. "Or that other man."

"So, Leo was supposed to die," Janey stated.

"Oscar and I were supposed to be married soon—as soon as the divorce went through." Nasturtium slumped in her chair and stared at the table.

"You will be charged with premeditated murder of a Sol citizen," Janey said.

Nasturtium didn't move.

"Unless..." She let that hang.

"Unless what?" Nasturtium sat up, straightened her shoulders, and held Janey's gaze. "Is there something I can do? I'll do whatever I can." Her eyes were full of tears. She wiped them away. "My life is over anyway."

"Maybe. Maybe not. What does Mrs. Montaigne have over you?" Janey said. "How did she get you to help her?"

Nasturtium spoke at the table. "There was a canister of tea, in Oscar's suite, part of the welcome basket. Inside were a few test tubes. I—I destroyed them...later...after." Nasturtium flew to her feet and paced the small room in mincing steps. She spun to face them. "What protection do I get if I help you?"

"You're willing to help us gather evidence against Lisa Montaigne?"

"Yes, okay," she said as if to herself. Then she focused on Janey. "It's complicated. I was researching the disappearance of Ji-woo Hwang, Oscar's little sister. By his father's third wife. Very young. Doesn't matter. And we were caught in a compromising position in Coban, Guatemala. Sex in a public park. We were secluded but still. They have such strict proprietary rules there." Nasturtium sighed.

"Mrs. Montaigne happened to be in the vicinity and came to our aid, expunging my record, and she kept the whole thing out of the public record and away from the media. A little thing really, but when she came calling for help with this *thing*, I couldn't say 'No.' She threatened to go public with our relationship. It would have been a scandal in the media to all the people who mattered. The media and the rumors would have ruined Oscar's reputation. I didn't care about my own. But Oscar—he'd always managed to stay out of the public eye, and he wanted it that way. He was a private man. I couldn't let him suffer. So, I said, 'Yes.' Biggest mistake of my life." She sniffed her tears away.

"Do you know why Mrs. Montaigne wanted to kill her husband?" Janey asked.

"She told me he had done some horrible things, including kidnapping people, like Oscar's sister. But she said, she just wanted to poison him, slow him down, to make him reconsider his ways, not be able to travel anymore."

"She told you that?"

"Yes, I asked her why she wanted him poisoned, just as you are asking me."

"You believed her?"

"I did."

"Did she help you find Oscar's sister?"

"She—no. She said she didn't know where his sister was. I believed her. We've been looking for Ji-woo for years."

"I'm so sorry," Prentice said.

"Thank you."

Janey waited a beat, then asked, "Did you ever actually find out what happened to Ji-woo?"

"No, we thought she was dead," Nasturtium said. "Mrs. Montaigne told us she tracked a handful of young women her husband had dealings with to a compound in the jungle, but when we pressed her for the exact location, she said that she would tell us after—after I helped her."

"We can use that," Janey said. "Have you had any contact with Mrs. Montaigne since this morning?"

Nasturtium shook her head. "I've been in shock."

"What was the plan?"

Nasturtium blinked. "Uh, sorry. What's that?"

"When were you to get the rest of the information from her?"

Nasturtium shook her head. "Ji-woo is dead. What does it matter?"

"Maybe she's not dead," Janey said. "You must believe that. Why else would you have gone along with Montaigne's plan?

"I told you. The blackmail."

"Did Mrs. Montaigne tell you that Ji-woo was dead?" Janey asked.

"No."

"You just guessed that," Janey pressed.

"Yes."

"And Mrs. Montaigne promised you this second bit of information." Janey wanted to go over it again, just to be clear.

"Yes."

"Anything else?" Janey asked.

"What do you mean?" Nasturtium blinked away more tears.

"Is there anything else you haven't told us about her, what she might have on you, or how she's paying you?" Janey leaned forward.

"And how were you to contact her?" Prentice asked. "You didn't answer the chief."

Nasturtium gave a little sigh. "I was supposed to meet her in a private meeting suite above the restaurant tonight in a disguise. Someone was supposed to give me that message with my afternoon tea. But I've been in here all afternoon. I don't know if the message was delivered."

"We took the high-alert surveillance off your suite once you came here, so I don't have the immediate answer to that," Janey said. "And?"

"There's nothing else. She wasn't paying me." Nasturtium stared at Janey, not seeing her, thinking. She stiffened, her cheeks reddening through the smudged white face powder. "She is one cold and heartless bitch, using me to do her dirty work."

First shock. Now came the anger. Janey had seen it, felt it.

"What did you do with the vials?" Janey asked. "How did you destroy them?"

"The recycler." Nasturtium glanced between her and Prentice.

"Damn," Janey said. "They're gone then."

Connecting the dots. Maybe that was what had been affecting the water filtration system. Everything got washed through it in the station as part of the self-contained powerful recycler. Then whatever couldn't be recycled was compressed and shot out of the station at regular intervals to the space junkers who came by to pick up the debris tumbling through space.

"How did you actually use the algae?"

"I put it in the air filter system."

"Disguised?"

"Yes, as a sanitation worker."

"That fits," Prentice said. "Housekeeping shows you were registered into cleaning detail when you arrived."

Nasturtium nodded. "From there, it was easy to get a uniform for the machine shop."

"Where did you get a pass to access the ninth level?" Janey asked.

"I didn't. I— Oscar and I had a rendezvous in the star-watching garden. He got the pass. So, I—" She stared at the table as if reliving the past. "When we went up there, I made an excuse about forgetting something back in our suite. But instead of returning there, I put the poison in the air filter system—the wall vents." She sobbed. "By my actions... I killed him. I don't deserve to live. I killed my one and only love. I thought I was saving him, protecting our future, by doing what Lisa wanted. But instead, I committed a cardinal sin. Besides, no one was supposed to die. She said it was fast-acting, only supposed make him sick."

Janey let the silence stretch out a few minutes. "Prentice will escort you back to your suite and help you get ready for your meeting with Mrs. Montaigne."

"You're not going to arrest her?"

"You said yourself, we have no evidence. Only your word against hers. You're going to help us get that evidence, Nasturtium," Janey said. "Are you up for it?"

"Yes, absolutely." Nasturtium then stood and looked around a little confused as if this was all a horrible dream. She eyed Janey. "I want to thank you for your kindness, Chief." She nodded to Prentice. "I am ready, and I will cooperate fully. You have my word. All I ask is that you be gentle."

"I will, ma'am. I was just doing my job back there with the interrogation," Prentice said.

"It worked," Nasturtium said. "I never did catch your name."

"Security Agent, Investigator in Training, Anahi Prentice."

At the door, Nasturtium turned to Janey. "I am sorry for your loss, Chief McCallister."

Janey blinked. "Thank you, Nasturtium."

"Call me Rose. Rose Nakashita—my real name." With a look of calm on her face, peace even, her back straight, the woman followed Prentice out of the room.

TWENTY-ONE

JANEY LET HERSELF INTO INTERROGATION ROOM
One. Lisa Montaigne was admiring her nails. Her manicurist
must be amazing. "Mrs. Montaigne, you're free to go."

"Finally." Lisa sniffed. "What took you so long to come to
your senses? You should be spending your resources on
catching my husband's killer and not wasting them on me."
She tsk-tsked. "No, don't tell me. I don't care. Just do it—and
fast. I want off this *maudit* station—sorry Frederick"—she
said his name with French-accented purr—"as soon as my
lawyer gets here and slaps you with an injunction."

Janey said nothing. What could she say to that?

Lisa strode to the door. "Well, aren't you going to open
it?"

"Mrs. Montaigne, just one thing," Janey said.

"Oh, only one." She lifted a finely shaped eyebrow.

"For now. When were you down in Tanchi, Guatemala?"

"There's nothing in Tanchi. You mean, Coban."

"I do?" Janey meant to misspeak.

"Oh, a few years ago, I don't know... Why? You think you
have something on me?" She laughed, a sharp tinkle that

seemed to reverberate off the grey interrogation room walls. She shook her head, as if in disbelief, and pivoted toward the door, tapping her foot, waiting for Janey to open it.

Janey did, and Lisa exited at a fast clip, heading for the elevators. Janey nodded at Prentice to follow. "Make sure she finds her way back to the public side. Then go help Antonia."

Prentice nodded and jogged to catch up.

Janey commed Meilani.

"Chief?" Shawhan replied.

"Stay in your greys and follow Lisa Montaigne on the hotel-casino side."

"And if she asks what I'm doing?

"Tell her that we're concerned for her safety."

"Is that true?"

"No. She's our prime suspect. But we don't have any direct evidence on her yet."

"Yes, Chief." Shawhan commed off.

Janey's stomach grumbled. It was dinnertime, but she still had work to do and a boss to deal with. Where was Schoeneman, and why wasn't he breathing down her neck, especially now that he was on the station?

Janey left the Interrogation Room and headed for the commissary for a bite to eat. She was about to comm Antonia to have a meeting over a meal when Kim commed.

"Yes?" Janey strode past the swinging doors.

"Chief, we have a problem."

"What is it?" Janey asked. "I was just about to grab a bite." The tantalizing smells of savory meats and spicy sauces had her salivating. The noise level comforted. Good company, a moment to rest.

"You need to get down to the weapons room," Kim said in a rush, tension in her voice." He's barricaded himself in there. Won't respond to my comm. The weapons turret —what if..."

"What has Orlando done this time?" Janey lost her appetite and headed back out of the hall, sidestepping staff pouring in for the dinner meal.

"Not Orlando. Schoeneman."

Venus hells.

"What? Why?" Janey moved toward the staff lift.

The weapons room at the very bottom of the station held an arsenal of weapons and rail gun turret. Schoeneman has installed the room in the early days when the space station was mostly an asteroid mining transit hub and he needed to defend his operations against pirates. His own staff maintained the room regularly.

"Someone has jettisoned in an escape pod."

"How? I didn't get any notification."

"It was hacked. They have skills," Kim said, surprise in her voice.

"Who's in that pod?"

"As far as I can tell it's Nasturtium, I mean Rose."

Venus hells and Jupiter's balls.

"What a stupid thing to do," Janey said. "Can you raise her on the comm?"

"We're trying," Kim said. "She won't answer either."

"We?"

"Orlando was in here," Kim said, "is here, talking to me about something, when this all went down."

"He's helping?"

"Yes."

Janey wanted to know more about their conversation, but now wasn't the time. "What is Schoeneman up to?"

"He stormed out of here muttering about the murderer, after we figured out the escape pod had been jettisoned. As if he knows who it is. Said something about Lisa 'was supposed to take care of it.'"

What did that mean? This was crazy. What was Lisa

supposed to take care of? Why was Schoeneman acting hot-headed and frankly crazy? He was normally cool-headed, getting what he wanted with skillful negotiations and heaps of charisma.

Janey had to decide—go after Rose or talk down Schoeneman from using the weapons. The weapons turret manned a powerful rail gun with a long reach.

She couldn't be in two places at once. She had to delegate.

Decision made, she spun and rushed for the nearest stairwell that would take her down to the pods. Faster than the staff elevator, if people were heading this way for the commissary.

Comm channel open, she talked fast. "Kim, have anyone who is available meet me at Rose's escape pod portal."

"Done. Sending Antonia. What about Schoeneman?"

"Get someone in there to delay him, distract him. Break down the damn door if you have to," Janey said. "Anything to stop him from using the weapons. If he gets his hands on the rail gun... What does he think he's doing firing on a guest?"

"Not firing yet," Kim said.

Orlando jumped in. "Maybe I can jimmy the lock there."

"Go. Once you're inside the weapons room," Janey said, "there's an override panel to shut down the weapons."

"He might shoot me," Orlando said.

"He might listen to me," Kim jumped in. "And I know where the panel is."

"Both of you, go. Avoid his goons. They're probably guarding the entrance. They'll warn him," Janey dashed into the stairwell and hopped the stairs two at a time. "Where's Prentice? She was guarding Rose."

"I haven't been able to raise her," Kim said. "Oh crap. Her ident is still in Rose's suite. Her vitals are lower than usual."

"Knocked out the probie." Janey swore. "Rose is wilier

than I thought." Janey arrived at the pod tunnel. "Her vitals are at least stable?"

"Yes, from what I can tell. I've sent medical there."

"Good, thanks." Janey slid down the ladder and jogged to the entrance. "I'm at the escape pod now."

"Janey, not sure what you think you can accomplish going after her," Orlando said. "Rose may have a bigger play here, trying to draw us out. Distracting us."

"I don't think so. She's on a suicide mission," Janey said. "I have to stop her."

"It's dangerous," Orlando said.

"I know." At least he didn't ask why Janey had to stop her. No more deaths on her watch, if she could help it, especially not for one with so much life ahead of her.

She ran through the safety checks, opened the hatch, and stepped into the pod, an oblong affair with enough amenities for three people to survive two days and one person to survive six. It even had space suits, self-repair kits, and full recycle food and water units. They weren't actually passive escape pods, having small cold plasma engines, enough to get someone to the next space station.

Did Rose know how to work the pod? They were pretty basic. Anyone with driver experience could easily figure it out, and anyone with the ability to read really could follow the manual or audio instructions. In fact, all hotel guests had to sign off on having read the instructions at least once. Staff, too. But Rose had bypassed all normal channels to board the station. Who knew how she'd managed to slip onto the StarEl space elevator? Probably bribed someone. Had she taken the time to learn how to drive the pods?

Janey fired up the engines. "Moving out," she said into the open comm to Kim and Orlando.

"We still can't raise her," Kim said.

"Orlando, I thought you were on your way to stop Schoeneman," Janey said.

"We are. I'm multitasking," Kim answered.

"Focus." Janey eyed the space suit but headed for the pilot's chair instead. "We have a small window."

"I know," Kim said.

"You have maybe no time at all, *mi corazon*," Orlando whispered.

"I see her on visual." Janey studied the screen. "Looks like she doesn't have the engines on."

"She doesn't. She launched on manual, the eject boost getting her off-station," Kim said. "That's how we knew she'd left."

"You shouldn't be talking to me," Janey said. "You should be talking to Schoeneman. Does he realize he plans to fire on a guest? Sort of a guest."

"He's not responding, even though his comm is open," Kim said.

"I need to trust that you can talk him down." Janey sat at the controls, strapping herself in, keeping her gaze on the control panels, ignoring the window screen showing the pinpricks of stars in the vast blackness of space. She blew out a breath. She could do this. Had to do this.

"Once I get in the door," Kim said. "I think I can. Best I can promise."

"I know, Kim," Janey said. "I'm firing the second booster, catching up to her."

"You're closing on her," Kim said. "Fifty feet."

"I got it. Eyes on the job, Kim," Janey said.

"I'm waiting for Orlando to do his thing," Kim said. "Thought he was a crack lockpick."

They had to be at the weapon's room entrance, which led to a small anteroom, and then to the secure weapons room.

"He is," Janey said. She could hear Orlando's grunt in reply.

"He's working on it," Kim said in a low voice. "You're gaining on her. Thirty feet. Easy."

"I see her," Janey said. On the control panels and eyeballing it on the window screen taking up the front of the pod.

She pulled back on the throttle halfway and eased beside Rose's pod. She sent out the grappling hook and it attached just fine to an outer strut. She reeled in the line and pulled it taut. The two pods moved in synchronous orbit side by side like two planets slowly dancing in orbit around each other. Janey fired up the engines on low and slowly turned them back toward the station.

She flipped the switch on the old radio comm. It was the only way she could think Rose might talk to her. The sound could bypass the digital channels Rose had turned off.

"Rose, what are you doing?" Janey said in an even tone as if it was another day in the park. One thousand feet back to the station. No sweat.

"What? Who's there?" Rose's tinny voice came back through.

"Janey McCallister, Investigator, Acting Chief. Check your rearview screen."

"I'm leaving. To meet Oscar."

Just as she thought. A suicide attempt.

"We need you, Rose. Now more than ever." Janey increased speed toward the station a notch. She didn't want to spook Rose. Seven hundred fifty feet away.

"It's no use." Rose's grief came through loud and clear.

"You're smarter than that," Janey said. "We need to catch her."

"I will do time, too. What's the point?"

"We need help to catch whoever is behind the kidnapping of Oscar's sister. What if we find her? She will need you."

"I am not family."

"How can you say that? Of course, you are. Family of the heart."

Six hundred feet.

"She has Oscar's wife."

"Does she?"

After a moment, Rose said, "That woman never liked Ji-woo."

"Ji-woo needs you. Don't give up now."

"I miss him." Rose's voice was faint and so sad.

Five hundred feet.

"I know. But your love still has a place to go, Rose."

Something jolted the pod. A streak of light passed the window.

"What was that?" Rose said, fear in her voice.

"Turn on your engines, one-quarter speed," Janey said. "We need to hurry."

"Why?"

"We're being shot at."

TWENTY-TWO

"Why are we being shot at?" Rose's voice edged up in panic. Good. Panic was better than not caring.

"I don't know," Janey said. She wasn't about to tell Rose that the station owner had gone crazy. "But I'm getting us back to the station in one piece. Count on it."

Janey's comm beeped the signal for a screen message. She waved the screen on the control panel to open the comm link, not wanting to startle Rose by talking to someone else. The readout from Orlando said: She's in.

Kim was in with Schoeneman down at the weapon's station.

Orlando sent: I can hear you.

Janey waved back a thanks.

"Rose, are you in a space suit?"

"No, should I be?" Rose's voice came through high and tight.

"Yes, just in case." Janey eyed the closet that held the suits on the escape pod. "But before you do, notch your front engines up to one-half impulse. I'm doing the same. By the time you have your suit on, we'll be back at the station, and then you can take it off."

"That doesn't make any sense, Ms. McCallister."

"It makes perfect sense. Something's going on. Better safe than sorry. And it's Janey. Are you putting on the suit?"

A moment later, Rose said. "Yes, Janey. Are you doing the same?" Good. She was caring about someone beyond herself.

"I am, Rose." Janey took the three steps to the closet and slipped into the two-part suit if only to be keeping her promise and to keep Rose company. Then the boots and gloves. Helmet was last. She left the faceplate open.

She shoved aside the flutter of fear in her chest. Putting on a space suit did that to her no matter how many times she donned it, no matter how many times she'd done psych sessions to eliminate the primal fear.

To take her mind off the suit, she focused on her next steps—getting the pods back to the station—her only way to mitigate the jitters flooding her body. Heart rate calming, thankfully, Janey finished the suit check and sat back in the pilot's chair, about to maneuver apart the pods—four hundred feet—when Kim burst through the comm.

"He won't listen to me." Kim's voice was controlled, "Something's got into him. I've never seen him like this," warbling only a little with fear at that part.

"Like what?" Janey asked but the question was drowned out by Schoeneman's voice.

"Who are you talking to?" Schoeneman barked, commanding and firm.

"Acting Security Chief McCallister," Kim said, firm in her tone, her control back. "She's bringing in the guest in the escape pod."

"Let me do my job, Mr. Schoeneman." Janey unhooked the grapples.

"She's a criminal," Schoeneman said. "She must pay."

There was something in his voice she'd never heard. Something wild, unhinged, fear. As if his burden had finally gotten to this powerful man and pushed him over the edge. Seemed so unlikely, yet there it was—unbelievable in its reality. Fear propelled people into a frenzy sometimes like a normally docile animal striking out in manic terror.

"That's not justice, Mr. Schoeneman," Janey said, trying to keep her voice level, calm. No need to poke the man further. "You hired me to do a job, remember?"

"She's— She must pay," he said.

"Pay for what?" Janey asked, but Schoeneman stayed silent.

"Kim, can you calm him?" Janey asked. "If he shoots again, he'll damage the station. We're too close."

"I'm not stupid," Schoeneman said, his tone back to level. "I'm not shooting at my station. Don't be ridiculous. Just get back the suspect ASAP. That's an order. She's a flight risk. Can't you see?" You're an idiot was implied in his tone.

"Yes, sir, I see." Janey kept her voice neutral. "Kim, I need to close the comm with you to bring the pods back. You got this?"

"Yes, go," Kim said, her voice tense.

Janey commed off.

"Why was he shooting at me?" Rose asked. "What does he think I know?" She'd overheard the whole conversation.

"Is there anything you know? A secret? One that could in some way ruin Schoeneman's reputation?" Janey asked.

"No, I don't think so. He called me a suspect. He thinks I'm the murderer?"

"I honestly don't know what he thinks," Janey said. "Can you maneuver into the bay ahead?"

"I don't know how."

"I'll direct you. Cut your engines on my mark—three, two, one, mark," Janey said. Rose did as she requested.

"Good. I'll nudge you in." They were close, coasting on momentum.

Janey cut her engines down to one-quarter impulse and nudged Rose's pod into the berth that had been hers. "You're in, Rose. I'm having my people meet you. Will you stay with them while I sort this out?"

"I will," Rose said, subdued.

"I'm switching to normal comms, so you won't hear from me until I'm back on board, okay?"

"I understand, Chief. And thank you. For bringing me back. I'm just so…sad."

"I know how you feel," Jancy said gently. "It's probably best if you're not alone for the time being."

"Yes, ma'am."

"You can do this, Rose. Besides, we need you," Janey said. "McCallister, out."

Janey steered her pod away from the station to get clearance for the other empty bay. She opened a channel to Kim. Her comm popped with static. Janey winced at its loudness.

Kim yelled, "No!"

A flash of light filled Janey's vision, then the pod shot upward and tilted seaboard. She grabbed hold of the control panel and slid off her seat—she'd forgotten in the excitement to strap in. She managed not to hit the deck. A hissing sound like a boiling tea kettle whistled inside behind one of the panels nearby. That must have been an explosion below and on the port-side of her pod.

"Stop him!" Janey said. "He almost hit the pod!"

"I'm trying!" Kim said. "Mr. Schoeneman, you're shooting at Janey, your acting chief. What has gotten into you! Stop right this instant."

The pod rattled. Something crackled. A zigzag popped in the window screen. Bolts jiggled in place.

Venus hells.

She gulped and snapped shut her suit's faceplate, ran through the suit-up checks, again, and switched to the comm inside the suit. Readout displays on her screen reported her own health vitals. Elevated heart rate, blood pressure rising, and external oxygen levels dropping.

"Kim, the pod's about to tear apart," Janey said, her throat tightening, heart racing. "I'm abandoning ship before it does, setting it on an away course from the station. Let the team know to triangulate my location and pick me up. I'm heading toward the station."

"What's happening, Janey?" Orlando cut in. "I can't hear a thing from Kim and Schoeneman."

That didn't make sense.

"Not good, Orlando. I'm abandoning the pod. He almost hit me. Man's gone crazy."

"I can arrest him on negligence," Orlando said, dark glee in his voice.

"Get in there then," Janey said.

"I can't. Kim locked it from the inside. Not sure why."

"Not good, but it sounded like she had a handle on things a few seconds ago."

Something else popped behind a panel, a tiny explosion. The panel flew off. She swerved, but the panel hit the opposite wall and cracked the wall.

In the space suit, she strode as fast as she could into the tiny depressurizing chamber, hit the right buttons, and was floating in space sixty seconds later. She kept her eye on the tiny escape pod zooming away from her toward the debris field. It would get picked up by the space junk nets and get recycled by the junkers.

High-pitched crackling filled her comm. She squeezed her eyes shut as if that would lessen the squeaks and squawks—from what she didn't know.

"Sitrep, Janey?" Orlando asked, booming in her ears. "I don't like the sounds of that."

"I'm fine," Janey said, finally remembering that she had volume controls on her wrist. She turned down the volume. "I'm free of the pod, heading toward the station." The jet boots nudged her in the right direction.

"I'm on my way," Orlando said.

"No, stay there." Janey bit back the panic that threatened to rise in her throat and focused on the pod distancing itself from her, now a red dot against the starfield. "I have Antonia and the team meeting me."

Kim broke through and said in a whisper, "Where are you?"

"Heading toward the station on momentum," Janey said. "Why?"

"Schoeneman is bent over the instruments and won't talk to me. He's muttering, but I can't understand a word of it."

"Well, there's nothing to shoot at," Janey said. "I should be out of view and in the shadow of the station. The pod is zooming out of range. Why don't you leave?"

"He might do something stupid."

"He already has, Kim," Janey said. "He'd only be destroying his precious station and his whole reputation. I thought he was too smart of a businessman for such behavior." No way he'd destroy the hotel-casino space station just for the insurance money and damage his reputation perhaps permanently.

Without warming, her visual field narrowed. She gulped. Or maybe she gasped because Kim spoke, urgent and worried.

"Janey, what's wrong?"

"Nothing. Fine."

"I'm sending Orlando."

"I'm already on my way," Orlando cut in.

"No, I got this. I'm fine," Janey said. "Just make sure our people are with Rose, two or three guards, and then we need to set up the sting for Mrs. Montaigne." Janey closed her eyes. Her throat was dry.

She must have moaned because Kim asked, "Janey, you're sure you're okay?"

"Yes, I should be in soon." She sipped from the water tube in the helmet.

"Hey!" Kim yelled.

"What?" Janey's heart rate increased. Her vision darkened at the edges.

"Mr. Schoeneman, I really wouldn't do that if I were you," Kim said calmly. "Give me that."

What the hell was happening? Her heartbeat was too loud in her ears. Her breathing sounded raspy, wispy, echo-y. She shivered, clammy in the space suit. Where was the station? Why couldn't she see the hulking silver metallic surface?

"There, there," Kim said. "Janey, he's sobbing in my arms. I unlocked the door. Get Orlando to cuff this man now. He pulled a sidearm on me. He's crazy."

Kim cut the comm.

Janey calmed the upheaval in her stomach enough to speak. "Orlando, get in there now. Cuff Schoeneman before he wigs out again and hurts someone else." What was wrong with the man? Maybe he was on something.

Orlando grunted. "In a minute. Busy."

Queasiness descended, then the shakes. Pain shot in her head. Then all went black.

TWENTY-THREE

JANEY BLINKED AND STARED INTO THE WORRIED eyes of Orlando. He had a shiner, a cracked lip, and was squinting at her, mouth tight. She was lying down in the escape pod anteroom, still in her space suit.

"Janey, are you okay?"

"You look awful." Janey lifted an arm, then winced at the pain in her chest. "I'm fine. What happened?" She managed to lumber to her feet, ignoring the roiling in her stomach, huffing entirely too much, Orlando at her side, a solid crutch. "How did you get that black and blue?"

"Are you hurt? You passed out." He scanned her from head to toe.

Her temples throbbed, and she sipped from the water Orlando handed her. "I don't know what happened." Janey frowned and undid the hook-ups on her suit. Jintao and Clark were stationed at the doorway, their backs to them, giving them privacy. "Where's Kim? Is she okay?"

"She's in medical with Schoeneman. His men rushed me at the weapons room door—hence the eye." Orlando smirked, then banked the feral glee. "How Kim got past them, I don't know."

"And the lip," Janey said.

"Oh." He touched it, winced. "But two against one. I like them odds. I handled them, then cuffed a docile Schoeneman." He shook his head. "Something's wrong with that man."

Janey frowned and struggled with one of her boots, fighting the dizziness.

"Sit, let me help you with that," Orlando said, "you need to get checked out."

"How long was I out?"

"Only a few minutes. Jintao and Clark were able to reel you in."

"Junker's trick," Clark said, over his shoulder. Right, Clark grew up on the space junkers' station.

"Cool trick," Jintao said quietly to his friend.

Janey pushed down a small jump seat and sat, sweating from the effort. "Doesn't seem right, his actions."

"Maybe he's sick." Orlando tugged off her boots. That was sweet of him. She didn't have the oomph right now.

"Maybe." Janey stood in her stockinged feet and tugged off the rest of her suit. She'd left her shoes on the pod. She swayed. Orlando was right there, slipping an arm around her waist.

"I got you," he said. "We really need to get you to medical."

"Yes, to interview Schoeneman."

Jintao stowed her suit in one of the lockers.

"No, so they can check you out. You haven't been at one hundred percent since...since... Then the blackout out there..."

"Since my mom passed away. I know, it's just the stress. I'm fine."

"You need a break. A real break."

"I need to solve this case, then I'll take my vacation."

Orlando grunted as he maneuvered with her through the doorway. Janey shook him off.

"I'm fine." But she strode beside the wall just in case she needed its support. Quite nice to have it there, friendly grey wall.

"It's okay to lean on someone," Orlando said.

"I know." Janey didn't lean on him again. Just didn't feel right. "I just need to walk it off, get my sea legs back. I'll be fine."

"You are so stubborn sometimes." Orlando looped an arm around her waist but kept his grip loose.

By the stars, it was nice having him close by. She could be adult enough to admit that to herself. She focused on deep breaths and one foot in front of the other all the way to the service elevator. Once inside the lift, she pulled out her holo and tried to get caught up with staff communiques, but the words swam before her eyes. Maybe she needed a little break. It was past dinner time. Her stomach grumbled its accord.

Orlando released her, opened his comm, and spoke into it softly without raising a privacy shield.

"Who are you calling?" Janey leaned against the elevator wall then straightened as the door opened near medical.

"Kim, for her to get us some dinner. I haven't eaten either."

"Thank you." Janey exited the elevator, turned toward medical. "How's Rose?"

"Your team is looking after her," Orlando said. "Wait. Stop."

"What? Why?"

"You're going the wrong way." Orlando turned her one hundred and eighty degrees.

"Oh dear," she said. "I am messed up. When my sense of direction goes, something is truly wrong."

"Now you admit it," Orlando said. "We'll get you straightened up in no time. You're probably just hungry, thirsty, and tired. Like the rest of us after a long day's work. You're human, after all."

Janey didn't know what to say to that. Did she act like she wasn't human?

Medical staff she didn't know well greeted her at the door and led her to a bed. They pulled a curtain around it.

"Sit." The nurse motioned.

Janey did. Seems like she'd been doing a lot of that lately, being ordered to sit. She'd been ordering others. Her thoughts shuffled in no apparent order. The smell of pungent coffee had her opening her eyes.

"There she is," Kim said.

"I'm here." Janey blinked. She was on her back again. Not this again. She sat up and winced at the dull pain across her chest. "Why do I feel like horses trampled across my chest?"

"Rae said you were low on electrolytes," Kim said.

"Where's Schoeneman?"

"He's under guard in a private room,"

"What's wrong with him?"

"From her initial scans, Alison says nothing is wrong with him. They're running more tox screens now."

"And Lisa Montaigne?"

"Confined to her suite. Though if she wants to have meetings, I suppose we can't stop her. Meilani is keeping an eye on her," Kim said. "And Rose is also under watch. We moved her to a new room, hoping that would help her state of mind."

"Great idea, Kim. You're a godsend."

"I know." Kim smiled. "How you feeling?"

A nurse, Rae—Janey saw her name on her ocular screen—

pushed aside the curtain and approached, tray in hand. "Dinner for our patient."

Janey moved to stand. "I'm better."

"Not by much," Rae said. "You're low on electrolytes. We're not done getting you up to normal levels." She motioned to Janey's wrist where a med box was hooked into her veins.

"I didn't even notice." Janey sat back in the bed and devoured the meal in front of her. Hearty bean soup and thick bread. "Where's Orlando?"

"Getting checked out, too." Kim sipped a steaming drink.

"And you? Are you okay? Did I ask that already?" Janey asked.

"No, you didn't." Kim smiled wryly. "But that's understandable. I'm fine. Just shook up. It's not every day that your boss goes crazy and points a gun at you."

"You disarmed him?"

"What do you think?"

"Badass."

"You bet. But I hope to never have to do that again. Put me behind a desk any day. Fieldwork." Kim made a face. "How do you do it?" She shuddered.

"We train well, just as you did. You were prepared."

"Training is one thing. Thank goodness you set those drills, but the reality is something else altogether." Kim shook her head.

"You did great," Janey said. "What's your evaluation of Schoeneman? Did he say anything to explain his behavior? How did he know Rose had launched? Does he have a grudge against her? He said something... 'She knows,' he said."

Kim sipped from her drink that smelled like spicy hot chocolate. "All good questions. Near as I can tell, he was raving about the network, the compound, how no one was supposed to find out. How Rose knows. But he didn't say what." Kim considered. "Remember how I told you the board was putting pressure on him, wanting to push him out, and cut him off his funding sources?"

"All except for that last part." Janey nodded, acting natural, but inside she was stunned. Schoeneman was one of the wealthiest and most powerful men in the Sol. How could his board cut him off?

"Maybe the Very Important Man act is cracking to reveal his true colors," Kim said, bitterness seeping out.

"What do you mean?"

Kim shook her head as if she didn't want to talk about it. She seemed to have deep insider knowledge of Schoeneman. "Back to the case... More questions. Like, how did he find out Rose left the station? He wasn't there when I detected the anomaly. Only Orlando was there..."

"Could Lisa Montaigne have told him?" Janey mused. "She does seem to be on a first-name basis with Schoeneman."

"But how would she know of Rose's whereabouts?" Kim sipped her tea, leaned back in the chair, and pulled a blue hospital blanket around herself.

"How indeed?" Orlando said, stepping around the curtain into Janey's alcove. Despite the healing goo around his eye and lip, he looked good to her. Was this true love? When you were both down and broken, you still saw the other as beautiful?

"Tracker?" Kim mused.

Janey shoved the tray aside, rattling the empty plate and cup, and stood. "Yes! Maybe she put a tracker on Rose, to monitor her." Her wrist IV beeped. She yanked it off. Her head spun only a little.

"Where are you going?" Rae rushed back into the alcove.

"Work to do," Janey said.

"Delegate," Kim said.

"Tell Antonia to do it," Orlando said.

"I need to get moving," Janey said. "I feel better."

"She's so stubborn," Orlando said.

"Don't I know it," Kim said.

"Guys, I'm right here," Janey said. "Okay, here's what we need to do. Wait, where is Antonia anyway?"

Kim smiled. "She's doing my job and her job for the moment, holding down the fort in the office."

Janey nodded and commed Antonia.

"Chief," she replied. "How are you?"

"Recovering. I need you to protect Rose."

"Already on it," Antonia said. "I sent Jintao and Clark. Meilani is still sitting on Lisa."

"Good job. I have an idea for a sting that I want Kim to run."

"Whatever you need, boss, just put me in," Antonia said. "Oh, a call's coming in." She commed off.

"What do you have in mind?" Kim asked.

"Where do you want me?" Orlando asked.

"Do you mind helping Antonia?"

"On it. And you know I'm game for the sting." Orlando grinned, kissed her on the lips, and was out of her alcove before she could say thanks.

Kim pulled out her holos, her headset, and primed her wrist comm. "Ready, Chief."

Janey spelled out her plan and watched in awe as Kim waved into one device, then another, as she sent orders to various team members and dug into coordinating the sting.

Janey pushed aside the tray and perched at the edge of the bed.

Now, where were her boots?

TWENTY-FOUR

"WHAT ARE THE ODDS OF FINDING YOU HERE, Chief?" Prentice poked around the curtain, sober, holding an ice pack to her head.

"High, given today's events," Janey said. "Good to see you're okay. Help me find my boots?"

"Certainly." The probie peered under the bed. She then lifted a jacket off a chair and held up Janey's boots like a trophy. "Here!"

"Thanks." Janey took her black stylish boots and shoved her stockinged feet into them. "Catch me up on what happened to you after you escorted Rose to her suite, and before she hijacked an escape pod, giving you that bump."

Hand on the back of her head, Prentice said matter-of-factly, "When we got to her suite, she seemed tired. She sat on the couch and asked me to get her a glass of water. I turned to go to the kitchen and, quick as a lightning bug, she clocked me with a vase when my back was turned." She grimaced. "I came to only a few seconds later when I heard the suite door open and close." She frowned. "But by the time I got my legs working and dashed to the door, she was nowhere in sight in the corridor. I went for the elevators, but they were in use. I ran down the stairwell and made it to the lobby level without seeing her there. She'd vanished."

Janey stood, without wobbling. That was a good sign. "I thought Kim sent medical to you."

"They did. I caught up with them when I went back to Rose's room to look for clues for where she could have gone. Or maybe to catch her there if she'd doubled back. That kind of thing." Prentice frowned. "Was that the right thing to do? The going back to look for clues part?"

Janey shouldered her jacket. "Yes. What did you find?"

"Nothing. All her clothes seemed to be there, her bags, too. Boy, she sure has a lot of slippers."

"What does that tell you?" Janey set her ocular implant to run a diagnostic, even though medical probably already ran one.

Prentice considered, her head tilted. "That wherever she was going she didn't need all her clothes, so not leaving the station. Or maybe she was fleeing..." She eyed Janey. "A suicide run. Now I see the signs. Kim filled me in. I didn't connect the dots before."

"How could you know? She surprised all of us," Janey said. "Anything else you noticed?"

"No, not that I can think of. Now what?" Prentice peered around the small medical bay as if the answers were lying about.

"We need to wrap up this case. Check in with Kim. She's coordinating the sting I planned against Lisa Montaigne. We'll need all hands on deck. I'm going to talk to Schoeneman."

"I want to come."

Janey shook her head. "No. This I need to do alone."

Prentice opened her mouth to protest, but then she seemed to think better of it when Janey gave her a stern look.

"Yes, Chief. Understood. I have enough to do." Prentice smiled, then winced and hustled out of Janey's alcove.

Janey checked her appearance in the mirror and was surprised that she looked all right. Inside she felt raw and empty, with a bone-deep fatigue she'd been pushing out of her awareness all day. She could sleep a week, but not until this case was wrapped up. She had to maintain for just a few more hours.

She shoved back the curtain and stopped Rae. "Where's Mr. Schoeneman?"

"He's in Med Bay One. I'll take you to him," Rae said.

Janey followed the nurse to a side wing, separate from the main room. She straightened her jacket, brushed her hair out of her face, and blew out a breath. She could face him.

Rae left her in front of a closed door guarded by two of her own staff, Natalia and Liberosa, pulled from machine shop duties.

"Chief." Each one nodded to her.

"Don't let anyone else in while I'm in there." Janey unlocked the door to a patient room.

Schoeneman sat in a chair, his back to the door. There was a bed, one more chair, a private bathroom, and wallscreens showing a gentle video landscape of snow-tipped mountains and bright, sunshiny grassy hillsides.

Was he watching the landscape flow by?

Janey came around to face him. "Mr. Schoeneman?"

Dressed in a tailored gray suit, he stared at her glassy-eyed and gave no expression that he noticed her.

"What did they give you?" Janey pulled out a chair from the wall and sat. "Are you alright?"

"Chief Medical Officer Horsely performed admirably," Schoeneman said mechanically, his gaze pointed over Janey's shoulder at the mountains landscape.

"Did she give you any medicine?" Janey moved her head to be in his sightline, but he still didn't focus on her.

"No."

"What's going on?" Janey crossed her arms. "Do you know where you are?"

He finally gave her a look as if she was dumb. "Of course, I do. I'm in medical on L'Étoile."

"Why are you in medical? Horsely says there's nothing wrong with you."

"She's wrong."

"She is? What's wrong?"

"Yes, it's all over." Schoeneman went back to staring through her.

"What is all over, sir? I don't understand," Janey said in a calm voice.

"All of it." He waved a hand in the air as if to encompass the room, the whole station, or maybe his entire life.

"This is really unlike you, sir." Janey straightened and opted for a command tone. "You're a fighter. A master negotiator, a cunning business mogul, always two steps ahead of the competition." Janey quoted his carefully cultivated propaganda. "What happened, Mr. Schoeneman?"

He peered at her blankly as if she was speaking unknown words, as if he were wiped clean, as if he'd been rebooted. So unlike the in-command man she'd encountered in all her other dealings with him. He had enhancements she'd guessed from their previous encounters but kept them well hidden. Maybe he had been hacked.

She studied him, waiting. One breath, two. Still nothing from him. She stood. She wasn't getting through to him. She needed to focus on the main case. "I'll be back later."

He didn't respond, just stared through her.

Janey left him like that, exited the room, and said to

Natalia and Liberosa, "No one in or out except for me or Chief Medical Officer Horsely. No one else. Understood?"

"Yes, sir." They nodded.

Janey waved a request to medical to send her Schoeneman's health file and headed for the exit. She rolled her shoulders and neck. She had a case to close.

"Chief McCallister," someone called after her. "Janey."

Janey turned. It was Alison Horsely.

"You haven't been discharged," the chief medical officer said.

"What's the verdict? Am I going to live?" Janey said, deadpan.

"Yes, but you're exhausted and are suffering from stress-related immunosuppression symptoms. If you don't get some real rest soon, the damage may not reverse." Alison placed a compassionate hand on Janey's arm as if to convey the seriousness of her words.

"I'll take another stimulant."

"You're not listening. That's the problem. You've had way too many stimulants today. It's taxing an already taxed system."

"What are you talking about, Horsely? It's just tea."

"It's not."

"But Gina's crew makes it for me special…"

"It's not good for you."

"I'll speak to her, get her to tweak the formula," Janey said.

"No more. And get a good night's sleep. Or you'll keep fainting and having blackouts."

"I can get a good night's sleep tonight."

"No, starting now," Horsely said.

"I can't," Janey said. "The case—"

"I am not clearing you for duty," Alison said in a light but firm tone, confident and backed by her years of training and experience. Though she was in her mid-thirties like Janey, Alison had been in medical clinics and hospitals for at least twenty years, starting young in her home region of the Tennessee Corporate.

"I feel fine."

Horsely glared at her, a glare worthy of one of Janey's old drill sergeants.

"You're so cheery," Janey said.

"I'm serious," Horsely said. "Want to collapse on the job again? Oh, and no more space walks until we do a full workup. I don't like how your blood pressure hormone levels were dangerously low."

"I'm not planning on it," Janey said. "Anything else?"

"You aren't indestructible, you know, Janey McCallister."

"I know," Janey said. "Can I please go back to work?"

Horsely frowned and ran her medical comm over Janey. Then Rae came from the main room carrying a tray.

"Roll up your sleeve, Chief," Rae said, calm, neutral, expecting obedience.

Janey sighed. "What for?"

"It's a medical dosing patch," Rae said.

Horsely said, "We want to monitor you closely and be able to dose you remotely as needed, wherever you are."

"Uppers? Downers?" Janey asked wryly.

"Only with your permission and approval," Rae said.

"Okay, fine." She rolled up her sleeve, and while Rae sterilized her shoulder, placed the patch, and calibrated it with her comm, Janey asked Horsely, "What is wrong with Mr. Schoeneman? He seems...drugged."

"There's nothing medically wrong with him," Horsely said. "He's in shock. My psychology training isn't my strongest suit, but he seems to have suffered a systemic identity crisis so unexpected that he's shut down. We'll keep an eye on him."

"Thank you. I have heard of that, studied it back at the academy," Janey said. "Please, no one except you or I can go in there."

"He's a security risk?" Horsely asked.

"Yes, I think so, don't you? Professional opinion?"

"Kim said he pulled a gun on her and shot at a guest and at you, so yes, I see where you're coming from. Medically, I have no good reason."

"I should put him in holding for what he did, but he's the boss," Janey said.

"We'll keep an eye on him, even though—"

"There's nothing wrong with him." Janey shook her head. "Medicine doesn't stretch to the emotional or self-identity ills, does it? Do we have a mental health professional aboard that can help us?"

Was he building an insanity case?

"Not at the moment," Horsely said. "We do have the religious staff for the meditation room…"

"Maybe one of them can help," Janey said. "What is Schoeneman's religion?"

Alison checked her holo, presumably Schoeneman's public hotel record. "Decline to state."

"Get a non-denominational or cross-religious person here then."

Alison nodded and put in the request.

Janey huffed a breath, releasing pressure that she'd been holding. She felt her shoulders release around her neck. "Now that I'm thinking clearly, and not having to deal with a runaway suspect while I'm in a space suit, I realize something doesn't add up. Need to get with my team and call the Sol Space Authority. I have a good case against Schoeneman for several violations of space security and human rights regulations and laws."

She'd been deep in a gravity well this entire case. Understandably so.

"See? This is why you need to take better care of yourself." Alison smiled. "For your work."

"I understand, Horsely." She sighed. "Am I free to leave? Please clear me."

Horsely gave her a stern look and waved toward the exit. "We'll be monitoring you."

"Thank you." Janey left medical and took the staff elevator for the security wing.

In the bullpen, she arrived to a scrum around Kim's desk. Kim was speaking, something about people's positions in the casino, but she broke off when she saw Janey.

"There you are, Chief." Kim waved her into the huddle.

Janey stayed on the outside of the circle. "Go on, Kim. You're doing great."

"That's about it. Everyone has their assignment?" Kim asked.

Staff nodded.

"Great. We get into position in one hour. Any last questions?" Kim asked.

No one said anything.

"Great, see you then, on comm channel two." Kim smiled. "I'll be right here." She waved her earpiece.

Staff disbursed, some leaving ops, some going down into the bullpen, many stopping by Janey to say they were glad she was okay and up on her feet again. They were focused. There was an undercurrent of excitement in the room. Good.

Kim grinned. "I like coordinating from the safety of my desk."

"Glad to hear it," Janey said. "Catch me up. Orlando is on board with the plan?"

"Yes, he's going undercover for us, just as you suggested. Disguise and all," Kim said. "Reeling Lisa in with a cover story on being an investor in one of her late husband's companies, who is offering his condolences and to discuss a lucrative business deal."

"Nice. Where is he?" Janey asked.

"Getting ready for his role, I presume." Kim wiggled her eyebrows, comedy style. "Using plenty of cover makeup for that shiner of his."

Janey groaned. "Oh no. Is he using his bolero gigolo outfit again?"

"He didn't say." Kim grinned.

"You're having way too much fun," Janey said.

"Gotta get my kicks how I can." Kim laughed and then sobered. "What's next for you?"

"You're doing great here. The team looks ready," Janey said. "I need to make some calls before the sting starts. I'll be in my office."

She got to work, preparing for her call to the Sol Space Authority to report Schoeneman's actions. Schoeneman was one of the most rich and powerful men in the Sol, one of the richest men on the planet, if not the richest. He'd made his massive fortune with his conquests in asteroid mining and had who knew how many holdings he had all over Earth, on the moon, in the asteroid belt, and beyond. With some of his vast fortune, he'd build Bijoux de L'Étoile, which had started as a waystation for asteroid miners. On the hangar level, there was still a bare-bones eat-and-sleep for them.

But even with all Schoeneman's wealth and holdings and the influence that came with it, he wasn't above Sol Unified Planets law—the governing body that regulated Earth's planet and off-planet-wide trade and the judicial system.

She drafted her report of the events in the escape pod and then commed Orlando. He didn't answer. She tracked him down on the station's tracking system. He was supposed to be in his quarters, preparing for the sting. This had better not be a repeat of his earlier disappearing act from this morning.

She sent him a message that she was about to file formal charges against Schoeneman to the Sol Space Authority for his actions against Rose and her and did he want to file a joint report. That should get his attention.

He didn't reply, so she commed Kim. "Where do you want me for the sting?"

"I've set up a listening post in the adjacent suite on the mezzanine level for you and Anahi. That's a good spot for you to coordinate, jump in, and do the arrest. Unless you want Antonia to do it," Kim replied.

"Where is Antonia? I didn't see her in the huddle?"

"I sent her to advance scout to the casino undercover. She was itching to get out of the bullpen. She sent you the updated case files. Did you see them?"

Janey waved up the files on her tablescreen. "Yes. Here they are."

"Did you want me to fill you in on who is doing what?" Kim asked, excitement in her voice.

"Sure."

"Orlando, Antonia, and Prentice, you know. Meilani will overtly trail them. Clark and Jintao will be servers, and Rose, well, let's just say she has a pivotal role. Natalia and Liberosa will be on standby undercover in the casino if we need them —one as a spotter at the bar and the other at the mid-level tables. We have some off-duty hanger security on Schoeneman. Even Milano has asked to play a role so he's at the slots watching the exits."

"Good job, Kim!"

Nice to know Milano was feeling better.

"Thanks!" Kim exclaimed. "You ready?"

"Always, but you're coordinating. I'll wait for your cue," Janey said. "Oh, I can't get Orlando on comms. Any word from him?"

"Yah, he's here, getting the tech straightened out. He

always has to have the last word, it seems. My specs are never good enough."

"Send him to me as soon as he's done," Janey said. "I need to brief him on Schoeneman,"

"One minute," Orlando said, over Kim's comm. "I saw your message. Don't file anything yet."

"You could respond, you know? Your comm says you're in your room."

"I'm going undercover. Had to do that… misdirect."

"Understood," Janey said. "But you could warn me first. I am chief of security." For the time being. She stiffened. "Wait—undercover? Lisa has met you already."

"I have it handled." Orlando chuckled. Then his tone grew serious. "I'll be right there. Don't take any action on Schoeneman until I get there."

Janey commed off. He wasn't the boss of her, but he did work for the Sol Police. She needed their backing to take any action against Schoeneman—like arresting him. The man who was actually her boss.

She had a few minutes, so she reviewed Antonia's files for the case against Lisa Montaigne. They were in order. Good job. But something was still bugging her about Schoeneman.

She dug into his personal files and searched for the medical files she'd requested. They were blocked. She commed Horsely.

"Chief McCallister, Janey, how are you feeling?" Horsely said. "Is everything okay? Your readings look good."

"I'm not calling about me but Mr. Schoeneman. I need to get into his medical files. Can you unlock them for me? I asked… Something isn't adding up."

"I can't. Sorry. They have a triple-layer legal privacy block on them. I can only show you the case file on the recent checkup I did earlier today."

"Fine. Send that. How do I get through to the rest of the files?"

"Checking." Horsely paused and then came back. "You need to call his lawyer to request to open the files."

"Any name specified?"

"No, sorry."

"I'll find it. Thanks. Wish me luck." Janey closed the comm.

The name and contact information for Schoeneman's legal firm was easy enough to find. It was public, on the investment page for the hotel-casino.

She put a call into the firm. Luckily, they had twenty-four-hour reception and junior lawyers on staff working somewhere around the world.

"I need to reach the person in charge," Janey said. "It's urgent. Please wake him or her up. This is the head of security and investigatory services from the Bijoux de L'Étoile Hotel-Casino calling on an urgent matter of security."

Having the mantle of the chief of security had real clout at times like these because less than a minute later the sleepy voice of the lawyer sounded in-ear. No vid.

"Chief McCallister here, sir. Sorry to wake you, but your boss is in trouble and thought you should know. I need your permission to—"

"Wait!" It was Orlando barging into her office. He'd heard what she said—somehow—and was vigorously shaking his head, making the cut motion with a finger across the neck.

She ignored him and focused on the lawyer who was talking.

"What happened to Chief Milano?" the lawyer asked. "What do you need my permission for?"

"This morning former Chief Daniel Milano took Mr. Schoeneman's offered retirement package," Janey said, "and stepped away from duties immediately for some much-needed leave,"

"I didn't get the memo," the lawyer said.

"Oh. We'll see that you do."

The lawyer asked. "Who are you?"

"I was lead security investigator, now I'm the chief. Janey McCallister. I don't think we've met."

"Well, no. Because I've not had the pleasure of coming to the Jewel in the Sky." He sounded bitter.

"Maybe you'll get a chance. Mr. Schoeneman, he—"

"Hey! Wait!" Orlando shouted.

"What's that?" the lawyer asked, worried.

"Just a disturbance." Janey turned her chair around so as not to see Orlando's frantic hand waving. She turned on her privacy filter.

"What's the matter?" The lawyer sounded awake now.

Janey opened her mouth to reply, but Orlando stood in front of her, frowning, a hand over her wrist. His intended action was clear. He was going to cut off her call, the height of rude, but at least was giving her a warning.

"Sorry, sir. I need to call you back. Get yourself some coffee in the meantime." She clicked her wrist band to cut the comm and glared up at Orlando. "What the hell?"

"What are you doing talking to Schoeneman's legal?" He glared back. "They're part of the problem."

"What problem?" Janey stood and crossed her arms.

"Schoeneman's insanity plea."

"I thought so," she muttered.

"See? We're closing in on him, and he goes and does something completely out of character. I bet he was acting weird when you went to interview him."

"Yes, he was. You have a point." Janey squinted at him. He was dressed in a dashing short black coat with a bright red silk lining. Black thigh-hugging leather riding breeches and shiny black Hessian boots completed the Bolero ensemble. She'd seen him work in this getup before. Quite effective for snaring certain kinds of people. "What about his guards? What did you do to them?"

"They're cuffed in the back room of the machine shop."

"I better send staff for them."

"I already had Kim do it. They're probably in holding. Kim didn't tell you?"

"No, she has her hands full coordinating the sting," Janey said.

"I know. I had in designing it with her."

Janey frowned. "You're taking charge around here?"

"No, cool it." Orlando gave her a stern look. "You don't have to do everything. You have capable people on your team, you know? Including me. Antonia. Kim. Everyone."

"I know. Sorry." Janey sat down and tried to relax.

"I get it. You have a lot of balls in the air." Orlando cocked his head.

"What is it?"

He waved his ear.

Right. He had an earpiece in, for the sting.

He focused on her. "Gotta go. It's time."

She stood. "I'm coming too."

A message scrolled on her holo from Kim: Places, everyone.

TWENTY-FIVE

Orlando rushed out of her office. She followed, keeping step.

"Stop admiring my backside," Orlando said, with a smile in his voice. "It's not my only thrilling quality."

Janey lengthened her stride to come alongside him. "I won't argue with that."

He gave her a sideways glance. "You up for this?"

"Are you?" Janey said as they arrived at the staff elevator.

"Of course."

"Let's run through it."

"No time." He kissed her on the lips, a quick peck, excited, thrilling. "You'll hear the whole thing on comms."

"Oh, I need my earpiece. Good luck." She turned around to head back to ops before he could make another enticing remark. She still heard his sexy chuckle as he stepped into the elevator.

As soon as she entered opps, Kim handed her the earpiece, all the while talking to staff on the comm, getting a sitrep, and checking her screens.

Janey waited, not shifting from foot to foot, even though she wanted to.

Thirty seconds later, Kim smiled up at her. "Suite Antilles. Casino mezzanine. Prentice is there, waiting for you."

"I'd think she'd want to be undercover for the big sting." Butterflies danced in her stomach and her chest.

"She asked to shadow you."

Janey breathed out, acknowledging the nerves. That didn't make them settle, only feel less frantic. "Sounds like getting knocked out by Rose has made her more cautious." Janey slipped in the earpiece. The background noise of the casino came through. "How do I look?"

She was in her black slacks, top, and jacket she'd donned hours ago. It felt like days ago when she went to interview Rose and Lisa Montaigne.

"Fine," Kim said, barely glancing at her, her attention on her screen. "Maybe a quick makeup refresher is all."

"Will do." Janey turned off the earpiece. "How are you? Have this in hand? I didn't even help you prep for this. It's your first high-stakes sting. Mine, too."

"Not my first. Just the biggest. I'm good. You go."

Janey hurried to the women's room to handle the makeup. A few minutes later, she switched on the earpiece, signaled her departure to Kim, and hustled out of opps.

Two minutes later, she exited the staff turbo to the main lobby level. Kim was calling in comm checks. The only one she hadn't heard from yet was Orlando. She strode down the corridor to the opulent lobby and made eye contact with Peter and Paula Redstone, the hospitality chiefs, who were chatting with guests. She spotted Antonia behind the desk, too. Good that she was active. Antonia was dressed as part of the hospitality staff in a sleek black suit jacket, the L'Étoile lapel pin shiny on her collar—a five-pointed gold star on a vibrant blue background.

Janey crossed the threshold into the casino. The cheerful clang of the slot machines greeted her. She headed for Sky Bar. The crowd was lively around the tables, and the holo warm-up band was playing requests at the other end of the large room. Men in tuxes or long jackets and women in elegant gowns or chic pantsuits drank as they mingled and gambled, laughing, and chattering in a multitude of languages around the Sol. To alleviate any suspicions about there being no departure or arrivals this evening, the casino was offering tier multipliers and bonus spa packages for winning hands.

Natalia was at the bar, a spotter, dressed up in an off-the-shoulder A-line black dress with sparkles across her decolletage and a fabricated diamond necklace. Clark and Jintao were servers, working the poker tables, looking smart in their all-black attire.

She arrived at the bar. Monty, a new hire, was manning the end of the bar, and he lifted a chin to indicate he was ready to take her order.

"Very dry martini," she said.

He didn't know what she was up to, but everyone on staff knew that if she wasn't in uniform, or in her leather jacket, she was undercover and to serve her whatever drink she ordered in nonalcoholic form.

Down at the other end of the bar, Natalie, also undercover as a guest, wore a little black number and a shimmery chunky layered strand of pearls, enough to fill an aquarium. Natalia's gaze passed over her.

Janey waved her comm bracelet over the bar to pay credits for the drink, took the faux-martini, and stared up at the wide star screen. The Orion Nebula was high, smack dab in the center of the wide floor-to-ceiling window. She hoped that meant good luck. She always loved the Orion Nebula, part of the Orion sword, which was itself part of the constellation Orion the Hunter. Best known for the three stars at a tilt, together, forever a team.

She sipped her drink, saluted the stars for good hunting luck, and headed for the stairs to the mezzanine. The stairs were partially hidden by the living wall and tinkling water. Interior design had just added the waterfall that prettily flowed down the living wall into a basin at the foot, recycling back into the system, as all the water did on the station.

That reminded her of the water filtration problem maintenance told her about. Later, she'd check up on that.

Janey took the musical stairs at a fast clip, making the music play at a quickening rate. A jaunty toon, haunting and lively, evoking the sea and singing. Maybe they should have turned off the stair's music. But then the change could alert guests to something going wrong, and she didn't need any undue attention.

At the top of the stairs, she hustled to Suite Antilles, let herself into a room done in cool greens and blues, a wide table in the center, lounging couches along the perimeter walls, and the gentle waves of the Caribbean Sea lapping on white sands on a moonlight night. Stars filled the wide night sky, shimmering as they did when seen through Earth's atmosphere.

Prentice was at the wide table, staring at a large holo screen. "There you are, Chief. Just waiting for the signal. I haven't heard the call yet. Have you?"

"Not yet."

Two seconds later, Kim said through their earpieces, "Get ready, everyone. Keep this channel open. We're a go shortly." Then, "It's time."

Janey slipped into a chair and watched the live feed on the holoscreen of the empty suite beside theirs, the site of their sting, Suite Maple—luxuriously appointed in velvety browns, warm yellows, and accents of red and oranges like a maple forest in fall. Soon, if all went well, Orlando would accompany Lisa Montaigne through the door into this suite.

Through the comm came a soft chime—the guest's suite door request. Orlando was in position at the door of Lisa's hotel suite. Orlando had hacked Leo's appointment book to show that his meeting with them had been scheduled even before they'd arrived. He was banking on Lisa being a bit disorganized and not knowing that Leo had booked the appointment.

Then his voice came on the comm, more high-pitched than usual, tinged with nasal sounds. "Ma'am, Señora Montaigne, Señor García here. As I messaged you earlier, I'm here for our meeting."

Prentice raised a holo screen from the table so they could see the action from the hallway ceiling vids. From the ceiling angle of the vid, Orlando seemed skewed, shorter somehow, even though that couldn't be right. Was that a wig? He had blond highlights mixed in with sparkles and blue streaks, signaling that he was part of the high-end party crowd. Even his nose, cheekbones, and jaw were different, though it was hard to tell how from the above angle.

"Yes, yes, let's go," Lisa spoke, imperious, cool. "I understand you have a business proposition for me."

"Let's discuss it in private, if you don't mind, ma'am. Your suite is fine," Orlando said, his Barcelona accent impeccable.

"I don't mind. I thought a drink first at SkyBar would be nice. Don't you?"

"I don't want to impose..." he said. "But what about"—he lowered his voice—"your guard?"

He meant Meilani who was stationed at the end of the hall.

"Oh, it's fine. She can follow us to the bar if she wants to." Lisa gave an elegant snort. "They act like I'm under house arrest. Ha! There's nowhere to go."

"Well, then, fine. It's quite nice to meet with you," Orlando said. "I have a suite reserved just for us. Absolute privacy and all the business hookups if you should care to review my portfolio in greater detail and even talk to my home office. Everyone is in Barcelona by now." He lisped the city name, sounding like the Barcelona native he was supposed to be.

"Very well, Mr. Garcia. Fine. I have my lawyers at the ready should we come to an agreement."

"You move quickly, Senora Montaigne."

"I am accustomed to getting what I want, Mr. Garcia, and you may call me Lisa."

Prentice flipped through the vids following them down the hall to the guest elevator bank, then out to the lobby and into the casino. A few minutes later, the low hum of the lobby and the sound of Lisa's clipping heels was soon followed by the clang of the slot machines, a jazz number the band was playing, and the tinkling laughter of someone in glee, exclaiming over their winnings and bonus prizes. They'd entered the casino.

"I don't know how to use the vids to follow them here," Prentice said, worry in her voice.

"That's fine," Janey said. "We know where they're going."

A moment later, at SkyBar, Monty was asking Orlando for his drink order. "Sir, what's your pleasure?"

"The lady, first, please, señor," Orlando said.

"A Manhattan on the rocks," Lisa said.

"A classic. I'll take the same," Orlando said. "I'll take care of it, señora, Lisa."

Janey's screen showed that his transaction went through.

No one spoke for a few minutes.

Waiting. The game of every sting and stakeout she'd been on. Janey stared at the window screen, wishing she could actually see the Orion Nebula, instead of the generic starscape with no discernible constellations.

"Are you ready for some business?" Orlando said, his voice high and excited.

Lisa said nothing. The musical stairs chimed. From both spotters, they got the signal that they were climbing the stairs past the living wall.

One camera showed the mezzanine hallway. There they were, Orlando in his flamboyant bolero get up and Lisa Montaigne in a magenta silk pantsuit arriving at the top of the stairs and heading toward the suite next door. Orlando had indeed added expert prosthetics to his nose, jaw, and cheekbones. He seemed taller, more foppish, his posture different.

Prentice gasped. "How did he do that?"

"Master of disguises," Janey said. "Incredible." He'd done his face prosthetics and added the wig in the elevator ride to meet Lisa.

The rug muffled their footfalls. The entry door to the neighboring Maple suite opened and closed on silent treads.

Inside the suite, Lisa held up her wrist holo and turned slowly in a circle.

"Are you concerned that the suite is bugged, Señora Lisa?" Orlando asked.

From one of the many super stealth cameras in the room, they could all see Lisa lift an elegant eyebrow. Apparently satisfied, she went to the wet bar and topped off her drink.

Tech had done a great job. Janey had a three-sixty view of the room. She knew Orlando had a hand in the excellent hidden nature of the tech.

"Refill for you, Señor García?" Lisa asked, her voice a lower seductive purr.

"When you ask like that…"

Lisa laughed, a throaty self-assured laugh. How could anyone ever say no to this woman?

Orlando strode to the wet bar and let Lisa serve him, standing close, initiating contact the way his shoulder brushed hers.

Facing her, he leaned on the wet bar and saluted her with his drink. "Here's to making lots of money for us both. I'm sure your husband would have been very proud of you."

Lisa stopped her glass at her lips. She pursed them. "I doubt it. He had no idea of my abilities."

"I'm sorry to hear that. From what I hear, you are a brilliant strategist. I wouldn't have called you otherwise." Orlando sipped his drink and set it down with a clack. "Come, let me admire your outfit. It's just lovely. Who made it? Givenchy?"

"Oh, yes, how did you know? The classics are always the best." Lisa let herself be led to the center of the room and was twirled by Orlando.

He smiled and led her over to the couch and table set. "I am friends with all the world's artists, Señora."

Lisa sat. "I just love the classical design houses. They know quality in a way the young, hip designers don't know."

Orlando smiled generously and waved over the table. "Shall we? Nothing makes me happier than making money with a beautiful woman."

"We shall." Lisa pulled a paper screen out of her small satchel. She scrolled it open across the table.

The door chimed, and Orlando glanced at her. "I took the liberty of ordering us a meal, Chef Gina's daily prix fixe. Hope you don't mind."

"Oh, no, that's fine. Gina is the best, isn't she?"

Orlando went to the door and manually opened it. Clark, undercover as a server, wheeled in a cart of delicacies.

"Here is fine," Orlando said.

Clark nodded. "Very well, sir. When would you like me to bring up the magnum?"

Lisa laughed. "Mighty confident, aren't you? We haven't even gone over the fine print."

"True, but one must always be prepared for success." Orlando nodded graciously. He turned to Clark. "Wait for my signal."

"Yes, sir." Clark exited the room.

Even though Kim hadn't briefed Janey on all the details, she gathered that was all code between Orlando and the server, to check in and to arrange Rose's entrance. Her stomach clenched, being out of the loop and all. But she'd delegated and had to trust her people, who so far were performing admirably.

"What signal would that be, Señor?" Lisa said with a coquettish smile.

"Our squeals of delight, no doubt." Orlando wheeled the cart closer to the table. He set small dishes on the table, all manner of Spanish tapas, many Janey didn't recognize.

Janey gnawed on an energy cube from a small bowl Prentice had placed on the table. Jell-O-like consistency only slightly sweet with all the nutritional components Horsely had no doubt approved and maybe even prescribed for her. A great way to get around her stubbornness. She'd lost track of mealtime. She'd eaten in medical, but that seemed long ago.

Orlando sat, nibbled, and listened to Lisa Montaigne read the contract under her breath. She paused occasionally to ask questions, which Orlando answered like the investor he was supposed to be.

Lisa sat back, apparently satisfied. "So, if I sign this, you'll be a silent partner, funding me to the tune of one hundred million credits, all for your hands on the Central American operations."

"Yes, that's right."

"Silent, huh? Why?"

"Straight talk. I appreciate that." He steadied his gaze on her. "Not exactly, silent, but close enough. I am looking for someone. Many someones in fact."

TWENTY-SIX

"OH? WHO ARE YOU LOOKING FOR?" LISA
Montaigne sipped her drink and eyed Orlando over the rim of
her glass.

Janey paused in chewing her cube. Lisa was quite the
cougar.

"It's a long story."

Lisa sat back on the couch and crossed her legs. "We have
time. The night is young."

Orlando frowned. "My sister. She—" He broke off,
choked up.

Lisa reached out and touched his leg. "We all have lost
someone to…ugly things."

"No, my sister is fine. It's her best friend. I won't bore
you with the details, but she's been missing for over a year,
and still, we can't find her." He shrugged, looking sad. Why
his story needed to be so elaborate, Janey didn't know. He
sounded convincing and that's what was needed. "We've
heard rumors, coming out of Central America, specifically the
cocoa and coffee production areas, girls and women missing.

I want to find her," he said fiercely. "And now with your help, I will finally have total access over those areas."

Lisa looked thoughtful and sipped her drink.

Orlando leaned forward. "In fact, I'm surprised you're willing to allow this buyout. It's such a rich region."

Lisa sat forward to match him and made it look seductive. "Bad memories."

"Oh?" Orlando said lightly and leaned back. "I sense a story... the night is young."

"My husband was a bad man."

"I am so sorry."

"I lived with it for so long. I just couldn't stand it anymore. One day I snapped. Caught him where he shouldn't have been with people he shouldn't have been with."

"What did you do?" Orlando asked.

Lisa shook her head, sipped her drink.

"Sounds different from his public persona," Orlando prompted.

"We all have secrets," Lisa said.

"Yes, we do." Orlando gave her a pointed look.

"What are yours?" Lisa leaned in.

"Too many to recount in one night," Orlando said softly.

"Well"—she put her hand on his chest—"I'm in no hurry."

Deftly moving out of her caress, Orlando reached around her for his drink and sipped. "Your husband's secrets, would they have anything to do with harems or young women who were bribed and coerced into becoming surrogate mothers?" He spoke mildly, watching Lisa over his drink, close to her as if they were already an intimate couple.

Janey spotted the subtle eye twitch of the older woman. But other than that, her expression was neutral.

"You've done your homework, Mr. Garcia."

"Do call me, Orlando." He smiled. "I always come to

meetings prepared. I take that as a yes," he continued mildly. A statement, not a question.

Lisa got up, padded to the wet bar, and mixed herself another drink. "Another for you?"

Orlando shook his head. "Are you ready to sign our contract?"

"You're eager. Somewhere to be?"

"I just want to know if I should call for our celebratory drinks."

"I'm almost ready. Let's eat first." She eyed him as if he was the meal she wanted and strode back to her seat and sat close to him.

"I do wonder about your husband." Orlando leaned back against the couch, again creating some distance from her, casually.

"What is there to wonder?" Lisa sat back too, her shoulder touching his.

Orlando glanced at her. "Don't you find it suspicious that he was in perfect health and then just up and died? Pretty rare, in this day and age."

"Suspicious, no. Rare, I suppose." Lisa shrugged. "Why do you ask?" She inched away from him to look him squarely in the face. "And how do you know my husband was even dead?"

"My sources tell me the on-board security staff was questioning you for a few hours."

She narrowed her eyes at him. "Who told you that?"

"This is a small station. People talk."

"My people don't talk."

"I meant hotel staff," Orlando said.

She tsk-tsked. "Most unprofessional. I must speak to Frederick."

"Frederick?"

"Mr. Schoeneman. You must know of him. He's the owner of the station. He keeps me informed of all matters.

"Which matters are those?"

"Why do I get the feeling I'm being interrogated?"

"Maybe because you are. I like to know who I'm doing business with. I speculate"—Orlando moved closer to Lisa and lowered his voice to a low rumble—"that you killed your husband and covered it up expertly." His eyes bright, he looked excited as if he enjoyed such salacious, macabre, and illegal action.

Lisa's eyes widened.

"What are you talking about?" Lisa stood and paced. Then turned to glare at Orlando. "What is this?"

"A business deal."

"A shakedown?"

Orlando sipped his drink.

"What do you want?" Lisa demanded.

"I need to know if you murdered your husband," Orlando said in an even tone as if he was asking for the weather report.

"There's no proof. None at all." She continued to pace, looking around the room frantically as if someone might jump out and grab her.

At the watch station next door, Janey said, "She slipped. We got her." Prentice nodded, watchful, not so sure.

"Oh?" Orlando said calmly, in direct opposition to Lisa's frantic pacing. "Shall we call for that magnum of champagne then?"

"Yes, indeed." Lisa glanced at him, relieved, smiling as if she'd just won a race. "Unless there's something you slipped into the fine print in the last few seconds..." Her expression shadowed, and she hurried back to sit on the couch, bending over to examine the contract, her fingers tapping the table in a staccato. "Where is it?"

"Where is what?" Orlando leaned back and crossed his legs.

"You're trying to bait me. For some reason."

"Why would I do that?"

"Everyone always wants more. I learned that from my husband. People are naturally greedy, naturally manipulative."

"And you think I'm doing that."

"Yes, why else would you talk to me of murdering my husband."

"Well, only someone guilty would claim there's no proof as you do."

"How could you say such a thing?" Her eyes widened, surprised. Or acting surprised.

"Did you know that two other men died this morning around the same time your husband did?" Orlando asked casually. "In the same mysterious way."

"How could you possibly know that?" Lisa panted, color high in her cheeks.

"I told you, I have my sources." He nibbled on one of the tapas, keeping his gaze on her.

"No one is that good." Lisa gulped her drink.

"Many people are that good." Orlando's voice was low, certain. "But I'm one of the best."

The door chimed, a discreet and melodic two-tone bell. Orlando crossed the room to answer it. Lisa stared at his back, a horrified expression on her face. She gathered her purse, stood. She was going to make a run for it. Janey's heart pattered loudly. What was Kim going to do to prevent that?

At the door was Rose dressed in a server's black uniform, sans white face powder. Instead of looking like a delicate doll, as she had in her white power, she appeared to be a comely woman, ordinary, if not for her intelligent eyes and firm expression of her mouth. With grace, she glided into the room, calm, carrying a tray.

Well-played.

"On the table, please," Orlando said.

Lisa rushed toward the door. "You!"

"Oh, so you two know each other," Orlando said in a calm tone as the door slid shut on its silent path. He stood in front of it like a club bouncer.

Lisa glanced between Orlando and Rose, her face pale, mottled with angry splotches of red. "What plot is this? Blackmail? That's my weapon. And you're not taking it away from me." Her voice was biting, mean, clipped.

"I need to know where Oscar's sister is," Rose said. "He's helping me. You said—"

"I know what I said." Lisa gulped her drink down. "You're supposed to be dead. Frederick said he'd take care of it..." Lisa set her glass on the table and discreetly slipped a knife into the sleeve of her tunic.

Janey wasn't sure why Lisa thought she hadn't been noticed. But then again, Janey had the god-view of the suite.

"I take it you two have done some business before," Orlando said.

"You were supposed to dispose of the evidence, and we'd be free," Lisa said through gritted teeth.

"I did as you said," Rose said. "But you had me kill Oscar and then tried to have me killed."

"I didn't know he'd be affected. And I had no hand in what happened to you on the escape pod."

Janey put it together. Lisa must have told Schoeneman about Rose's run for the escape pod. Maybe she even had a hand in pushing the young woman in that direction.

"You said the poison was tailored to your husband," Rose said, her cheeks red, her voice wobbly.

"How could I know it would affect Oscar?" Lisa screeched.

"And the poison killed another innocent man," Rose said, anguish in her voice.

"That's not my fault. The scientist said nothing about affecting other people. I don't think..."

"You don't think," Rose repeated with a knife edge to her voice and stood straighter. "Science is imperfect, and your scientist is a criminal, just as you are."

"You're implicated in this too, Rose." Lisa stepped around the table and stalked toward Rose.

Rose paled.

Orlando moved out of the way but not too far. He positioned himself close enough to intervene before any harm could be done.

Lisa glared at Rose as if she'd forgotten about Orlando and her pending business deal with him.

"I just want the truth about Ji-woo." Rose stood her ground, the heavy tray in her hands, a large magnum bottle in its center.

"How should I know?" Lisa stopped.

"You told me you spied on your husband."

"I said no such thing. Don't put words in my mouth." Lisa glared at Rose.

"Ladies, ladies, as much as I'm enjoying the show, we have business to conclude and celebrate. Champagne?" Orlando uncorked the large magnum. He grinned as the cork shot to the far wall with a loud thud. Totally unprofessional. "¡Salud!"

"That's our cue." Prentice shot to her feet.

TWENTY-SEVEN

"RIGHT. LET'S GO." JANEY RUSHED OUT INTO THE mezzanine hallway and unlocked the neighboring door with her security override and hustled in.

Lisa stared at Janey and backed away. "What is the meaning of this? You can't barge into a private suite." She folded her arms, caressing the knife. "We're having a confidential meeting." She sniffed and glared at Janey and Prentice. "I'm lodging a formal complaint with Frederick. If this is how he runs his station—"

"You're welcome to do that, Mrs. Montaigne," Janey said. "But you'll find Mr. Schoeneman indisposed."

Lisa stared at her as if not comprehending.

She'd understand soon enough.

Janey strode over to the stunned woman and plucked the knife from her sleeve.

As if coming out of a trance, Lisa glared at her. "What are you talking about?" She then glanced to Orlando as if he had the answers.

"Here's what I'm talking about." Janey tossed the knife to the couch and pulled out her handcuffs. "Lisa Montaigne, you're under arrest for first-degree murder of three people, including your husband. And your brother."

"My brother? I haven't seen him in years. What are you doing? Unhand me."

What was this? The nineteenth-century? Janey read that kind of language only in old books.

She continued. "You have the right to an attorney. If you cannot afford one—"

"Of course, I can afford one. She's arriving soon, in fact, and will sue you for all you're worth." Lisa wriggled, half-heartedly.

"—One will be provided for you. Anything you say can be used in a court of law."

"We are the law. How dare you!" Lisa slumped. "I will report you to Frederick."

"As I said, he's indisposed right now," Janey said. He was suffering from an identity crisis or an emotional breakdown, the doctor wasn't sure. But she wasn't going to tell Lisa that. "So good luck with that."

"What? What's going on?" Lisa came to life, jerked sideways, and kicked Janey—or attempted to.

Janey side-stepped a sharp heel heading for her shin but unbalanced and wobbled on one foot. But only for a second. Then she grabbed Lisa's arms and slapped cuffs on her wrists.

Rose chose that moment to dart for the knife on the couch. Janey eyed Orlando. He strode to the couch, got there before the young woman did, scooped up the knife, and slipped it into his fancy boots.

Rose glared at him and then spat at Lisa. "She should die for what she did."

At least the woman's rage wasn't turned inward anymore.

"She'll probably go away for a long, long time," Janey said. "Prentice, take her," she added, nodding to the probie.

Prentice took hold of Lisa by an arm and her cuffs and nudged her toward the door.

From the middle of the suite, shoulders drooped, Rose looked tiny. "That won't bring my Oscar back," she said in a small voice.

"No, it won't." Janey strode to her. Maybe her presence would lend the young woman some comfort.

"You have nothing on me," Lisa said to no one in particular.

"But we do," Prentice said. "We have your confession on vid and audio, the whole thing."

"What? But I scanned the room." Lisa glanced about the suite.

"We are very good," Orlando said.

"You!" Lisa said, accusation heavy in her voice, her face screwed up with distaste.

"Me." Orlando sketched a bow. "Orlando Valdez, Sol Police Investigator, Special Branch."

"Oh!" Lisa said. "You are despicable."

"And you, my dear, are a murderer," Orlando said.

Lisa turned to Janey, glanced at Rose, then looked back to Janey. "You tricked me."

"We did," Janey said. "Prentice, take her away to holding. Two of you on her at all times. Watch her."

"Yes, Chief. Like a hawk."

Prentice led Lisa out of the suite. Meilani arrived, and Janey asked her to escort Rose to a safe room in the staff wing and make sure there was a permanent guard on duty. Rose was to be under room arrest until leaving the station to be brought up on trespassing and accessory to murder.

"I'm to be prosecuted?" Rose asked.

"Yes, as we already explained," Janey said. "I'll make sure the judge knows of all the mitigating circumstances, the blackmail, and how you helped us catch Lisa Montaigne. As an accessory to three counts of murder, you may only be charged with a lighter sentence."

Rose looked at her clear-eyed, no tears. "You'll make sure she'll pay, won't you?"

"We will," Janey said.

"Do you think we'll find Oscar's sister?"

"I think there's a possibility, what with all the information Mrs. Montaigne revealed," Janey said.

"The Sol police will seize Montaigne's assets, and a team will be sent to raid the area in question," Orlando said. "If she's there or has been there, we'll find her."

"Thank you, Mr. Valdez," Rose said and to Janey: "Chief Janey McCallister." Rose turned back to Meilani and nodded. "I'm ready."

Rose left with her escort, her back straight.

Orlando reached for his glass on the low table. It was empty. "Want anything?" He headed for the wet bar.

"No, wait. Don't touch anything."

"Why?"

"I want Soren to sweep the room. Lisa's contract is still on the table. We'll get her fingerprints and any trace. You may need them for your case."

"We have her confession. That should be enough."

"For someone like her, I doubt it."

"You're right. What was I thinking?"

"Post-case jitters?" She smiled at him.

"Could be. It's been a few months since I've done the undercover thing and a bit longer since I've been the García persona."

"It doesn't come back to you like riding a bike?"

"I never learned to ride a bike."

"No?"

"Nope. Poor kid from the wrong side of the tracks." He

stalked toward her. "Bet you're from the right side of the tracks."

"You've seen where I'm from." She shrugged. "We all were from the tracks."

Kim commed her.

Janey answered, "Orlando's here with me."

"I know. I can see you both on the vid feed."

Orlando chuckled.

"Everybody settled on your side?" Janey asked.

"That's what I wanted to check in with you about," Kim said, her voice tight.

"What's going on?" Janey asked, her throat closing.

"Rose attacked Mrs. Montaigne in the security wing corridor."

Janey swore under her breath. "I spaced their exits on purpose."

Kim didn't continue right away. "And?" Janey asked

"Mrs. Montaigne suffered scratches and a bloody nose. Rose is now handcuffed in one of the interrogation rooms since we only have one holding cell. Medical is treating Mrs. Montaigne in holding."

"That happened fast," Orlando said.

"Rose is fast," Kim said. "We have it all on vid."

"We'll be right down. Send Antonia and Soren to the room to bag and tag. I want all the evidence cataloged and handed over to Orlando by tomorrow. It's late." Janey eyed Orlando. He nodded. "Take the station off lockdown. We have our murderer and accomplice."

"Yes, Chief." Kim had a smile in her voice. "You did it."

"We did it," Janey said and closed the comm. They were confident the algae were fast-acting and no longer in their air system. To be doubly safe, the environmental systems were being scrubbed and should soon receive a clean bill of health.

New environmental protocols were being put in place from all the relevant departments.

"I didn't get my glass of champagne," Orlando said.

Janey raised an eyebrow. "Case is over, Orlando."

"Both cases, looks like."

"How do you figure?"

He shifted from boot to boot. "Is there any rush?"

"What do you mean? What's wrong? What other case?"

He grimaced. "Looking this pretty is not as easy as it looks. I need to get out of these boots, and you look like you could do with a quick pick-me-up shower." He wiped something off her cheek.

She did feel wrung out. He still hadn't answered her question about his case.

"Sure, let's reconvene in thirty minutes for the debrief. It's been a long day."

"The longest." Orlando scrubbed his face, gave her a kiss on the cheek, and strode out of the room.

That was it? What about a hug? A real kiss? Something, anything. Janey shook her head. Maybe she could corner him in the elevator. She rubbed her cheek and hurried after him.

TWENTY-EIGHT

THIRTY MINUTES LATER ON THE DOT, FRESHLY
showered, Janey entered the conference room and was
greeted by wonderful scents of dinner. She sighed.

"Glad you like it," Mai said, uncovering the last of the
dishes at the counter.

"Smells wonderful." Janey smiled. "All my favorites."
Would this be her last case on L'Étoile? And maybe one of
her last wonderful meals from Mai.

"Where's everyone else?" Mai asked.

"Maybe they don't know we're meeting here," Janey said.

"They should know. Kim told me to set up here."

"Oh, wow," Prentice said, entering the room. "You're the
best, Ms. Chen."

Orlando was next and made appreciative noises at the
spread. He winked at Janey and headed for the fizzy drinks
and punch Mai had set out. He searched for something,
making considering noises.

Janey's chest heated as she watched him. They'd had their
moment in the elevator—all hot kissing and no words. Then
it was over, and they'd sprinted for their respective quarters

for shower and a change, alone. Maybe she could have a life with him, but how would that work?

"Sorry, no alcohol since Kim told me this is a working meal," Mai said to Orlando.

Orlando groaned dramatically. "Be sad my champagne heart."

"Shall I have a bottle sent to your room later, big spender?" Mai chuckled.

Orlando glanced at Janey. She shook her head.

"Not tonight, dear," Orlando said to Mai. "It's a school night."

"If there was ever a day that needed celebrating for surviving, it was today," Mai said. "I don't know about you, but I've been up since 5 a.m."

"You have us beat," Janey said. "But it feels like I've lived at least four lifetimes today."

And no Mom to share her week with and celebrate the close of such a big case. That was too odd.

"But Kim tells me you closed the case!" Mai said in awe. "You ought to celebrate with champagne!"

"Two cases," Orlando said. "We closed two cases."

Janey filled her plate with a little bit of everything. "How is that true? You were going to tell me."

"I will, just waiting for Kim and the rest of the team," Orlando said, filling his own plate.

At that moment, Antonia and Soren arrived.

"Evidence is ready for you from the latest kerfuffle," Soren said and headed for the buffet table.

Antonia grabbed a plate. "I could eat. And the case report has been updated with the latest."

"Good job, Antonia," Janey said. "Really good job. Soon you'll be chief."

"Nah, boss," Antonia replied. "I'm just getting the feel for being lead. The team did a lot of the work, as did you. Whoa, and it's a lot."

Jintao, Clark, and Natalia arrived, laughing as they entered the conference room, oohing and ahhing over the food.

Doc wasn't likely to make an appearance, and Janey didn't know if anyone else had been invited. Maybe Milano would show up. As if on cue, her comm buzzed against her wrist with a message of congratulations from Milano. She sighed. What a day.

"Where is our sting operator?" Prentice asked, also in the buffet line, looking toward the door.

Janey set her plate down at the end of the table by the star-field window and was about to hit her comm to call Kim, when there she was, walking into the conference room.

"The woman of the hour," Orlando said.

Janey clapped, and the others joined in the applause.

Kim blushed. "Oh stop. Janey, you came up with the idea. I just—"

"Just nothing," Janey cut in. "You ran a successful sting operation, and now we have a confession, an arrest, and have solved three murders. Major kudos are yours."

"Where's the champagne?" Kim laughed.

"That's what I want to know!" Orlando chimed in.

"It's a working dinner," Janey said.

"More like midnight feast." Prentice sat at the table and smacked her lips.

Right. It was late.

"Call the kitchen if you need anything else. I'm done for the day, and I have an early start." Mai waved and headed for the door.

Everyone sang out choruses of thank you and stay, but Mai just smiled and left.

"Let's dig in, everyone," Janey said. "And then we'll talk."

Kim served herself from the amazing buffet and sat at the star end of the table with Janey, Orlando, and Prentice. The rest of the team gathered around. Sometime later, belly happy, Janey leaned back and surveyed her team.

Prentice, Soren, Antonia, and Meilani were listening to Orlando regale them with one of his undercover tales on one of the other space stations. Clark, Jintao, and Natalia had their heads together laughing. Kim was studying her holo.

Janey yawned. She'd be up for eighteen hours. A very long day indeed. Fatigue pressed her down against the chair. Just a bit more to go on this longest day, and then she could sleep. Hit the reset button on her life, was more like it. Now she could decide what she wanted to do next now that she no longer needed to stay at the station for her mother.

Grief washed over her for a moment and flowed away. She rubbed her face.

Janey had leave coming to take care of her mother's affairs and say a proper goodbye to the one who'd raised her well, so she could fly from the nest into a life of her own choosing. As Janey had partially done. Mom hadn't wanted it any other way. Soon she'd decide what to do next with her life. Teresa promised she'd tell her when the funeral rites were. In a few days, most likely.

"Chief, you okay?" Prentice asked.

Janey blinked back the tears and scrubbed her face again. "Just exhausted, as I'm sure you all are."

Kim looked at her with concern as if she was thinking about Janey's mom, too.

Janey stood and strode to the window. The starfield displayed the actual Orion constellation.

Orlando stood beside her. "Gorgeous."

"It never gets old." She gazed at him. He was staring at her, appreciation in his eyes.

He was there for her, but what about until the next case?

Even though he'd proven himself, why did she still doubt him Maybe it was herself she doubted. Maybe she didn't trust herself, trust her judgment. Maybe she worried too much about the future. She'd always taken the safe path. Maybe it was time to take more risks, go after what she really wanted. But she had no idea what that was, and she had no idea where these thoughts were coming from. She was tired was all. And there Orlando was, a warm presence beside her. Now. Solid. Real.

She'd take the now, leaned against him, and rested her head on his shoulder.

Somebody rustled behind her.

Janey straightened, breaking contact.

Orlando made a small sound of protest.

"Right. Time to do our debrief." She strode to the middle of the conference room and waved to a wallscreen to activate it. It went from a starfield sleep mode to showing the security department's roster, work rotations, and open cases. Janey waved open the Nel, Montaigne, Hwang murder files, and the details filled the screen.

"Shall we?" she announced.

The team gathered around her.

"Antonia, please do the honors. Update us on next steps," Janey said.

"Sure. Tomorrow morning, a Sol security jet will arrive to take Lisa Montaigne into custody for the murder of her husband, Leo Montaigne, and two other guests—Oscar Hwang and Hampton Nel. Another agent will escort Rose into custody on the same jet." Antonia waved to the screen, revealing the flight manifest. "They're due to arrive at oh-eight-hundred? Everything's in order with that flight, right?"

"That's right," Orlando said. "I'll be the one to bring Montaigne into custody and get her testimony about what she knows about where the girls are kept."

"Is that how we solved your case?" Prentice asked.

"You helped. You all helped," Orlando said. "I've had my eye on Schoeneman for a long time—"

"Really?" Prentice said.

Janey gave her a look.

"Sorry, I'm just surprised is all," Prentice said.

"I'm not," Kim said. "The man acts like he can do anything and get anything, with impunity. I'm done with it." What was their history?

Something clicked into place. Janey sucked in a breath.

She said to Kim, "You've been helping Orlando compile a file on Schoeneman."

"Yes, I meant to tell you, Janey. I'm sorry." Kim sighed. "All the odd requests Schoeneman's made for clients, and their odd requests on his say-so." Kim shrugged sadly as if it was a burden to spy on her boss of a decade.

"Like what?" Antonia asked.

"Off-book entertainers, for one," Kim said.

"That's not odd," Janey said.

"Schoeneman asked me to tell no one, not even Milano," Kim said.

"That *is* odd," Antonia said.

"I checked all their backgrounds. Something was often fishy about those ident files, but I couldn't put my finger on it." Kim frowned. "Nothing added up until recently when I tracked down Rose's identities."

"Connect the dots for us," Janey said.

"Well, Rose had a different identity when she arrived," Kim said.

"Yes, I uncovered that with housekeeping," Prentice said.

"Whoever did her ident..." Kim said. "There was something in the code that looked similar to the others I'd seen over the years."

"When I untangled my code mess from my snitching on

Chief Milano," Orlando jumped in and nodded at Janey's reaction of surprise. "Yes, that was one of the ways I scooped up information for my case—Kim and I got to talking about weird code, and she told me about the similarities. That jogged a memory about the girls we've rescued over the years." Orlando waved the board to bring up files. Janey couldn't see where he grabbed them from. Probably one of his top-secret databases. "I tracked down some of their new identities and followed the thread to an outfit in Coban, Guatemala, near where many of the girls had worked and where Oscar's sister, among others, had disappeared." He turned to Janey. "Sorry I didn't let you know I had recruited some of your team to help me. I should have."

Janey nodded. "Yes, you should have. And I get it... today has been—" She shook her head, words not arriving for the moment.

Orlando put a hand on her shoulder.

Antonia jumped in. "How does this all connect to Schoeneman and to today's murders?"

"Getting to that," Orlando said. "What I discovered in my digging is that Schoeneman has several holdings in that area, all in the coffee industry, including plantation grounds, processing plants, warehouses, shipping, and hiring. The area is heavily guarded and masked from our most powerful sensors and satellites, and financially hidden by several layers of shell corporations."

"So, he owns one of the few coffee plantations left. So what?" Prentice said. "I thought many of the big industrialists owned a few or a piece of a coffee plantation."

"Actually, he owns a majority share in all of them, and he makes a pretty penny off all of us coffee addicts." Orlando gave Janey a look.

"He's controlling the market prices," Meilani said.

Orlando nodded. "He has been, from behind the scenes, for a few years now."

"I thought such monopolies were illegal," Prentice added.

"They are," Orlando said. "I have him on monopoly charges, in addition to human trafficking charges."

Many of the team murmured, shocked. This was the first time they'd probably heard about the charges against Schoeneman.

"He owns all the coffee plantations in the world?" Clark asked. "I really like coffee."

"Pretty much," Orlando said.

"Me, too." Meilani sighed. Natalia nodded and sighed, too.

"I only drink coffee provided by the station," Clark said, voicing what was true for all of them. "Otherwise, I couldn't afford it."

"Thank goodness I only like tea," Jintao said.

Kim shook her head. "I don't know what I'd do without my two cups a day."

"We'd adapt. Be more like Jintao," Janey said and turned to Orlando. "But what makes you certain that you have enough to arrest Schoeneman?"

"And what will happen to the hotel-casino when he gets arrested?" Prentice asked, looking to Kim and then Janey. She was the newest agent hired. Restarting somewhere else would be the hardest for her.

The others jumped in with ideas and speculations.

"No one is arresting me today or ever," Schoeneman boomed from the entrance of the conference room. What was he doing here?

Everyone went quiet.

Schoeneman entered. In the silence, the door slid shut behind him with a louder than usual snick.

TWENTY-NINE

JANEY STIFFENED. "SIR—"

Orlando broke away from the group and strode toward Schoeneman, fists at his sides. "You are behind all the missing person cases I've been investigating for years. I finally have the evidence."

"What are you talking about, young man?" In the center of the conference room, Schoeneman towered over Orlando by a good seven or eight inches. Then he brushed past Orlando, approached the murder board, and slapped it. "What do you have here? Update, McCallister. Posthaste." Schoeneman peered down at her, a commanding broad-shouldered presence, charisma oozing off him, a sharpness in his gaze.

Janey huffed out a breath, heat in her face. "The timelines for the murders today—"

Orlando got in Schoeneman's face, steel in his voice. "I'll tell you what it is." He glanced at Janey for a moment, full of determination, and a glimmer of protectiveness. "It's about circumventing our child labor laws to work your plantation. It's about hiding your majority ownership. It's about monopolistic practices. All to control the coffee supply. You're keeping the prices high, your profits high, too. All on the backs of illegal labor."

"I run legitimate businesses." He glared at Orlando. Then he turned to Kim, ignoring the rest of the team, who had stepped away as soon as Schoeneman stormed in, taking up all the air in the room. "You know what I do."

"I-I...As far as I know, I do." Pale, Kim glanced away. She wouldn't look at Janey.

What was going on with her? She seemed to turn into another person, meek and cowed.

Janey addressed Schoeneman. "Sir, what are you doing here? Are you okay?"

"Of course, I am, Chief McCallister. Why wouldn't I be? I'm in the peak of health." He patted his trim stomach under his silk shirt, looking mighty pleased with himself.

"But you were under medical observation, under guard. You were—something was wrong," Janey said, relaxing her stance. What happened to the people guarding him? Maybe if she was nonthreatening in her voice and physical presence, he'd explain his odd behavior from earlier. Maybe he'd do the right thing and turn himself in.

"Oh, please." Schoeneman waved a hand in the air. "Water under the bridge. And the guards are fine. Only a little...hmmm...confused." He pivoted and strode back to the door.

Had he attacked them? She glanced at Antonia, who waved in a message hopefully to check in on medical and their people.

"I can't let you leave, sir," Janey strode after Schoeneman, hands at her side, ready for anything. "You shot at me and at another in the escape pods. Sol Space Authority will want to speak to you. Regs, you know."

"That was—" Schoeneman spun back and narrowed his eyes at her when she reached for her gun.

Janey gripped the gun handle. "Unjustified, and not water under the bridge."

"You can't. You better not." He puffed his chest out. "This is my station. You work for me, and you do as I say. I came to tell you to your face."

"You put me and others in danger for no reason." Janey approached. "Turn around, sir, I'm arresting you for station endangerment."

"Is that a thing?" Prentice whispered.

Antonia whispered, "Come on."

Without turning around, Janey could hear her team approaching, backing her up.

"Yes," Orlando said loudly and approached Schoeneman from the other side. "I'd prefer to charge him with at least fifty counts of human trafficking and child labor infringement and breaking the monopoly laws." He gazed at Janey with a fierceness. He wanted Schoeneman bad. The man was his collar after all.

Schoeneman took that moment of her attention on Orlando to do a sweep kick toward Janey. She saw it out of the corner of her eye but too late. Janey toppled on her butt before she could do a thing about it. What was this, the schoolyard?

Schoeneman shoved Orlando hard in the chest and dashed out of the conference room.

"Hey!" Antonia shouted and dashed after him, but she wasn't quick enough. The door slid shut. "What's wrong with the door? It's not opening." She stepped back and then forward. The door wouldn't open.

Janey scrambled to her feet. "Get to the override."

"Where is it?" Antonia asked, looking around.

"The main system," Kim said.

"Which is where?" Antonia asked and swore under her breath. She'd been outmaneuvered. They'd all been outmaneuvered.

"My office." Kim frowned. She turned to Janey. "Sorry for siding with him. It's-it's a long story, and I'm so ashamed. I'm not that person anymore."

Janey shook her head. She couldn't address that right now. She strode back to the murder board. A red dot flashed in the upper right-hand corner, a security warning. She waved a corner to call up the dashboard.

"No, wait!" Orlando yelled.

Too late. The board flashed the white screen of death, and all data was wiped from view. The screen glared red numbers counting down from three minutes and beeped a high-pitched whine, over and over, urgent and shrill.

"What happened?" Prentice shouted over a shrill whine. She rushed over and tried resetting but nothing worked.

"A bomb!" Janey yelled at the same time as Orlando did. "Take cover," she added. "The breakroom."

Not again.

The team all made a run for the small room behind the board. The last time they had a bomb, the whole safety of the station had been threatened.

Prentice was first in, then Kim, then Meilani, Soren, Clark, and Jintao. Orlando stood at the doorway. "Come on, Janey! Antonia, come on!"

Antonia rushed in, bringing up the rear, making sure the team got all herded into the small break room. "Come on, boss!"

"Maybe I can disarm it," Janey said still staring at the board, touching it all over to no effect. She glanced at her holo. It was working but not syncing with the board.

What was Schoeneman playing at? It made no sense at all.

"No time," Orlando said.

One minute thirty seconds left. "I can do it!" she yelled over the whine, studying the security readouts on her holo.

"You can't," Orlando shouted. "Now get in here."

One minute twenty seconds. He was right. She dashed for the break room. Orlando closed the door behind her.

Janey panted in the center of the small room.

Kim sat on the bed, tapping away on one of her several holos she was never without. The rest of the team was squeezed into the corner, staring at their comms in disbelief.

Kim growled. "What just happened? My systems don't show a bomb."

Prentice stared at her, pale, afraid, and for once, with nothing to say.

Antonia shook her head as if disappointed at herself. The rest of the team looked glum.

"What is Schoeneman's endgame?" Janey asked to no one in particular. "Has he truly gone crazy? What is he protecting?"

"Well, he can't destroy the files. They're all auto-backed up, triple redundancy," Kim said.

"Thank the stars," Janey said.

"So, my employer wants to kill us." Antonia paced the small room, anger coloring her cheeks. When no one spoke, she added, "Hey, I don't hear anything. Three minutes should be up by now."

Orlando was fiddling with his holo wrist comm and spoke without looking up. "I think it was a diversion."

"So, we wouldn't try to follow him. But to where?" Janey paced. "Where is he going?"

"I got it." Orlando turned toward the door.

"Off-station," Janey said at the same time Orlando did.

"Obviously," Kim said.

Antonia chuckled. "Oh, the hunt." And the lead investigator was back.

"Yes!" Prentice said, her enthusiasm and hopefulness back.

"But if he wanted to get off-station," Jintao said at the closed door, "why bother to show in the conference room? He could have just locked the door and took off."

Beside him, Clark scratched his head. "Maybe he wanted something in the conference room."

Janey waved open the door and it slid open.

"Wait. Don't go out there," Kim said. "It might not be safe."

"It's okay, Kim. He just needed a head start," Janey left the break room. She paused and turned back to Antonia.

"Check to see if any space jets have taken off." Antonia nodded.

"Good," Janey said.

"Didn't know any had arrived." Prentice bent to the task on her holo, as did the rest of the team.

"Two have docked," Meilani said.

"He's leaving," Janey said. "We have to stop him. He has how many secret hideaways? He could get out to the asteroid belt and be scot-free. Maybe even disappear and start a new life on Mars."

"And leave everything behind?" Clark asked.

"The man is richer than God," Jintao said. "Doesn't make sense he'd leave all this behind and run."

"Exactly. He could easily start a new life at the asteroid frontier," Orlando said. "We have to go."

Janey put a hand on his arm to still his impatience and eyed Kim. "The data is safe?"

Kim examined her holo. "Yes, thank goodness. Schoeneman is smart, but I know the station systems better than he does. I overrode his lock. He'd set it for an hour." Kim grinned. "Sorry about before. It's just that—"

"Kim, later." Janey rushed toward the exit, Orlando

matching her stride for stride, Antonia and the rest of the team on their heels.

This time the door opened as it should.

"No jets have left, Chief." Antonia was ready to follow her out. So were the rest.

Janey turned and held up a hand to stop her new lead investigator. "No, you stay in the security wing. Keep an eye on Montaigne and Rose, and help Kim, if she needs it. Assign jobs. What I used to do."

"Chief, fieldwork is for field agents," Antonia said. "The chief is supposed to stay behind. Regs."

"Orlando and I are the only rated field agents here," Janey said. "I need you at this post."

"We just did the sting," Antonia protested.

"Controlled circumstances," Janey said. Antonia looked like she was about to protest again. Janey held up a hand. "Be ready with a backup team. Lockdown the station again. Tell the hangar security now."

"Yes, Chief," Antonia said.

"Good, everyone. Stay sharp. Antonia's got you in hand."

"Yes, Chief," everyone chorused. Prentice nodded when Janey eyed her. The young probie looked like she was happy to learn from Antonia now and not hang on Janey's every word.

Janey dashed for the elevator.

At its door, she shifted from foot to foot and said to Orlando, "How far out are your guys?"

"They haven't left yet. They're arriving at oh-eight-hundred, I told you."

"Can you get them here sooner? If they left now, they could be here in thirty to forty minutes port-to-port, tops."

"I'll try. What reason shall I give?"

"How about Schoeneman making a run for it, resisting arrest?"

BETH BARANY

"I'll put in the request but can't guarantee it."

"Really?" Janey shook her head. "Sol bureaucracy."

The elevator door slid open, and they stepped in. Janey clicked the button for the lowest level, below the hangar.

"Where are we going?" Orlando asked.

"I can't fly one of those jets. Can you?"

"No." He peered at her. "Weapons station?"

She firmed her lips. "Do you see any other way he'll listen?"

"Not sure he will anyway."

Janey waved into her holo for Schoeneman's position on the secret vid system. She couldn't find him anywhere.

She checked the vid for the hangar. Two jets were docked, engines off, as Kim said. No one was on the hangar floor. It was after midnight, after all.

She commed Kim. "Any trace of Schoeneman in your system?"

"None. I even did a visual security check of his quarters, his favorite private suite, the kitchen, the works. No sign of him. You?"

"Not in the hangar, and not on the ident system," Janey said. "Please monitor the jets. First sign of engines on, let me know."

He must have turned off his ident or was in a cloaked area.

"Of course. Want me to wake the dockmaster?"

"Yes. Any trace of anyone down there? Strange. I don't show anyone."

"Confirmed. Quiet as a pip."

"Thanks, Kim." Janey commed off.

The elevator came to a stop at the lowest level. She exited and strode down the narrow hallway that led to the weapons room, Orlando right behind her. "You don't have to come with me."

270

"Oh, but I do," Orlando said. "Where else would I be?"

"Some solo stunt, going after Schoeneman at the hangar."

"No, I'm sticking with you," Orlando said.

Janey stopped at the weapons room entrance. "The weapons room barely holds two. It's not made for human comfort."

"I know. Been here earlier today. Remember?" He stopped beside her, close, and eyed her lips.

"No, I was in an escape pod then, tumbling through space. Remember?" Janey tore her gaze away from him and punched in her security code. The door honked and didn't open.

"This is why I'm here, *mi corazon*," Orlando said. "Step aside and let me do my magic. Schoeneman's probably done something to the door."

If he was even in there.

"Another delay." Janey got out of his way and let him work.

How did things come to this? Entering a weapons room to shoot down her boss who was running from his Jewel in the Sky? What was his ultimate game?

Orlando unlocked the door and it opened. They entered the small anteroom to the weapons room, about eight feet cubed. Dull grey metallic unfinished graphene walls, low ceilings, and no windows.

Janey commed Schoeneman. "Janey McCallister here. Pick up. Let's work this out. You don't need to run."

"Who said anything about running?" His voice came from right behind her. He must have been behind the door, cloaked.

Janey spun. An explosion of gunfire, close. Acrid. Choking. Orlando screamed and shook his hand, blood streaming from it.

"You shot me!" Orlando roared at Schoeneman.

Schoeneman was fast. He advanced toward Janey. She pulled her laser-sighted pistol. But he thwacked the gun out of her hand before she had the time to aim. Her gun skittered across the grey-recyclo floor to lodge under a bolted-down desk.

She danced around Schoeneman, putting herself between him and Orlando. Her heart pounded, and sweat beaded on her forehead. She panted. Keeping her gaze on Schoeneman, she slipped the ceramic-graphene handgun out of one boot, and the sheathed four-inch black carbon steel blade out of the other.

Probably overkill, but Venus hells, she was pissed.

She aimed her handgun, spun the knife in the other hand, gripped it strong, and steadied her breath. "Freeze, Schoeneman. Drop it."

He laughed, a jolly full laugh as if he had heard a great joke. He pointed his slim laser gun at her. "Feisty. I like it."

THIRTY

JANEY STARED AT SCHOENEMAN. HAVING A GUN pointed at her was not her idea of a successful end of a case.

She tried for a calm voice, but instead, it cracked. She cleared her throat and tried again. "Is this really all about coffee?"

Orlando moaned softly.

Janey didn't take her eyes off Schoeneman but spoke to Orlando. "You alright?"

"Yah, fine. Do your thing. I'll do mine." Orlando's voice was tight with pain.

Schoeneman laughed again, a full throaty laugh that pitched high as if the crazy was edging in. "Your boy toy is broke."

"Shut up." Janey aimed her gun at Schoeneman's center mass.

"Ah, a mouth on you. I always liked that about you, Janey McCallister. Mouthy as shit. Too bad we can't keep you on staff." He lifted his gun toward her head. "You're fired."

"Stop!" Janey shouted.

But he didn't. She blinked to zoom in and could see in

precise detail of his trigger finger depressing the trigger as if in slow motion.

She shot the gun out of his hand.

He glared at her and reached back with his other hand, possibly for another weapon. She shot his shoulder.

He staggered back and swore, putting down all women in his curse. He got his feet under him and charged at her, head down like a bull.

Taking advantage of his momentum, Janey shoved him to one side.

Schoeneman crashed into the wall and bounced to the floor. He struggled to his feet but got as far as his knees.

"Schoeneman, stop!" Janey shouted again, her gun pressed against his temple. "Is this what you want? What the Venus hells is wrong with you?"

He cradled his bloodied hand in the other, grimacing. "This is my station. You can't have it."

Schoeneman didn't sound like the business mogul she knew.

"I don't want it," Janey said. "I'm going home." She called over her shoulder. "Orlando."

"McCallister." He was right beside her.

"Cuffs, please."

"With pleasure." Orlando cuffed him, somehow managing that one-handed. "Frederick D. Schoeneman, you are under arrest under the Sol Unified Planets Accords for fifty-plus counts of kidnapping, human trafficking, monopoly control, and attempted murder."

"I'll have your boss on a platter before breakfast," Schoeneman said, but he winced when Orlando tugged him to his feet.

"You give that a try," Orlando said, his bloody hand wrapped in a piece of his shirt.

Janey barked into her wrist comm: "Kim, send down a

security team to the weapons room entrance. And medical. No, better yet, have them meet us at the nearest elevator."

"Got it, Chief. Antonia's already on her way."

"Traitor!" Schoeneman yelled at Janey's comm. "Kim, I took you out of a gutter, and look what you became. You owe me."

"I owe you nothing, Frederick. If anything, you owe me hazard pay," Kim said and commed off.

Schoeneman yelled more obscenities against women.

Orlando yanked the cuffs, and Schoeneman winced in pain again.

Janey motioned with her gun, still beaded on his head. "Let's go."

———

SEVEN HOURS LATER, JANEY WAS SWAYING WITH exhaustion as she watched four Sol Special Police frog-walk Schoeneman into the space jet. Montaigne and Rose had already been loaded.

Orlando stood on the hangar floor conferring with his boss, Captain Sebastien Kavya. Everything had to be done by the book.

Schoeneman had to stay locked up.

He'd attacked her, Orlando, and Rose. Overnight, Janey personally guarded Schoeneman in medical, even though there was no way he could have broken out of that small, locked room. Four of her agents had backed her up with stun guns at the ready. They hadn't taken any chances. She hadn't been able to sleep, even though he hadn't tried anything.

Thank the Stars Aligned.

In the enormous hangar, Orlando strode over to her and stood close without touching. "I'll join you at your mom's place as soon as this case wraps up. Just a few days. You're taking leave, right?"

"Soon. I need a few days to wrap up a few things here, too," Janey said.

He moved closer and whispered in her ear, "Are we good? It's just a few days…"

"I thought I was just one of your women in one of your ports," she joked lamely.

"You're my woman in every port. Come with me. Work for the Sol. Special Investigations could really use you. We can visit all the space stations and other exotic locales together, fighting crime on a global scale. High glamor." He smiled roguishly.

"I don't know, Orlando. I can't decide anything until after Mom's funeral rites."

Kavya called after him, "Last call for boarding, Investigator." Kavya nodded at Janey. "Chief."

Orlando waved off his boss, lifted Janey's chin, and bent for a gentle kiss. "Be sure to tell me when that is. I'm coming." He kissed her, sweet and soothing. "Whatever you decide, *mi corazon*, I'll be there for you."

She stared at him, his dark eyes giving her love. He caressed her cheek, turned, and strode away to board the space jet. The Sol Security Office's jet taxied down the runway and took off out of the hangar, the engines leaving a blue burn at exit.

She took a deep breath and headed for the elevator.

Prentice jogged over to her. "I missed the hand-off."

"Walk with me."

"Yes, Chief."

"I need you to take point on the security team, under Kim's watch, of course."

"Really?"

"Really."

"Where are you going?"

"To bed."

Prentice nodded, fresh after her six hours of shut-eye. "I understand, Chief. Does this mean I won't be a probie anymore?"

"We'll talk about it in the morning."

Twelve minutes later, Janey was in her quarters and fell onto her bed, fully clothed.

Her comm beeped. "Orlando."

"Janey."

She closed her eyes.

"Janey."

"What?"

"Take off your boots."

She moaned her fatigue.

"Do it, McCallister."

She sat up and tugged off her work boots and lay back down.

"Did you do it?"

She grunted.

"Good." There was a smile in his voice.

She grunted again, this time in comfort. "Good night, Orlando."

"Good night, *mi corazon*."

Orlando commed off.

He was there for her.

She could do this job anywhere, do anything she wanted. Working side by side with Orlando fighting crime around the globe. Yah, maybe. But she'd decide after her longest day was over.

ACKNOWLEDGMENTS

It takes a village to create the world that lives and breathes in this book.

A very Special Thanks to my Kickstarter backers for the paperback edition: Adam Gaffen, Amanda Arthur Krill, Cheryl Liquori, Bella Barany, Ezra Barany, Jon, Khadija Hussain, Laurie A. Green, Megan Cain, Rhel ná DecVandé, Snellopy.

In the early stages, many people helped me create this fourth book in the Janey McCallister Mystery series. A huge thank you to my Early Reader and Beta Reader team: Beth Perry, Briana Burgess, Bob Morton, Carol Malone, Catriona Bain, Dodie Coe, Kay LaLone, Marilyn Lugner, Mary Van Everbroeck, R.K.H. Ndong, Helen Picone, Melanie Shinkaruk, Sally Stackhouse, and Shelly Small.

To my Patreon supporters: Chloe Adler, Elayne Griffith, Janet Patterson, and Lisa Boragine.

To F.S. for his ongoing support and for his lending his name for a character in this book.

To Leah Ellias, for asking me to do the honors of naming a recurring character after her husband who passed away in 2019. He would have loved it, she said. Thank you for the permission.

To my students for giving me feedback during our One Hundred-Word Critique classes. You rock!

To my first cover designer, the talented Elayne Griffith, who helped me refine the cover concept and shape the book titles.

To my amazing, diligent, and ever-patient critique partners, Patricia Simpson and Kay Keppler, for their support, encouragement, and critical eye. Bottle of wine and gobs of chocolate coming.

To my mastermind group, Leanne Regalla and Bonnie Johnston, for their moral support and cover feedback.

To my Blurb Babes, Lea Kirk and Tess Rider, for never ever tiring of refining my book blurbs and for the fun brainstorming sessions.

To my proofreader, Paul Martin of Paul Martin Editorial, for his eagle eye.

A massive double thank you to Bonnie Johnston for her friendship, amazing brainstorming sessions, and incredible, tireless support.

To my brother Sam Zoesch for his just-in-time expert input on all things biology and chemistry.

And a multiverse-sized thanks to my husband and fellow creative nebula, Ezra Barany, for all the re-reads, edits, and more edits, geeking out on science right alongside me, and supporting my storytelling instincts every step of the way. You rock!

——————

And a huge thank you to you, dear reader. If you enjoyed this book, please tell a friend about space station investigator, Janey McCallister. And if you're so moved, please leave a review at your vendor of choice. Readers who share with me their reviews get announced in my Readers' Newsletter: http://bethb.net/acknow.

ABOUT THE AUTHOR

Award winning author, Beth Barany writes in several genres including young adult adventure fantasy, paranormal romance, and science fiction mysteries. Inspired by living abroad in France and Quebec, she loves creating magical tales of romance, mystery, and adventure that empower women and girls to be the heroes of their own lives.

For fun, Beth enjoys walking her neighborhood, gardening on her patio, and watching movies and traveling with her husband, author Ezra Barany. They live in Oakland, California with a piano, cats, and over 1,000 books.

For more information:
author.bethbarany.com
beth@bethbarany.com

READERS' NEWSLETTER:
http://bethb.net/redrunningdeep

Made in United States
Troutdale, OR
03/07/2024

18285392R00181